Becoming Alva

By John Muller

Published in the United States
by Piscataqua Press
32 Daniel Street
Portsmouth, NH 03801

ISBN: 978-1-950381-33-3

For Diane Kelly.
For her generosity of spirit.
For her intelligence of the heart.

Chapter 1

Built just after the First World War, the house at the corner of Stockton and Weaver had initially served as the residence of the university's chancellor. Following World War II, owing to the significant number of ex-servicemen taking advantage of the GI Bill, the size of the student body spiked considerably resulting in a housing crisis. As part of the solution, the Chancellor moved to more palatial digs off campus and the house was converted for use as student housing. Over the years that followed, it was home first for ex-GIs, then forestry students, then the varsity football team, and then for students majoring in French. In its most recent incarnation, it became a residence for women who were either grad students or in their senior year at the university.

To someone walking by, it still had the appearance of a home of someone of significant means. It consisted of three stories. The top floor had a sloping roof with a dormer on both sides. Stairs with banisters on either side as well as one up the center led to a porch with a roof and a railing that ran the length of it. The front door was a massive piece of heavy wood with two panels of etched glass. On either side of it there was a substantial picture window. A three-by-two-foot sign was mounted on the railing to the right of the front steps. It read, simply, 'THE COTTAGE.'

Alva Parsons' room was on the top floor. For Alva, now a senior, this was the first year that she was actually going to live on campus. The previous year she had shared an apartment with her older brother Arvel, a senior at that time. The two years prior to that both she and her brother had lived with their Uncle Ward and Aunt Lillian. Uncle Ward was the head of the religion department at the university. Alva and Arvel would have lived with their aunt and uncle that year also, but their uncle had gone on a sabbatical to the Holy Land, and their house had been assigned to a visiting lecturer for that year.

Having graduated, Arvel was now at a seminary back home in Kentucky. Alva had planned to keep the apartment for the coming year, but her parents would have none of that, insisting that she move back in with her aunt and uncle. Alva tried to stand her ground on the matter, claiming that she was old enough now to be on her own, especially after having had the apartment the previous year, but, pressed on the issue, her parents refused to pay the rent for her, and that was that. It was at that point that Uncle Ward stepped in with a compromise, saying he knew of a 'suitable' residence on campus, the Cottage, which, he made a point to emphasize, was just for women, and that the premises were under adult supervision. It was also, he told Alva's mother, his wife's sister, on campus and conveniently located next to a dining hall where Alva could take her meals. Surprisingly enough to Alva, her parents agreed, even offering to foot her board bill for the year.

"Watch your head," her uncle warned, opening the door to her room that first day as she moved in. "The ceilings slope some," he continued, setting her first box of things on the floor.

Standing up, he took a handkerchief from his pocket and wiped his brow. "Sure is a hot one." He turned to Alva. "So…what do you think?"

Standing there in the doorway, holding a second box of her things, Alva took a deep breath. It was, she thought, wonderful. 'Mine. Mine. My place. My room. Mine.' For a brief moment she thought she might cry.

"Alva?"

She turned quickly to her uncle, smiled, and nodded emphatically. "It's nice," she said. "It's really nice."

"You're sure?"

Alva nodded again. "Oh yes."

Stepping towards her, her uncle took the box that she was holding and set it down next to the first.

"You know, of course, that if this doesn't…if this doesn't work out for you, your Aunt Lillian and I would…well, we would like to have you come back and stay with us. You're always welcome. Always."

"Thank you, Uncle Ward. Thank you. I…I think this will work out. I really do."

Her uncle smiled and nodded. "So do I. It is time, isn't it?"

Without even thinking about doing so, Alva rushed up to her uncle and hugged him, pressing the side of her head against his chest.

"Your parents," he said, putting his arms around her, "your parents love you, you know, and…well…they're parents. They worry."

Stepping back, Alva nodded.

"And it's not *about* you," her uncle went on. "They just tend to focus on…on certain, let's call them, *aspects* of life here at the university, things that they've heard about and…well, you know. They worry. Your mother worries."

Alva nodded.

"I think this is a good compromise," her uncle said making a gesture with one hand, encompassing the room. "A good first step away."

"Yes," Alva said with a slight sigh of relief. "Yes."

"Good. Let's go get the rest of your things and get you settled. Your Aunt Lillian will have dinner waiting for us by the time we get back."

Alva would have preferred to decline the *invitation*, her preference being to stay there in the room, to relish just being there, but, after all that her uncle had done arranging for these new accommodations and working everything out with her parents, she knew that she had to go. It had, she knew, been a real kindness on his part, and her gratitude was both genuine and heartfelt.

Still, she did so want to remain here in *her* room, to take *her* time putting it together *just so*, arranging the furniture (what little of it that there was), putting her things away, all of it. But mostly, she wanted just to be there. Still, she knew that all of that could wait a little longer. She would be back, and knowing that pleased her. It pleased her very much.

Chapter 2

Dinner that evening seemed, to Alva, to take far longer than necessary. It was almost dark when she finally returned to the Cottage and she knew that, despite the smallness of the room and the fewness of her possessions, there was little left of the day to get much done. This annoyed her, but she reminded herself that there was no hurry, that, in fact, the putting together of the room would probably end up being an on-going process. Realizing this pleased her. Her annoyance passed. She would, she decided, be satisfied to do what she could get to this evening, and that would be good enough *for now*.

"My life starts here," she said quietly to herself, and although she found the *preciousness* of her comment slightly embarrassing, the idea of it, the *truth* of it, pleased her, and with that she went to work.

Since it was only a few days before Labor Day, summer continued to hold sway. The day had been a warm one, a humid one, and some residual warmth hung in this upper room giving it a close feel, as if there was only so much oxygen available. Although far from unbearable, it was warm enough that Alva walked over to the dormer and raised the window several inches.

Yes, the room was small. In terms of furniture placement, there weren't many options. As few pieces as there were, the room still had a bit of a cramped aspect to it, a condition that was exacerbated by the slope of the ceilings. Still, this appealed to Alva; she preferred to think of it as *cozy*. It would, she felt, be that way even more so once the days of cold weather and snow settled in. This pleased her very much.

The first thing she addressed was the placement of the bed.

"Perpendicular," she said. "Perpendicular to the north wall." Glancing towards the window, she visualized the street layout beyond in reference to where the sun rose and where it set. Then, picking up her pillow, she tossed it to one end of her bed. "West of Polaris," she said and, with a smile of satisfaction, adjusted the bed accordingly. With that done, Alva crawled onto the mattress, lying back and resting her head on the pillow.

With her eyes on the ceiling, she thought of nights ahead, the many long winter nights that made up most of the school year. Closing her eyes, she thought of how, climbing into bed, burrowing beneath her heavy quilt, the one that had been her grandmother's, she would lie there and feel not only the warmth, but also the quilt's weight. In this bed, she would envision the sky beyond the sloping ceiling. There would be stars, a sky full of stars, the *sky-full* that one gets on cold winter nights with no moon, on nights of bitter cold. Lying there, she would come to know and see in her mind that one particular star, Polaris, there above her head. She would, in her mind, see it and it would be as real to her as the weight of the quilt and the warmth beneath it.

"Yes," she said quietly to herself knowing that the bed was where she wanted it and where it should be. With that she opened her eyes and got up.

The other item that Alva wanted to get squared away that evening was the desk. It was a small enough item as desks go, which, with the smallness of the room, was a good thing. It reminded her of those desks that she sat at as a young girl at the parochial school she attended. She didn't mind its smallness. In fact, she was concerned that it wouldn't be small enough to fit where she wanted to place it—in the dormer, which contained the room's only window. Her plan was to situate the desk so that, sitting at it, she could look up from her writing or whatever else she happened to be working on and gaze outside. She pushed the desk towards the dormer, worried that it might be too big. Her relief was palpable when it slid right in with almost an inch to spare on either side. Better still, as she pushed the desk right up to the window, she noticed the top of it matched the height of the windowsill so that the view was not obstructed in any way.

"Perfect," Alva said. "Perfectly, perfectly perfect."

Standing at the desk, Alva took in the view. She was mildly disappointed to find that the window looked out and down upon the roof of the dining hall next door. On the roof, closest to her window were the AC vents and the machinery and exhaust units of the dining hall's kitchen. The view was something definitely less than picturesque. Alva frowned. But then she realized that, with the dining hall being only one story, its roof was considerably beneath her window. Grabbing the room's one chair, she placed it at the desk and sat down. To her delight and relief she could see nothing of the roof of the dining hall. What she saw were the upper limbs and branches of an old oak that grew next to the house. Off in the distance were the lights of the houses along what was known on campus as Fraternity Row. And above all of that there was only sky.

"Perfect," she said again. "Perfectly, perfectly, *perfectly* perfect."

Although there was still much to do in terms of setting up the room, a sense both of satisfaction and completeness came over her and she felt, for the moment, content to just sit there at her desk. Things, she felt, were falling into place. This was it. This was the right place for her. It was where she would return each day – her place, her place where she would study, sleep, and live.

It was also the place where she would write, yes, write, and write well, well and true and with honesty. She would write things that counted, that said something worth saying. And doing so, she would become the person that she wanted to be, the person that she truly felt she was.

"Finally," she said softly as she sat there looking at the leaves of the old oak beyond the panes of glass, the lights across the way, and the night sky. Alva sighed. "Finally."

Chapter 3

Alva's reverie was broken by a knock at her door. It wasn't a loud knock, but it startled her, enough so that, for a moment, all she could do was just sit there, holding her breath. A moment later the knock repeated, this time with more force. Sliding the chair back, Alva got up and went quickly to the door. Outside her door, she found a short, stocky woman standing there. The woman had brown hair that was closely cropped, almost a crew cut. Although not old, Alva thought that she was a couple years beyond being a senior. The woman wore a pair of faded denim cut-offs, and a large, loose sweatshirt of a certain vintage, which Alva thought odd considering how warm it was. From each ear dangled a large gold hoop. She was barefoot. In one hand she held a clipboard, in the other a pencil.

"Hi," the woman said before looking down at the sheet of paper affixed to the clipboard. "Alva?" she asked, looking up and then looking Alva over, "Alva Parsons?"

"Yes."

"Then Alva Parsons it is," the woman said, looking at her clipboard and putting a check mark next to Alva's name. With that she stuck her pencil behind one ear, smiled, and extended a hand.

"Bernie," the woman said as they shook hands. "Bernie Holden. And if you ever call me Bernice, I'll give you a black eye."

"What?" Alva said, startled.

"Just kidding. I'm the RA here."

"RA?"

The woman gave Alva an odd look. "Resident Advisor."

"Oh. Yes. Of course," and then, without knowing why, "I'm Alva."

"Yeah, I got that." The woman looked past Alva. "Still settling in?"

Alva nodded.

"So far so good?"

Alva nodded again.

"Good. Well, let me know if you need anything. You got a fan?"

Alva shook her head.

"You'll want to get one. As you can tell, it gets warm up here. Anyway, my room is on the first floor, used to be the living room. Don't be a stranger."

"Thank you."

Bernie looked past Alva into the room again. "You're going to want to get some curtains too. For your window."

"I'm sorry?"

"That's Fraternity Row over there across the way."

"Yes?"

"Well, you've heard of Galileo, haven't you?"

Alva shrugged. "Sorry?"

"The inventor of the telescope?"

"Sorry?" Alva said again.

The woman rolled her eyes. "This may be 1973 and all, but there are still neanderthals around, especially over there in fratland. Just get some curtains." With that she turned to go. She had only taken a step before she stopped and turned back. "Seen anything of your neighbor?" she asked, gesturing with a nod of her head towards a room across the landing from Alva's, the only other one on the top floor.

Alva shook her head.

The woman smiled. "You don't say much, do you?"

Alva smiled and shrugged.

The woman smiled, shaking her head. "I guess you don't. Well, okay Alva The Silent. Later." And with that she crossed the landing and started down the stairs.

Chapter 4

Alva stepped back through her doorway, and watched as Bernie descended the stairs, her head disappearing beneath the level of the floor. She listened as Bernie's footsteps faded away, and, when she no longer heard them, she turned to head back into her room. Yet, before disappearing, she glanced across the landing to the room across the way, and wondered what her neighbor would be like. She felt tempted to cross the landing and see if the door was unlocked. Then, suddenly shocked that she would even consider doing such a thing, she turned and quickly stepped back into her room, hastily closing the door behind her.

With the door now closed, the warmth in the room seemed even more pronounced than it had earlier, to the point of being oppressive. She stepped across to the desk and placed a hand on it to support herself, then leaned forward and raised the window as far as it would go. It was then that she remembered the RA's comment about getting curtains. She felt herself grow annoyed with the prospect of creating an impediment to the one view, now *her* view, that the room afforded, to say nothing of, especially in this heat, restricting the flow of fresh air. Why, she asked herself, would she want to do that?

"Fraternity Row," she said quietly, looking out over the roof of the dining hall to the fraternity houses beyond. Why had Bernie brought up Galileo? Yes, Alva knew about him, about the Leaning Tower of Pisa and gravity, about the Inquisition. And yes, she knew about him inventing the...

"Telescope," she said, her voice hushed. "The telescope." It finally dawned on her what Bernie had been driving at. As she stood there, this realization sank in so profoundly that she found herself trembling, not so much with fear, but with anger. She felt exposed. It wasn't so much out of a sense of modesty, as it was one of intrusion, of trespass, of trespass into this room that was hers, her room, her place to be and no one else's. The idea, and then the image, of someone unknown peering into her room from 'out there' angered her. The longer she stood there, the angrier she grew.

"No," she said. "No," she said again, making up her mind right then and there to *not* put up curtains, to *not* allow persons unknown to have that kind or any kind of influence here in her room. She would offer them nothing when it came to that, no 'reward' whatsoever for their efforts. And that, she knew, would require no change on her part as to how she went about things. If anyone did indeed spy on her from 'out there,' all they would get for their efforts would be the sight of her at her desk studying, that and nothing else. Eventually, she told herself, they would realize that they were wasting their time. "Yes. Yes, they would. Yes, they will." It was only when she decided that this was how it would be, that Alva's anger abated, and her trembling ceased.

"No," she said quietly, "no curtains."

Alva felt both pleased with and proud of herself. It was a novel experience for her. This was, she felt, right. This was the way she was supposed to be. This was how, she told herself, that she would be from now on.

That feeling of confidence stayed with her for the remainder of the evening as she continued to put her things away and arrange the room to her liking. It was still with her later when she decided that she had done enough for one evening and that it was time for bed.

After first getting her nightgown from the dresser and laying it on the bed, Alva stepped to the wall switch and shut off the light. She had just started to unbutton her blouse when, noticing that the room was not completely dark, she stopped. Glancing towards the window, she saw that the light was entering the room from outside. She stepped up to the dormer and leaned over her desk, then looked out and saw the loading dock for the dining hall below and just off to the right. Near the steps leading up to it there was a dumpster with a compacter attached. The entire area was well illuminated. Seeing this, Alva realized that this was probably as dark as it was ever going to get in her room. Although mildly disappointed, Alva shrugged it off. She stepped back from the window and looked around her room; it was certainly dark enough. With that she once again started to unbutton her blouse.

Folding each item of clothing as she removed it, Alva placed each on her bed. When all that she remained wearing were her panties, she took up her nightgown and was just about to raise her arms to put it on when she suddenly stopped. There before her, in the mirror mounted on the closet door, was her reflection looking back at her.

Even with the room as dark as it was, Alva could see herself there in the glass, but the vision was a modified one owing to the dimness of the room. It was her, but not, to her eye, her as she had ever seen herself. Never happy with her skinniness and the tall, lankiness of her figure, Alva did not make a habit of spending much time before any mirror, but the image reflected now was different. With the semi-darkness, there was something indistinct to the image, something more like an impression than an actual likeness. It was, she thought, almost like looking at a painting, a portrait of her. Absently, she let her hands fall to her sides.

She stood there, entranced by the image in the mirror, and considered the possibility that this was some hidden self, one only seen, like now, under special circumstances, from a new perspective, in a different light. She wondered what it would be like to actually pose in such a manner, to pose in such a manner in front of someone.

Almost simultaneously with this notion, Alva suddenly felt a sharp pang of embarrassment coupled with shame. The feeling became even more acute and took on a heavy dose of guilt when she realized that the idea thrilled her. Panicked, she quickly covered herself with her nightgown, but even with that, she couldn't take her eyes off her reflection.

Standing there, she realized that she was trembling, especially her legs. It felt as if she had no control over them, and that they might collapse beneath her. The trembling increased but her fascination with what she saw before her did so also. It was almost as if she were in a trance, paralyzed by the vision before her.

"Possessed," a voice whispered hoarsely.

Panicking even more Alva looked quickly about the room, drawing her nightgown up to her chin, looking to see who had spoken. It was a moment before she realized that the voice she had heard had been her own.

"Possessed. Yes. Possessed." A wave of guilt washed over her. Quickly she turned away from the mirror and hastily put on her nightgown. Again, there was the guilt. Again, there was the shame, to the extent that tears welled up in her eyes. She was on the point of actually sobbing when the sound of a door being gently closed made her catch her breath and hold it.

Alva stood there listening. The sound came from the other side of her door, either, she thought, from the room across the way or from the small bathroom that the two rooms shared. For several minutes there was nothing, but then she heard a toilet flush. Stepping to her own door, Alva leaned her ear near it. There was the sound of water running into a sink. When that stopped there was a moment of silence followed by the sound of the bathroom door opening. A few moments later she heard the sound of a different door being closed. Alva knew it must be that of the room across the way. After waiting several moments and hearing nothing, Alva carefully and as quietly as she could, opened her door enough to allow her to look out onto the landing.

By a dim light, which later proved to be from a nightlight in the bathroom, Alva could make out the door across the way. A strip of light ran across the bottom of the door. She heard a faint whirring sound coming from the room.

As quietly as she could, Alva stepped out onto the landing. Crossing quickly to the bathroom, she hastily stepped in, carefully closing the door behind her. Since the room was quite small, the nightlight provided enough light to see by, and Alva felt it unnecessary to turn the overhead light on.

Several moments later, emerging from the bathroom, Alva heard again the faint whirring sound from the room across the way. She also noticed that there was no longer a strip of light across the bottom of the door. Alva tiptoed quickly back to her room. Once inside she closed her door behind her as quietly as she could. Turning, she stood with her back resting against the door. A sense of relief came over her, and she stood there, breathing easily and smiling.

But then, as she continued to stand there, she wondered what this sense of relief meant. It didn't take her long to realize and admit to herself that she was relieved not to have had to deal with meeting her neighbor at that moment. With that, a feeling of disappointment came over her. What, she asked herself, was there to be so timid about? This was not the Alva that she wanted to be. This was the rabbit-like trait of hers that, in the past, made her think less of herself. She resolved to make this the last time that she would let herself act this way.

"It's time," she said softly. "It's time."

It was with this thought in mind that she went to bed.

Chapter 5

A resounding clang broke the silence of the following morning. Startled out of her sleep, it felt to Alva like her entire room reverberated with it. So, startled and with a sense of disorientation at waking in an unfamiliar place, she lay there clutching the bedclothes to her chin. A brief moment of silence was followed by the whine of a large engine. So suddenly and severe was this awakening that it was several moments before she was able to sort out where she was and what was going on. Eventually, determining that this was her room, that this was the start of her first full day here, that this was the first morning of many that she would, hopefully with less clamor, be waking up here this coming school year, Alva smiled. She was just settling into a pleasant calm when…

CLANG!

She threw off the bedclothes, and bolted upright. She sat there holding her breath, waiting.

A hissing sound followed that she recognized as one that large trucks and buses sometimes made. Following that there was the rising roar of an engine, one that after a moment started to slowly fade away.

Sliding out of bed, Alva made her way quickly to the dormer.

She placed both hands on the desk to brace herself, and leaned forward to look out the window just in time to see a garbage truck back away from the dumpster near the loading dock below.

A middle-aged black man wearing a white, paper cap and a white short-sleeve shirt was standing on the dock, smoking a cigarette and watching the garbage truck back down the drive.

"Well, hello there, Robert," someone called out.

Alva looked to the left. A young man walked along the alley that ran between the back of the dining hall and the Cottage. His hair was shoulder length and he wore a t-shirt, jeans, and black, high-top sneakers – the kind, Alva remembered, that boys used to refer to as Chuckie T's. The man on the loading dock turned to look at him.

"Well," he said, "if it ain't the prodigal son hisself."

"As prophesied," said the young man as he climbed to the top of the stairs and held out a hand.

"As prophesied," Robert repeated skeptically as they shook hands.

"As expected then," said the young man.

"As expected," Robert repeated even more skeptically. "I'd know better than to ever *expect* you on any day at any time."

Alva saw the young man nod his head and smile. "Okay. Yeah, okay. So, anyway, how're you doing?"

Robert inhaled on his cigarette. "Fine," he said, slowly exhaling a small cloud of smoke. "Like old man river. Just rollin' along."

"Good summer?"

Robert looked down the drive. The garbage truck had backed into the street and was pulling away. "Not bad. They kept us open right through it." He looked at the young man. "So," he said, "you working this morning or what?"

"I'm not scheduled. Just thought I'd stop by and see if anything was going on, if there was anything to do."

"Anything to do," Robert repeated. "Of course, there is. There always is. Plenty."

"Business as usual."

"Business as usual," Robert repeated, proceeding to take another drag on his cigarette. "Mrs. Patel was already asking if anyone had seen you."

"She was? How nice."

"Hmpf. Go figure."

"Well, Robert, that just goes to show that when you're good, you're good. You know how it is."

"Yeah," Robert said sarcastically. "That's if you show up on time, which is rare. Hell, that is if you show up at all."

"Well, I'm here now. Maybe this will be the start of something. A new me. You never know."

"A new you", Robert repeated doubtfully. "Yeah, well, we'll see how that goes. To be on the safe side, I'll just keep my expectations low." With that he dropped his cigarette, stepped on it and kicked it off the loading dock. "Let's get to work."

"I'm right behind you."

Alva watched them both go inside.

Although she hadn't gotten a very good look at him, there was something about the young man, particularly his voice and manner that seemed familiar, something that she was sure that she recognized. Standing there, still leaning over the desk, still looking out the window, she tried to place him, but couldn't.

Her reverie was broken by the sound of a toilet flushing.

Turning back from the dormer, Alva tiptoed to her door and stood there listening. A moment later she heard the bathroom door open. This was followed by the sound of someone stepping hurriedly across the landing and down the stairs. She glanced over at her alarm clock. It was only half past six. She wondered, since registration didn't start until nine, why anyone would be up already and heading out at this hour.

The sound of the footsteps faded away to nothing. For a moment there was silence, and then Alva heard, somewhere below, the sound of a door closing. Cautiously, Alva opened her door and looked out. Seeing no one around, Alva took a step out onto the landing. To her surprise, Alva saw that the door to the room across the way was open and that the interior was dark. Like the evening before, Alva felt drawn by curiosity to the room across the way. With the door open, her curiosity was even stronger than the night before. This time she was unable to shake off the allure of taking a look inside, and found herself gliding across the landing towards the other room.

Alva knew that this was wrong. She knew that what she was doing was an intrusion, a trespass, but, as strongly as she felt this, she felt drawn on. The open door was just too great a temptation. She didn't hesitate; she didn't stop until she got to the door.

In case someone might still be inside, Alva stood back a step and to one side. Leaning her head around the jamb, she looked in. She was relieved to find no one there. It seemed odd to her that the room's occupant had left the door open. Alva took a step into the room and stood there looking it over.

Although she hadn't approached the room with any notion of what she expected to find, it was with some disappointment that she found nothing inside of any particular interest. Like her room, there was a bed, a desk, a chair, a dresser, a small table next to the bed, and, like her room, there was a dormer. It was all, she found, spectacularly ordinary. It was nice, but it was just a room.

Only two things caught her eye as being different from the way her own room was furnished. One was the fan in the window, which explained the whirring noise that she had heard the previous evening. The other was a small, cushioned chair set at an angle in the dormer. That was it. Nothing exciting. Yes, Alva was disappointed. Disappointed and even annoyed that this *trespass* yielded nothing notable.

Then, like the evening before, a sense of guilt came over her. Standing there, she once again felt ashamed of herself. Along with this there was anger. She was angry with herself for yielding this time to the temptation to trespass. More than that, she was angry with herself for not doing right by her resolve of the evening before to be better, to do better, to start being the person that she knew she should be. "What's wrong with you?" she chastised herself. "You've got to do better. You've got to."

Turning, she walked back slowly to her room.

Chapter 6

Because each year her parents had always insisted that she take the maximum number of courses allowed per semester in order to *'get your* (meaning 'their') *money's worth,'* Alva, now a senior, was far enough along in the number of credits earned to graduate. As far as her major, religion, and minor, English, were concerned, all she needed was to take an elective in each in the two semesters that remained. Also, since she had been able to preregister for her courses the previous spring, she didn't need to go through the usual registration rigors this fall. With registration taking two days and classes not starting until the following Tuesday, Alva had what amounted to a four-day weekend ahead of her. She was grateful for this, as there were a couple items that she wished to attend to before the semester got underway.

One item on her agenda was to put the finishing touches on two poems that she had been working on over the summer, poems that she intended to submit for admittance to a creative writing course that was being given that fall by the university's 'Poet In Residence,' Edmund Phillips.

Applying for a slot in one of his courses had become a matter of persistence on her part. Not being an English major, she was not eligible for acceptance in the creative writing program. The only opportunity possible for her to take any of the courses offered in the program depended on there being a slot open at the beginning of any given semester. Even then, open slots went to English majors first. Beyond that, one had to submit examples of one's written work for evaluation. Except for a preliminary poetry writing course open to all students in their sophomore year, she had not been able to take another, despite submitting samples of her work every semester.

The previous spring, after hearing that Mr. Phillips would be back this fall from sabbatical, she had selected two of her poems, two that she had the most confidence in, and mailed them directly to him along with a letter in which she wrote that they were attempts on her part at developing her 'voice,' her 'Southern' voice, in her work – something she hoped to pursue that fall within the parameters of the creative writing program at the university, namely… as a student of his.

This was, she knew, not without some guile on her part as, after doing some background research about him and his work, she had come across an essay of his in a literary journal in which he stated how important his own New England voice was to his work. She dismissed any qualms she may have felt in being cagey, reasoning that she had written the truth, that her 'voice' was an important aspect of her writing, one, she felt, made it unique and, as she noted in her letter, 'necessary in order to insure her work's honesty.' If she felt any unease, it was the thought that he would see through this *transparency*. But, after two years of rejection and with time running out, she felt both desperate and that she had nothing to lose by writing to him. So, she sent the letter along with the poems, and waited and prayed.

Three weeks passed with, despite her prayers, no response and Alva had given up all hope of receiving a reply when one morning a letter postmarked Stonington, Maine arrived. Her hands were trembling as she opened the envelope with an overpowering mix of hope and dread.

Ms. Parsons,

I'm writing to let you know that I did receive your letter and poems.

As I'm sure you are aware by this time that the creative writing courses at the university are highly competitive and, unfortunately, admissions to them are limited. I'm sorry to say that all available slots for the fall semester have been filled.

Having read your poems I would agree with your assessment that your 'voice' is an important aspect of your writing, as it well should be. I would encourage you to continue to be conscious of it as you write.

I would also encourage you to keep writing. Obviously, you have something to say (one of the marks of good writing), and that you strive for honesty in what you write (excellent, keep a good hold on that). Do not be discouraged. Admission to the courses is mostly a question of numbers and not in any way a final comment on the value of your work.

With that said, please stop by my office sometime during the semester, as I would be interested to see what progress you are making with your writing.

Sincerely,

Edmund Phillips

Although disappointed at being *rejected* yet again, the fact that Mr. Phillips had responded at all made the disappointment less harsh. Also, when she considered that he had actually taken the time to read her poems, and had even suggested meeting her this fall, she found herself excited, to the point that her hands continued to tremble even as she read the letter a second and third time. As rejection letters went, she reasoned, this one wasn't that bad at all.

During the remainder of the summer Alva continued to work on the two poems she had sent to Mr. Phillips; revising, tweaking, even doing complete rewrites. The letter from him had given her momentum, and any time that it showed any signs of lagging, she would take the letter out and read it again. With that, her impetus would be restored. She would remind herself that this letter was from a noted poet, someone who had been in his own college career a student of Robert Frost, and that, come this fall, she would be sitting down with him to discuss not just poetry, but her poetry.

Still, along with all of that there was an element of doubt. She worried that her *persistence* after so many rejections might be viewed as obsessive. She worried that maybe this was actually the case, and, worse, that her persistence was not warranted by anything that she had written or was even capable of writing. She worried that, rather than an assessment of what talent she may or may not possess, Mr. Phillips's letter was just an act of kindness on his part, a gentle *letting down*. Beyond all of that, she worried that all of this worrying was a symptom of some internal neurosis of hers.

"You're doing it again," she would say to herself when this worrying jag would come upon her. She would remind herself that all that worrying didn't matter, that what mattered was that this fall she would have the opportunity to meet with Mr. Phillips and discuss her writing, and that it was an opportunity not to be undervalued and certainly not to be missed.

Another item on her agenda that morning had to do with getting a job. She wanted to find work, a part time job, so that she could earn some money, some money that was actually hers. It wasn't that she was in dire financial straits or that some major expense loomed on the horizon. She wasn't and there wasn't. For one, her parents kept a close eye on her checking account never letting the amount in it fall beneath a certain level, and, she admitted to herself, it was a comfortable level at that. But this, to her way of thinking, was *their* money, and she wanted to earn *her* money, money that was *unsupervised*, money that she could control and spend as she saw fit without having to account for it to anyone – 'anyone' meaning her parents. Over the last three years any time she made any purchase that didn't come under the heading of daily necessities or of being school related, they would *mention* it the next time that they called or wrote. What she wanted was just to have the means to shop without feeling that someone was looking over her shoulder.

This idea of having a job and earning money appealed to her on another level as well. She could finally lead a life of her own, and, by doing so, redefine her life, redefine how she was perceived not only by others, but by herself. This was even more important to her than the money aspect of it.

This was, she knew, also something that it wouldn't do to bring up with her parents, knowing full well what their response would be. They would forbid it, informing her, in no uncertain terms, that it was unnecessary, that her financial needs were provided for, and that she was there at the university to study and only to study. Alva knew that any argument of hers to the contrary would be futile. She even admitted to herself that, from a practical standpoint, their position was not entirely devoid of merit.

Still, Alva reminded herself that she had always done well with a full course load, making the Dean's List each of the previous six semesters, well enough to not only satisfy her parents but to actually earn their praise. She felt confident that, with this semester's lighter course load, she would have no problem at all managing a part time job and that this decision to seek employment was a good one as well as hers to make. But, she reminded herself, the less said about the matter to her parents, the better.

There was, Alva knew, a bulletin board at the student center that listed, along with apartment rentals, roommate opportunities, and ride shares, employment opportunities both on campus and off. She also knew that the financial aid office kept a list of campus job opportunities. Both were near the Hall Of English where Mr. Phillips had his office. Her plan was to stop in there while she made her rounds and see when his office hours were.

With a sense of purpose, ready to *get things done*, Alva put on a skirt, a white blouse, and her sensible shoes and started out, her first stop being the dining hall next door for a quick breakfast.

Chapter 7

If it was nothing else, the dining hall was "well-windowed". With the exception of the kitchen area in the back, the walls were glass, floor to ceiling. Because of this Alva could see the entire interior of the dining area as she approached the entrance. What struck her first was how empty it seemed – a vast, open area of rows of tables and chairs. Its emptiness led her to believe that the dining hall was closed. Coming up to the outer set of double glass doors, she half expected to find them locked. She was pleased and relieved when, taking one of the door handles and giving it a pull, the door opened. It was then that she noticed an older woman standing at a small table just inside the inner set of double doors. The woman was wearing a neat, modest dress with a subdued floral pattern. The woman, noticing Alva's approach, pushed one of the inner doors open for her.

Alva smiled and stepped in. "Thank you," she said, walking past the woman.

"ID please", the woman said in a peremptory tone

"Oh," Alva said, startled. She stopped immediately. It took her a moment of fumbling through her purse before she found her student ID and handed it to the woman. Tilting her head back in order to look through the bottom portion of her glasses, the woman examined the card carefully before handing it back to Alva.

"You'll need to take that over to food services," the woman said brusquely. "You need to get it stamped." Seeing the confused look on Alva's face, the woman went on. "You've signed up for a meal plan, haven't you?"

This was all new to Alva. "No. No, I haven't. Not yet. But I guess I will."

"I guess you'll have to if you expect to eat here, dearie."

Alva nodded. "Yes, of course. Thank you." With that she turned to go.

"Hold on, darling," the woman said laying a hand on Alva's arm.

"Ma'am?"

"Ma'am," the woman repeated, surprised, but also, as Alva could tell from her smile, pleased. "You can go on in this time sweetheart and have your breakfast. Just attend to that stamp and do it right away."

"Yes, ma'am. Thank you."

The woman shook her head. "You know, normally I'd give a person a swift kick for that."

"Ma'am?"

"Exactly. For that. That 'ma'am' stuff."

"I'm sorry, I…"

"That's okay, honey. That's quite all right. It fits right in with that lovely touch of an accent of yours."

"Yes, ma'am."

"Exactly. Now go have your breakfast before they close the hot line."

Glancing about the dining hall as she made her way to the serving area, Alva saw that there were actually a handful of diners present. Since they were spread out among the tables, which far outnumbered them, the place seemed emptier to Alva than if there had been no one there at all.

Eager to get going on her tasks for the day, Alva opted for a quick meal of shredded wheat and orange juice. She placed the items on a tray, and made her way to a far corner of the dining hall, to a small table for two that was situated next to one of the windows. After setting her tray on the table and draping her purse over the back of her chair, Alva sat down. As she poured milk onto her shredded wheat, she glanced up.

Along the same window, a couple tables away, a young man and woman were seated. The young woman, who sat with her back to Alva, was wearing a light pink smock, and had her hair tied up in a blue bandana. The young man sitting across from her had on a white, short-sleeve shirt, like the one worn by the man, Robert, she had seen on the loading dock earlier that morning. Alva noticed a white paper hat, again, like Robert's, on the table next to the young man's tray. Because he had his hair pulled back into a ponytail, Alva couldn't be sure, but she thought that he was the same young man that she had seen earlier that morning. She looked down, and noticed that he wore black, high-top sneakers; she knew that it must be him. Again, like earlier that morning, Alva thought she recognized him from somewhere.

The young woman sat straight up, her hands folded around a white coffee cup. The young man had his chair pushed back. He sat at a slight angle to the table, slouching, with his legs stretched out straight in front of him and slightly in the aisle. His ankles were crossed. His hands were in his pockets. He was doing most

31

of the talking. For the most part, the young woman sat there, listening, nodding her head occasionally.

As she ate her cereal, it occurred to Alva that they were probably both students. It was then that she first considered the possibility of getting a job there at the dining hall. Certainly, its proximity to where she lived would be ideal. That in itself was a major selling point. She wondered what tasks were involved in working there. She felt sure that she could handle something simple like washing dishes or any other type of cleaning chore, and maybe even serving food. Anything more complicated, like cooking itself, would be a stretch for her in terms of experience. Not that she felt that she couldn't learn, Alva told herself, but she doubted that they would want to take the time to train anyone for a part-time and temporary cooking position.

Considering this, she glanced over at the couple from time to time as she ate. It occurred to Alva that she should just go over ask them what a job working in the dining hall entailed. They, of course, would know. Yes, she told herself, she could just get up and walk over and smile, and, with an 'excuse me…' introduce herself, and with an 'I was wondering…' get right to the point and find out what's what with working there. But then, as she continued to sit there, she knew that she couldn't, that she couldn't *just* walk over to people she didn't know and intrude like that. She had never been able to just go up cold like that to people she didn't know, not ever.

Suddenly, with a spoonful of shredded wheat poised over her bowl, Alva felt extremely annoyed with herself. Of course, she could do it, she told herself. She could and should do it because it was something that a person, anybody, could and should be able to do. More to the point, it was the kind of thing that the person that she wanted to be, had made her mind up to be, could and should be able to do. They were just people, she told herself. They were just students like herself. "Do it," she said under her breath and set her spoon in the bowl. "Just do it, for crying out loud. Just get up and do it."

"Yes," she said, pushing back her chair.

And she might have actually done it except that, just as she was about to stand up and go over, the couple got up to go.

Alva sat there watching them as the young man put on his paper hat and he and the young woman picked up their trays. Alva sat there as the young man allowed the young woman to go ahead of him and the two of them started towards the kitchen area at the back of the dining hall.

Alva sat there watching them go. Then, slowly, pulling her chair back up to the table, she picked up her spoon. But instead of eating, she just sat there. She sat there feeling annoyed, annoyed about the opportunity missed, annoyed with herself. When she finally ate her spoonful of shredded wheat, it was soggy. This annoyed her too. Everything annoyed her.

Once breakfast was over and she was on her way, Alva felt better again. Although not without some trepidation, she found herself looking forward to the tasks ahead. She reminded herself that, even though she hadn't connected with the couple in the dining hall, she *HAD* made up her mind to do so and would have done so had they not chosen to get up and leave when they did. This, she told herself, was a step forward for her. A definite step forward, and this pleased her. It pleased her very much. She felt that from that point on, the morning would go well, or, at least, well enough.

Chapter 8

Her first stop was the job board at the Student Union, the school's student center. There wasn't much posted: some high school tutoring assignments, some typing. Alva felt capable of doing both, but neither option appealed to her. Since breakfast, since watching the couple there at the dining hall, she had been thinking about how, because they worked together, they were also '*connected*,' connected enough to have breakfast together. That notion appealed to her. Now, finding a job had taken on an added dimension. Now, it wasn't solely a matter of making extra money. Now, she wanted to find something that would involve her with other people. Alva thought of this as she stood there surveying the postings on the board.

"Not much yet."

Startled, Alva turned to find a young woman standing next to her.

She was on the short side, the kind of short that always made Alva conscious of her own height, which was a few inches shy of six feet. The young woman was also a touch on what Alva's mother would have referred to as the *full-figured* size. In comparison, Alva knew she must look both scrawny and gangly.

The young woman had long, straight brown hair parted off to one side. A pair of aviator style glasses prevented her hair from covering her eyes. She wore bellbottoms, the fabric a paisley pattern in muted yellows and oranges. Her top was a short-sleeve, beige, knit affair with three small buttons descending from the collar.

"Will there be more later?" Alva asked.

"Oh sure," the young woman said, turning towards her. "This time next week it'll be full. Big time. There's not much point committing to anything, not before your schedule is set."

Being pre-registered for her courses, Alva knew that this wasn't an issue for her, but she saw no need to say so. "Do they post dining hall jobs?"

"You want to work in the dining hall?" Alva couldn't tell if it was just a question or if the young woman was thinking along the lines of 'why would you, why would anyone.'

"I was thinking about it."

The young woman shrugged. "I think you have to go through food services for that, or maybe financial aid. I got a friend where I live that does that, but I think she's on work study."

Alva nodded. "Well… thank you."

"Sure thing. Good luck."

With that the young woman turned and strode off.

Alva stood there watching her go, thinking how it would be good to be like that, to know what's what about things, to be, not just intelligent, but experienced and smart, smart enough to be able to pass things along to others with confidence, with ease. She even felt a bit envious of the young woman. The notion of someone viewing her in a similar light was not an unpleasant one.

Yes, she thought to herself, working would be a good thing, *will* be a good thing. Her parents just didn't realize that. That's all.

"Food services," she said to herself, and to food services she went.

Chapter 9

After getting her student ID stamped for dining hall access, Alva asked the woman manning the front desk about job opportunities. She was told that, aside from those for returning students and new students on financial aid, they wouldn't know what openings there might be, or where, there being several dining halls on campus, until later the following week at the earliest.

"You might want to check in with financial services," the woman behind the desk suggested. "There are other types of jobs available, like library work, or..." the woman looked Alva over and smiled skeptically, "or, maybe, on the ground's crew."

Alva thanked her. Even though she hadn't, for the time being, come up with anything, Alva felt that just going through this process had given her momentum, with that she marched right over to financial aid. Although they had nothing there at the moment, they took her name and contact information.

"There's always work, honey," the woman there told her. "You can expect to hear from us in a week or so."

Again, nothing definite had come about, but, again, Alva felt that she was making progress.

Chapter 10

Unfortunately, it didn't last. Walking back to the Cottage, the old, innate insecurity of hers came back, leaving her feeling disappointed and frustrated. It almost seemed as if things were conspiring against her just as she was on the verge of finally making her own way at last. A sense of the impossibility of it all descended upon her, a sense of hopelessness, of helplessness. She found herself seriously considering that maybe she should be back with her aunt and uncle and go on being just a student.

"No," she said, loud enough to actually startle herself. Quickly she looked around and was relieved to find that there was no one within earshot. "No," she said quietly, "you can do this. You are doing this. You *have* to do this."

Turning the corner by the dining hall, she saw the Cottage up ahead. Noting the dormer of her room, she stopped to look up at it. She took a deep breath, and let it out slowly, savoring the moment. Suddenly and more so than ever before, she felt that she was indeed on her way, her own way. There would be no turning back, she told herself, no matter what. She would do what she had to do.

"Yes, you can," she said to herself. "Yes… you… can."

And with that she continued.

Climbing the front stairs, she crossed to the front door, opened it and went in. She was just about to start up the stairs to the second floor when…

"Hey you!"

Startled by being accosted so, Alva stopped suddenly and looked up. Above her, on the top step, a young woman sat holding a book open in her hands. With the light behind her, the young woman was in silhouette, and Alva could not make out anything of her features.

"You again," the young woman said, closing her book.

"Hello?" Alva said tentatively.

"Hello yourself." The young woman stood up and took a step back. "C'mon up."

It was then that Alva recognized the young woman as being the same one that she had met earlier at the Student Union.

"Oh," Alva said, starting up the stairs. "I couldn't tell it was you, with the light behind you."

"You live here?" the young woman asked as Alva reached the landing.

Alva nodded. "On the top floor."

"Oh. You're up there with Sandra," the young woman said, surprised. "Lucky you."

Not being sure whether the young woman was being serious or sarcastic, Alva just shrugged.

"You haven't met her yet?"

Alva shook her head. "No. Not yet."

"Well, that's not surprising. She isn't here all that much. Talk about conscientious. That's her middle name. If she's not working at the dining hall next door, she's at the library studying, and if she's not there, she's student teaching or tutoring or doing something with old folks. Hey!" She went on, suddenly brightening, "She's the one I was telling you about earlier, about dining hall work and all. You'll like her. She's aces. Tall and skinny like you. On the quiet side, too. At least not a motor mouth like me. By the way, I'm Lily, Lily Miel."

"Alva. Alva Parsons."

"Alva," Lily repeated. "You don't run into that one much nowadays."

"No, I guess not."

"Southern, right?"

Alva nodded.

"I could hear a trace of that in your voice. Different."

"I guess so."

"Hey, don't mind me. It's cool. Real cool. What's your major?"

"Religion."

"Religion?" Lily repeated. "Well, that's different. I took a religion course one semester. The Gospels. Can you believe that? I only did it to fulfill a freshman requirement. It was pretty good though. It was taught by the department head."

"My uncle."

"What's that?"

"My uncle is the head of the religion department."

"No shit."

Slightly taken aback by the obscenity, Alva blinked.

"Well," Lily went on, "good thing I said it was good, huh. I'm pretty prone to foot in mouth disease. So, what's your minor?"

"English. Poetry."

"Ouch. I mean, talk about a double whammy. Religion and

poetry. Not much of a buck in either of those rackets."

"I guess not."

"Hey, don't pay any attention to me. What do I know? I'm poli-sci and psych. Like where am I going with those two, huh, unless I do a tsunami amount of grad work. Anyway, like I said, don't pay attention to me. Nobody does around here. Like, what do I know?"

"With political science you could go to law school."

Lily started. And then she smiled. "Wow."

"Wow what?"

"Most people... I usually have to explain that to people. I'm impressed. Usually when I tell people my major is poli-sci they react like... well, like I did with you and your English and religion thing. You'd think I'd know better, huh."

Alva shrugged. "It's okay."

"Anyway, Alva Parsons. Welcome on board."

"Thank you."

"And let's go see if Sandra is in so I can introduce you."

"Sure."

Chapter 11

"Hey Sandra," Lily called out as they reached the landing on the top floor. "You decent?" Lily turned to Alva. "Yeah like anyone around here cares about that."

Alva's eyes went wide at the comment, but Lily, who was already headed across the landing, didn't notice.

"Hey Sandra," Lily repeated, knocking on the door, which was open, and entering at the same time. "Meet your new neighbor."

Alva hesitated and paused before entering.

"C'mon in," Lily said to her. "Don't be shy."

Alva entered the room. A young woman was seated at the desk writing, her back towards Alva and Lily. Putting down her pen, she turned towards them.

"Sandra, Alva. Alva, Sandra," Lily said by way of an introduction.

Alva recognized her immediately as the young woman that she had seen that morning at the dining hall, the one in the pink smock having breakfast with the young man in the high-top sneakers.

Getting up, Sandra came over to where Alva and Lily stood. "Hi," she said, holding out a hand.

"Hi."

They shook hands.

"Alva wants to work in the dining hall."

Sandra gave Alva a questioning look.

"I'm looking for work, something part-time," Alva said.

"They got any openings?" Lily asked.

Sandra shrugged. "Probably not at the moment. But they will."

Alva nodded. "That's what they told me at food services."

"You might want to check back with them next week."

"I will. Thank you."

"Do you think they're gonna take that Jerry guy back this year?" Lily asked.

"Kerry," Sandra corrected.

"Jerry. Kerry." Lily shrugged. "Whatever."

"He was there this morning."

"The first day? Really? Wow. And on time?"

"I think so."

"Wow. He must have had a sober night for a change." Lily turned to Alva. "The guy gets away with murder. Always late if he shows up at all." She turned back to Sandra. "Right?"

"Not always," Sandra said quietly.

"Not always," Lily repeated. "Often enough. More often than not. And usually with a hangover." She turned to Alva. "It's like the guy can do no wrong with 'what's her name' that manages the place. He probably screws her in the back storeroom."

Alva could feel her face flush vividly. She saw Sandra frown and shake her head slightly.

"Or something," Lily went on, turning to Alva. "And this woman," here she gestured towards Sandra, "this woman is a study in patience and tolerance. Didn't I tell you she was aces? Anyway, I've got laundry in the dryer," she said brusquely.

"Laundry?" Sandra repeated. "Already?"

"Came in straight from the mountains."

Sandra nodded.

"Well," Lily said, "I'll see you two later." With that she turned to go. Alva, who had been standing in the doorway, took a step back to let her by. "Aces," Lily whispered as she went past. "Absolutely aces."

Alva watched as Lily crossed the landing and started down the stairs. Once she was out of sight, she turned to Sandra.

"She's something," Sandra said softly.

Alva nodded.

"Come in," said Sandra. "Come in and have a seat," she said, gesturing towards the cushioned chair in the dormer.

"Thank you. But I don't want to interrupt your writing."

"Oh," Sandra said. "It's just a letter. It can wait. Come in."

"Thanks. But I really should go. I've got some things I need to attend to."

This wasn't true, and Alva immediately regretted having said it.

"Okay," Sandra said with a friendly smile. "Later then."

"Sure," Alva said, feeling guilty, feeling really guilty as there was, she felt, something real... something real and nice, genuinely nice about Sandra. It was, Alva felt, stupid, so stupid, on her part not to respond in kind and worse to lie.

"Well, I won't keep you," Sandra said. "And welcome to the Cottage, Alva."

"Thank you."

They shook hands again.

"Stop by when you can," Sandra said, "so we can get

acquainted."

"I will. I will definitely do that."

"Good."

Turning, Alva left the room. She had only gone a few steps when...

"Hey Alva," Sandra called after her. Alva stopped and turned back. "I've got a fan in the window here. If you'd like, you can leave your door open to get a cross breeze going. It can get pretty stuffy up here when it's warm. If I'm not around, just come in and turn it on. It does help."

"Thanks. That would be great."

"Sure thing. See you." With that Sandra turned and went back in.

Chapter 12

Back in her room, Alva quietly closed the door. As guilty as she had felt, she felt even more guilty now with Sandra being so considerate about the fan and all, guilty and also angry with herself for not being more open to things. She could justify some reluctance on her part as far as Lily was concerned. In her assessment, she was, well, *different.* But with Sandra, even admitting that it was very much just a first impression, Alva was convinced that she was someone easy to be with and worth knowing. What could her reluctance to accept Sandra's invitation to just come in and sit be indicative of other than her own inability to open up and be comfortable with others. Here, again, an opportunity had presented itself in which she could work to overcome some of that, and once again she had failed to make something of it. She was left feeling angry and disappointed with herself.

And what was she to do now, hide out in her room, or leave with no idea of a destination just for appearances sake? All this *drama* she thought, and just because she panicked and for no justifiable reason at all. She could feel herself getting all worked up about it when, glancing at her desk, she noticed the sheets of her poetry lying there. Seeing them, she realized that she had forgotten to stop by Mr. Phillips's office to see when his office hours would be this semester.

After what had just transpired, she felt a palpable sense of relief that she had forgotten about this errand as it now provided her with a means to graciously and honestly get through the current situation. Honestly? No, she admitted to herself, not honestly. Yes, she had been dishonest. She couldn't deny that, and wouldn't. But now she felt that she would do better the next time. Certainly, she felt she would try.

"Yes," she said to herself. "Yes."

With that, she gathered up the two poems she had been working on and slid them into a notebook. Picking up her purse, she headed out, back to campus, her destination the Hall Of English. Key in hand, she closed her door and was on the point of locking it when, remembering Sandra and her fan and the cross breeze, she stopped. "No," she said to herself. She put the key back in her purse, and pushed the door gently until it was open completely. Feeling better, she turned and headed down the stairs.

Chapter 13

Erected in the latter part of the 19th century, the Hall Of English was the oldest building on campus. An imposing three-story structure, it was made up mostly of large granite blocks. Because of this, the building managed to stay somewhat cool, even on warmest of days. This was especially true of the basement level where there was a small lounge, a couple of small classrooms, and a handful of faculty offices including Mr. Phillips's.

Alva was jotting down the hours in her notebook when she suddenly became aware of voices on the other side of the door. Possibly owing to the door being an old and substantial one, or to those on the other side speaking in low voices, or to a combination of both, she couldn't make out what they were saying, but she did note an occasional round of laughter.

Closing her notebook and returning her pen to her purse, she was just about to turn and leave when it occurred to her that there was no reason why she couldn't interrupt for just a moment to introduce herself and maybe set up a time that she could meet with Mr. Phillips, or, if nothing else, to drop off the two poems that she had with her. Normally she would never consider intruding in such a manner, far from it, but there was something about the laughter beyond the door that sounded friendly and relaxed.

"Just do it," she told herself. "Just do it before you change your mind and talk yourself out of it."

She knocked softly three times. As soon as she did so, everything went quiet on the other side of the door. When the silence persisted, she hesitated and just stood where she was fighting off an urge to turn and walk quickly away.

"Don't," she told herself. "Don't." And with that she knocked again, this time a little harder.

"Come in. Come in. Come in," a welcoming voice called from the other side of the door.

Alva turned the doorknob, and slowly pushed the door open. When it was open wide enough, she poked her head in and found a group of four people standing in the middle of the room, looking her way. Three of them, one young woman and two young men, were obviously students.

The fourth was a tall, middle-aged man with thinning hair and wire rim glasses. He was tall and with a solid build. He looked, Alva thought, like someone who cut and split his own firewood. From a photograph that she had seen of him in a poetry journal, she knew that he was Edmund Phillips.

"Don't be shy," Mr. Phillips said with a warm smile. "Please, come in."

Stepping into the room, Alva closed the door behind her and stood still.

"I'm sorry to interrupt."

"Not at all," Mr. Phillips said, separating himself from the others and coming towards her. "Come in. Come in."

"It's not important. I can come later. I really don't want to interrupt."

Mr. Phillips stopped and stood for a moment, looking at her. He smiled. "Ms. Parsons?" he asked.

Alva nodded.

"I can hear that slight touch of southern in your *voice*. It's what I would have expected from your poems." He turned to the others. "This is Alva Parsons, a fellow poet." The others nodded and smiled. "Alas," Mr. Phillips went on, "a fellow poet who, unfortunately, is not an English major." The smiles turned to frowns of commiseration. He turned back to Alva and pointed at her notebook. "More poems?"

Alva nodded, but then quickly shook her head. "No. Rewrites. Rewrites of what I've already sent you."

"Rewrites," Mr. Phillips repeated thoughtfully. "I'm surprised. The ones you sent my way seemed complete already. Now you've piqued my curiosity." He pointed again to Alva's notebook. "Can you leave them with me? I'd interested to see what kind of changes you felt were necessary."

Alva removed the two updated poems from her notebook and handed them to Mr. Phillips. "They're copies. You don't need to return them."

Taking them, Mr. Phillips glanced at them quickly and noticed that they were handwritten. "They're not typed."

"Oh. I'm sorry. I should have typed them."

"Not at all. But I do think, since they are in your own hand, that you should have them back, for posterity's sake. Rule number one, always hold on to your originals." He looked at her with a serious expression. "I'll make sure that these and their previous *incarnations* get back to you unharmed, that is if you're comfortable leaving them with me."

Alva nodded vigorously. "Oh yes. That would be fine."

Mr. Phillips smiled. "Good. But I must tell you that I'll only be on campus two days each week this semester. As I think you might know, I was on sabbatical last semester and now the 'publish or perish' Philistines are on my trail for some sort of *finished product*. So, it may be a while, maybe not until the end of the semester, before I can get them back to you. Again, if you're not comfortable with that, just say so."

"No. No, that's fine. Really."

Mr. Phillips nodded. "Thank you." He held up the poems. "And thank you for stopping by. It was a very nice *interruption*." They shook hands.

Chapter 14

Once outside of Mr. Phillips's office, Alva decided to leave through one of the rear exits that led out onto the quad. Pushing open the heavy wooden door and stepping out of the building's cool interior, she was immediately made aware of just how warm a day it was. She knew that it would only be warmer back in her top floor room; she stopped for a moment on the steps to consider her options.

Although everywhere else on campus was bustling with students moving in for the year, the quad was empty, and it occurred to her that, if she could find a shady spot, it would be nice to spend the remainder of the afternoon there. Looking about, her gaze fell on the university chapel building, the main stairs of which, facing east, were now in the shade.

"Perfect," she said to herself as she started off in that direction. She climbed to the top step, and situated herself with one of the columns as back support. Finally, she took out a pen and opened her notebook, turning to a blank page with the intention of starting a new poem. With nothing coming to her right away, Alva felt a sense of frustration settle in. After ten minutes or so of this, the hardness of the step on which she sat became both noticeable and impossible to ignore. Also, even though in the shade, it was still very warm where she sat. Alva started to think about finding someplace cooler and with more comfortable seating. The only idea she came up with was the main library, and she wondered, with classes not having started yet, if it would be open. Since, with only a slight detour, it was on the way back to the Cottage, she decided to walk over that way and find out.

On the way there it occurred to Alva that it might be worth her while to better familiarize herself with the work of Mr. Phillips and that this would be a good opportunity to do so.

As she approached the library, things did not look all that promising; no one was in the immediate area. Seeing as she had come this far anyway, she went up to the main entrance and, trying the door, was both pleased and relieved to find it unlocked. Stepping inside, she was even more pleased and more relieved to find that the air conditioning was on.

With the exception of a security guard reading a newspaper at the entrance and a young woman at the main desk, the place was empty. The guard looked up from his paper as she approached. Even seated behind his desk, Alva could tell that he was a large young man, like he might be on the varsity football team.

"Are you open?" she asked.

"No," he said with a smile that had something of a smirk to it. "Someone lost the keys and we can't lock the doors. So, I have to sit here until they turn up."

"Oh," Alva said, startled.

"I'm kidding. We're open until eight."

"Thank you."

Since she was well acquainted with the library and its layout, Alva had no trouble finding the poetry section. As the poet in residence at the university, she was not surprised to find several volumes of Mr. Phillips's poetry there, including a sizeable anthology. Selecting the anthology, Alva made her way to a cushioned chair in a quiet, out of the way corner, expecting to spend the remainder of the afternoon there. Making herself comfortable, she opened the anthology and started to slowly leaf through its pages.

As she sat there a calm came over her. After all the stimulation of the day, it felt good to just sit and not have to deal with anything or anybody. With that and the quiet and stillness of the library, her calm slipped into a languor. Letting her head lie back, Alva closed her eyes and just sat there relishing the silence, the coolness of the air, the tranquility of the moment.

"Excuse me," a voice said quietly.

Alva stirred.

"Hey. Sleeping Beauty."

Alva started, her eyes snapping open. Looming over her, the guard from the front door smiled. From where she sat, he looked like a giant.

"The library will be closing in fifteen minutes."

"Oh," Alva said, sitting up quickly. For a brief moment she sat there, and then she hastily gathered up her things. "I fell asleep. Sorry."

"Not a problem." He gestured towards the anthology of poems that she held. "Must be a real page turner."

Alva shrugged, smiling weakly as she stood up.

"If you're not checking that out, just leave it at the front desk. They prefer to have the staff re-shelve items."

"Yes. Of course."

"Take your time. You have fifteen minutes."

Alva nodded and made something of a smile. "Thank you."

"Have a good evening, Sleeping Beauty." With that the guard turned and continued on his rounds.

The main desk was unmanned when Alva got there. Leaving the book, she headed for the main entrance. The young woman who had been at the main desk was now seated at the guard's station reading the school paper. She looked up and smiled as Alva approached.

"I fell asleep," Alva said quickly and with some embarrassment,

"Well that's a first," the young woman said with mild sarcasm, nodding her head slowly. "Goodnight."

"Goodnight."

On exiting the building, Alva found the evening well along, with the streetlights on and the first stars showing. She was surprised to find that it was still considerably warm out. After the cool comfort of the library it felt somewhat oppressive. Still, she thought, it was a nice evening, a good one to be out, to be out walking, and, finding it so, she slowed her pace to enjoy a nice walk home.

"Home," she said quietly and with a smile. "Yes, home."

Chapter 15

Alva glanced at her watch as she climbed the last set of stairs to her room. As she approached the top step, she could hear the soft whirr of Sandra's window fan. For one brief moment she wondered if the sound would serve as cover for her so that she could slip into her room undetected. Holding her breath, she started across the landing to her room. But then...

"No," she said suddenly, "not again." And with that she turned right around and walked quickly to Sandra's room.

Sandra was there at her desk, her back to the door. It looked as if she was playing solitaire.

Alva knocked gently. "Hello," she said tentatively.

Sandra turned in her chair. She smiled. "Hello. Come in."

"Am I interrupting?" It was then that she noticed that the cards spread out on Sandra's desk were not like any playing cards she had seen before.

"Not at all," Sandra said, turning her chair around to face Alva. "Just amusing myself on a warm evening." She gestured towards the cushioned chair. "Have a seat."

"It is warm," Alva said, crossing the room and sitting down.

Sandra adjusted her chair accordingly. "That it is. And so..."

She took the neck of the top she was wearing between two fingers and pulled it away from her slightly.

Alva noticed Sandra's attire. The top, a sort of tank top with spaghetti straps, was white, the fabric sheer enough so that Alva could see that Sandra had nothing on underneath it. The only other thing that she had on was a pair of pale blue panties.

"Please excuse my skimpy duds," Sandra said starting to get up. "Let me put something more modest on."

"No," Alva said quickly. "You're fine. Really."

"You're sure?"

Alva nodded vigorously. "Yes. Really."

Sandra smiled as she settled back in her chair. "Thanks. And thanks for leaving your door open," Sandra said. "Although it's hard to tell on an evening as warm as this, it does help. So, how did your day go?"

"Well. It went well. Except that I fell asleep at the library."

"I took a nap myself. Not intentionally. Over in the park."

"The park?"

"Horton Park, one block up the hill. I brought a blanket, found a shady spot, opened the book I brought along, and..." Slouching, Sandra tilted her head to one side and closed her eyes. "Boom, boom, out go the lights." Opening her eyes, she sat back up and smiled.

Alva laughed. "It sounds nice."

"It was. I can give you a heads up the next time I go there if you'd like to join."

"I would. I'd like that."

"Good."

As engaged as she was in the conversation, Alva was also trying to pay attention to what she was doing, to what she was saying, to how she was saying it. She was paying attention to this 'who she was' that was sitting there in this room at this moment, sitting like this with Sandra. It felt as if she were playing someone else's part. But she wasn't, she told herself. This was the 'who she was' in this moment. And she liked it. She liked it very much.

They sat there together for a little while longer, talking. Then, not even feeling all that tired, Alva suddenly yawned.

"Excuse me," she said, covering her mouth.

With a smile, Sandra nodded. "It's late. And it's warm. And *I* have to be at work early tomorrow." And then, "This was nice."

"It was," Alva said, smiling, nodding her head and genuinely meaning it.

"We'll do this again."

"Yes."

With that they called it an evening.

Later, lying in bed, Alva listened to the whirr of the fan across the way. With just a sheet covering her, she could feel the motion of the air. It wasn't much, but it was something. *This is good*, she thought, and so was the day. And then she remembered the last thing Sandra had said. "We'll do this again."

"Yes," Alva said quietly. "And… and," she smiled thinking that she'd have to ask Sandra where she bought the top that she was wearing. With that thought in mind she fell to sleep.

Chapter 16

At church that Sunday, Alva sat with her aunt and uncle. After the service they went to a small café for a light brunch.

"You know," her Aunt Lillian said at one point, breaking off a piece of her croissant, "even though it's been over a year since you stayed with us, I find myself still not used to your absence, and I…"

"Lillian," Alva's Uncle Ward broke in gently but with firmness, "Alva…"

"I know, I know," her aunt said quickly, "I know, but… but with Arvel gone," she turned to Alva, "I just worry about your being all alone, and…"

"She is hardly alone, Lillian," her uncle broke in.

For a moment there was silence. Alva felt that she should say something, but she wasn't sure what. Something reassuring for her aunt, but also something definite, something, hopefully, to bring this particular subject of conversation to a close.

"Thank you, Aunt Lillian. And I do miss being with you, with both of you, but I just think it's time…"

"And it is," her uncle agreed.

Alva saw her aunt give her uncle a quick look of reproach.

"I know, I know. But you're so young and…"

"Lillian," her Uncle cut in, and not as gently as before. "She's twenty-one. It's right that she should want some independence. At her age we were already married."

"And I'm not alone," Alva added in a soft, reassuring tone. "I've met some really nice people."

Saying this, she thought of Sandra.

"Already?" her uncle asked, smiling. "Good for you. Any young men? If you don't mind my asking."

Alva felt herself flush. And for some reason it made her think of the young man who was having breakfast with Sandra at the dining hall that first morning and then the guard at the library.

"No," she said shyly. "Not really. Not yet." Alva, seeing her aunt look at her sharply, immediately regretted the 'not yet.'

"Well there's plenty of time for that," her uncle said.

"Don't be one of those… those women," her aunt added quickly, "who are only here to get their MRS."

"Lillian," her uncle said with a frown.

"Their what?" Alva asked.

Putting her left hand flat on the table, Alva's aunt tapped her wedding band three times.

"Lillian," her uncle said, rolling his eyes and then shaking his head. "One doesn't run into that kind of thing nowadays."

"Oh no?" her aunt said skeptically.

"I very much doubt it."

"Maybe not. I guess bra burning is more the order of the day."

Once again Alva's uncle just shook his head.

Sitting there, Alva tried to think of anyone she had met the previous three years who in any way indicated that they were looking for a husband before graduation rolled around. No one came to mind. And as far as bra burning was concerned... just the thought of such a thing struck her as embarrassingly ludicrous, enough so that she laughed at the idea of it, which caused her aunt to give her a sharp look.

"Sorry," Alva said.

"Anyway," her uncle stepped in, looking at Alva and smiling. "This is nice, being here with you."

Alva nodded. "It is."

"Would you care to make this a weekly Sunday thing? No pressure here, just if you would like to."

"I would like that."

"Good."

"Can't she come over and have Sunday dinner with us?" her aunt asked with some asperity.

"Of course, she can. But you know very well that we are often out on a Sunday, like today with that faculty get-together this afternoon. Let's just do this after church brunch for the time being and allow things to work out as they will." He turned to Alva. "How does that sound to you?"

Alva nodded.

"Fine," her aunt said with finality and with only a little trace of pleasantness. She turned to Alva. "Any friend or friends that you would like to bring along..."

"Including any gentleman," her uncle interjected.

"Including any gentleman," her aunt repeated giving Alva's uncle *a look* and then, turning to Alva again, "would be more than welcome."

Her uncle nodded his head and gave her aunt a wry look. Alva turned to her aunt and smiled. "Thank you."

As much as Alva felt that her aunt's offer was a genuinely

generous one and something that she, Alva, appreciated, she also knew that it was also an attempt on her aunt's part to keep an eye on her. This did not rankle Alva. This *mothering* of her aunt's was just *her way*. It was the way with practically all the women of the family of that generation, including Alva's mother.

"Thank you," Alva said again.

For the first time that morning her aunt smiled. For the remainder of the brunch she dominated the conversation with news of Arvel and the rest of the family, offering a variety of opinions and sometimes eliciting an '*I beg to differ*' remark from her Uncle.

Outside the café, preparing to part ways, her uncle gave Alva a big hug, after which her aunt took her firmly by the shoulders and gave her a kiss on the cheek.

"Any plans for the day?" her uncle asked. Alva shook her head. "Well, it looks to be another hot one."

"It already is," her aunt said.

"That room of yours," her uncle went on, "it must be hot up there in weather like this."

Alva shrugged. "It's not bad. I keep my door open and Sandra does too, and she has a window fan, so there's something of a cross breeze."

"Sandra?" her aunt asked.

Alva nodded. "Her room is across the way from mine. She's really nice."

"This heat won't last much longer," her uncle said. "We'll be up to our... *knees* in the old *partly cloudy* soon enough. But we do have an extra floor fan lying around. If you'd like it, just say the word."

"Thank you. And thank you both for the brunch."

With last good-byes, Alva's aunt and uncle turned and started home. Smiling to herself, Alva did likewise.

It was a warm one, and humid. Feeling a light touch of perspiration along her brow, Alva brushed back her bangs with one hand as she walked back to the Cottage. Even with a light blouse on she could feel the moisture between her shoulder blades. Although sunny, there was something pallid to the sky, giving one the sense that there was an impending change in the offing, possibly even a thunderstorm sometime soon.

Walking along, Alva thought about her Aunt Lillian and her 'earning an MRS' comment. This was a new one for Alva. She found the notion amusing. Marriage, she had always thought, would be just another logical step at some point, the next in a series of logical steps, each one following the completion of some other previous logical step the way high school followed grammar school and college followed that.. There was, she felt, something automatic about it all. Marriage? Yes, that would follow college for some, but she saw herself doing graduate work first, maybe even going for a doctorate. Although she did entertain ideas about a future husband, it was not with any degree of detail. Mostly she just accepted that, at the right time, when it would be appropriate, her *intended* would just appear, again, automatically, as part of another next logical step. But now, with her aunt having broached the subject, Alva started to wonder if things maybe wouldn't be as *just so* as she had always expected. Considering this, Alva felt a slight sense of unease. Taking it a step further, maybe the proverbial *Mr. Right* would never come along. This notion she found particularly distressful, especially when she thought that there just might be some degree of likelihood in it. Certainly, there had been nothing in her life so far to indicate that there was a *someone* out there somewhere for her. Here she was, twenty-one years old, without ever having had a boyfriend in any real sense.

But then it occurred to her that maybe this *step* was just waiting on other logical steps to occur first. Maybe, now that she was finally out on her own, the time was right or that the right time was approaching, that it was only waiting on what she was doing now, being off on her own, living in her own place, living *her* life for the first time. Maybe now there would be room enough, the space necessary, for that *someone* to come along. "Why not?" she said to herself. "Why not?"

It was at this point in her thoughts that, turning a last corner, the Cottage came into view, its wide steps leading up to the spacious front porch, and there, on the roof, the dormer, the dormer of her room on the top floor. She felt her spirits lift. Yes, she thought to herself, why not. Things were changing for her, step by step they were changing, definite steps that she genuinely believed were in the right direction for her.

"Yes," she said quietly as she made her way up the walk to the front steps. "Yes."

Chapter 17

On opening the front door, Alva was confronted with a commotion that, if not pandemonium itself, was something close to it. Folks were rushing about, yelling to one another, banging doors and pounding up and down the stairs. This was something Alva would never have expected, particularly on a Sunday, and a hot and humid one at that.

She was just about to head up the first set of stairs when the sound of someone bounding down towards her caused her to stop and step back out of the way. Lily, suddenly appearing at the top step, stopped short when she saw Alva standing there below. She was wearing a pair of cut-offs and a blouse that looked as if it had seen more than its share of washings. She was barefoot. In one hand she held a pair of flip-flops, in the other a long towel that must have been brightly colored at one time. Certainly, this was not exactly what Alva would have deemed appropriate attire for a Sunday.

"Hey!" Lily shouted. "There you are." Turning slightly, she looked back over her shoulder. "I found her!" she yelled. With that she hustled down the stairs to where Alva stood. "We've been looking all over for you, Ms. Parsons. We're all…" She stopped abruptly mid-sentence and looked Alva up and down. "Wow. Talk about dressed up. Where you been? Church?"

Alva nodded.

Lily blinked. "You're kidding, right? I mean you…" Then she caught herself. "O…kay. I mean… sure. Church. That's cool, I guess." She shrugged. "Whatever. But hey, everybody's going to the quarry for a swim. Get your suit on and grab a towel."

At that point Sandra appeared on the landing above. "Hey Alva," she said with a smile as she started slowly down the stairs. She was also wearing cut-offs, but with a faded pink t-shirt for a top. On her feet was an old pair of leather sandals. A towel was draped around her neck. "Are you up for a swim?"

"I… I can't," Alva said.

"What?" Lily asked. "Why not? You on the rag or something?"

Alva saw Sandra give Lily a *look* and shake her head.

"What?" Alva asked.

"What is it? Your time of the month?"

Frowning, Alva shook her head quickly. "No," she said with some heat. "No, just…"

"Can't you swim?" Lily cut in.

"Lily," Sandra admonished quietly, placing a hand on Lily's shoulder.

"What?" Lily asked turning to her.

"Let it…"

"I can swim," Alva protested. "I just… I just don't have a bathing suit. Not with me."

"You're kidding," Lily said with some astonishment.

Alva shook her head. "No. I didn't bring one with me."

"Well, okay," Lily said stepping past her. "Stay cool if you can. This weather sucks. Sucks big time. C'mon Sandra." With that she crossed the foyer and went out the front door.

Sandra turned to Alva. "I wish you'd come along. Throw on some shorts and something old."

Alva frowned. Taking a deep breath, she let it out slowly. "I don't have any shorts or anything like that."

Sandra nodded. "I bet you don't have anything old either," she said with a smile.

Alva, knowing that Sandra meant nothing mean by what she said, shrugged and nodded. "I'm sorry."

"Don't be," Sandra said. "It's nothing, just a swim. I'll stop by later when we get back. Maybe we can go for a walk in the park or something."

"Okay," Alva said.

"And turn on the fan," Sandra said. "It's hot up there. Just turn it off if you go out or if it starts to rain."

"I will. Thanks."

"You bet." Just then a car horn blared. "Well, I should go. We'll meet up later."

Alva nodded. And with that Sandra left.

Going up the stairs, Alva reasoned, but with limited success, that it wasn't that strange that she didn't have a bathing suit with her. Yes, from the past three years she knew that at this time of year there would still be warm days like this one. But they didn't last long, nothing compared to the length of time when winter had its grip on things. Going somewhere for a swim besides the pool at the women's gym where one had to wear the suits provided there, wasn't something that she had ever considered before. No one had ever invited her along for something like this, so there was no reason why bringing a bathing suit would have occurred to her. She had never seen the need for doing so, not before today. So no, it wasn't *that* strange, she told herself.

And yes, she thought, I most certainly can swim. And wouldn't they be surprised to know that I actually teach swimming. She thought of the bible summer camp that she worked at. *And diving too.* But then, she thought, it probably wouldn't do to bring up the fact that it was a bible camp, at least not around Lily.

But for all of that reasoning, by the time she reached her room, what she felt most of all was disappointed, and she dropped down on the edge of her bed and just sat there slouched, her head slightly down, her hands folded in her lap.

"Hello?"

Alva bolted up so quickly that she almost slipped off the bed.

"Sorry," Sandra said. "I didn't mean to startle you."

"I thought you had left." Alva saw that Sandra was holding some articles of clothing in her hand.

"I thought I'd drive myself." She held up the articles of clothing. "We can go together. These should fit you." She handed them to Alva. "They're washed."

Alva looked at the items: a bathing suit and a pair of plaid boxer shorts. She looked up at Sandra. "I…"

"It'll be fun. And it is hot. C'mon. Suit up."

"Okay," Alva said tentatively.

"Great. I'll wait for you downstairs."

After Sandra left, Alva sat there for a moment. She suddenly felt good, good about the prospect of going out with Sandra and with everyone else, good about going for a swim. She was nervous. There was no denying that, but not to the point of being uncomfortable. And this sudden good feeling lasted until she held up the bathing suit.

It was then that she noticed that it consisted of two pieces.

Worse, it was... "A bikini," she said in a whisper, "a... *bikini*."

All of that sudden good feeling quickly evaporated, replaced with dismay, and, worse, even some panic. Her first inclination was to hide, or to escape. But neither option, she knew, was viable. There was nowhere to hide. There was no way to *escape* without passing by where Sandra would be waiting.

The thought occurred to Alva to make up some excuse about something she had forgotten to do, or someone that she had agreed to meet, but immediately she remembered that time before on that first day that she had met Sandra, how she had made up an excuse, and how, afterwards, she had made up her mind never to do that again. She could not, no matter how much she wanted to do so, bring herself to *lie* to Sandra again.

Dropping the shorts on the bed and holding up a piece of the bathing suit in each hand, she was shocked by how little fabric there was to them, but, with some irony, she reminded herself that, except for being tall, there really wasn't that much of her to cover. She always considered herself skinny and pretty much flat-chested. This latter aspect of her physique prompted her to give the bra a closer look. It looked as if it might be too *roomy* for her, and, for a brief moment, she thought that this might provide the excuse she needed to get out of going. Quickly she got up and closed her door. After hurriedly getting undressed, she donned the bathing suit.

Turning to look at her reflection in the full-length mirror on the closet door, she inhaled sharply, feeling, at once, both ashamed and excited by her reflection. No, she didn't completely fill the bra, but it was close, close enough not to matter. Although the bottom piece didn't fit perfectly snug either, it was, again, close enough. No, she admitted to herself, she couldn't use the suit's not fitting as an excuse for not going. Oddly enough, although it would have been a relief to be able to bow out, Alva did feel pleased at the prospect of going, pleased and even excited. She looked at her reflection in the mirror, and she found that there was also something there that appealed to her. What, she wondered with a slight laugh, would the folks back at bible camp say if she showed up wearing such a suit? What would her parents say? It gave her something of a thrill to consider that, to the point that a slight knock on the door made her jump.

"Everything okay?" Sandra asked from the other side of the door.

"Y-yes," Alva answered. She hastily gathered up her blouse, put it on, and held the front closed.

"Can I come in?"

"Yes," Alva said, stepping back as the door slowly swung open.

Sandra peeked around the door. "Can I see?"

Grinning shyly, Alva opened her blouse slowly.

Sandra smiled. "That looks snug enough."

"Are you sure?" Alva asked doubtfully.

Sandra nodded. "It's fine. Really. Turn around. Let's see the bottom." Alva turned. "That's good too. Looks like we're all set."

Alva picked up the shorts from her bed, and put them on, then she started buttoning her blouse. Her hands trembled as she did so, but this didn't upset her. She could *feel* herself smiling; she couldn't help doing so. This was a big deal to her. This was exciting. It felt like the start of an adventure.

"Grab a towel. Do you have sandals?"

Alva shook her head. "I have tennis shoes," she said hopefully.

"Perfect. Put 'em on and let's go."

Downstairs, just as they were about to leave the building, the front door swung open. Bernie the house RA walked in. With her was another woman of about the same height and build, but whose hair, which, like Bernie's, was cut short, was decidedly on the gray side.

"Where you folks off to?" Bernie asked.

"The quarry," Sandra said. "For a swim."

"Now that sounds ideal. Anyone else going?"

"Pretty much everybody."

"No shit." Bernie turned to her companion. "You up for a swim?"

Her companion shrugged. "Maybe. You know… after…"

Bernie nodded.

Standing there, Alva got the impression that the companion was sizing up both she and Sandra.

"Well," Bernie said turning back to Alva and Sandra, "enjoy your swim. Maybe we'll catch up with you there later." With that she and her companion proceeded past them and headed across the living room to the RA's room.

Instead of turning to go, Sandra stood there watching them. Alva was surprised to see her give them a strange look and was about to say something when, with a quick shrug, she turned and smiled.

"Ready?"

"Yes."

"Let's go."

Chapter 18

"So, where are we going?" Alva asked as she and Sandra pulled out of the student parking garage.

"The quarry. Actually, it was a quarry. It's a park now. Greendale Park."

"Is it far?"

"A couple towns east of here. Not far really. Do you know where Deiter's is, the German restaurant?"

"No."

"Three Trees Pizza? Abdul's Donuts?"

"No."

Sandra gave Alva a quick glance and smiled. "You don't get around much."

"No. I guess not."

"Well, we can certainly change that, can't we."

"I'd like that."

Sandra glanced at her again and nodded. "Sure. Hey, look at you right now."

Alva brightened. "Right."

"This area has a lot to offer besides what goes on around campus. And I don't know all of it. We should do some exploring together."

"I'd like that too."

"Good. We'll do just that."

Alva liked hearing all of this and the good feeling that it engendered stayed with her even as, driving along, their conversation moved on to other topics. Between their talking and her own reveries, Alva was so caught up in it all that she had all but forgot about the swim and the quarry. So much so that it startled her when Sandra suddenly pulled off the main road and on to one of gravel.

As they made the turn, Alva noticed a brown sign with yellow letters.

"Greendale Park," she read out loud.

It was only then that she noticed that they were no longer in an urban or even suburban environment. It was all trees now and heavily wooded at that.

"So, there's a lake out here?" she asked.

"Not technically. It's just this old quarry that flooded. Supposedly there's still equipment and things down at the bottom of it, but that's way down… way, way down."

"Is it dangerous?"

Sandra shrugged. "No. I wouldn't say so." She glanced at Alva. "I don't sound very reassuring, do I?"

Alva smiled. "Not totally."

"Like a lot of places, things are fine if you exercise some caution and some smarts."

"I guess."

"You don't sound reassured."

"I'm okay. Really. I'm good at being careful." She turned to look out the window. "Maybe too good."

The road grew gradually narrower as they rode along, with

tree limbs and branches reaching out and arcing out over it. *It's almost*, Alva thought to herself, *as if we are being absorbed into the woods.*

"Is it much further?" she asked.

"Almost there."

"What happens if we meet someone coming the other way?"

Sandra glanced over at her. "We inhale deeply and hope for the best."

Alva laughed, but not with any heartiness. "This makes me think of Flannery O'Connor and that short story of hers where the grandmother talks the family into taking an old dirt road to look for a house with treasure in it."

"Uh-oh," Sandra said jokingly. "You mean 'A Good Man Is Hard To Find'."

"I think that's it."

"Southern psychopathic killers."

"So, I'm safe up north here?"

"Oh sure. Well… kind of. Things happen more at a community level up here."

"Like witch trials."

"Mmm. That's way east of here. I was thinking more of Shirley Jackson."

"'The Lottery'," Alva clarified.

"Yes. Great writing."

"I think so too, but…"

"But it can creep a person out."

Alva nodded once. "It sure can."

"Well, strange things, bad things, can happen anywhere. Remember the young woman who disappeared last year."

"The one who had posted for a ride share home for vacation?"

"Yes. A car pulls up, some guy driving, the car takes off, and she's never seen again. And that's all that anybody knows. Things like that can happen anywhere. Even…" Sandra paused to glance at her passenger and found Alva sitting there, head down, her hands folded together in her lap, and her eyes closed. She also saw that Alva's lips were moving.

"Hey," Sandra said quickly. "You okay?"

Lifting her head and opening her eyes, Alva nodded, but Sandra could see that she wasn't.

"How about a new topic?" Sandra offered.

Alva nodded again, but for several minutes neither of them said anything.

Chapter 19

The road ended at an open grassy area large enough for a dozen or so vehicles to park. Owing to the warmth of the day, there were more cars than spaces and folks had doubled up in places.

"It looks like there's no place to park," Alva said as Sandra maneuvered slowly through the lot.

"Actually, we're in luck. I see Stu over there."

Alva looked around but couldn't see whom Sandra was referring to. "Who?"

Sandra smiled. "You'll see." A moment later she pulled up behind a white car. Alva noted that the car was of no recent vintage, that it had some serious rust to it and that the paint had that dull, faded aspect, indicative of too little wax and too much sun.

"Stu," Sandra said coming to a stop inches from the white car's back bumper. "As in Studebaker."

Setting the brake, she shut off engine, opened her door, and climbed out. Alva followed suit.

"How are they going to get out?"

"I know Stu's owner. If he has to leave, we'll jockey the cars or just switch keys."

"Really? You'd just let someone take your car?"

Sandra shrugged. "Sure."

"That's pretty trusting of you."

"I'm insured." Sandra glanced at Stu and frowned. "Unlike certain people. See the license plate."

Alva looked. The back plate was a dark green with white numbers. Small letters spelled out 'VERMONT' beneath the plate number.

"Your friend is from Vermont?"

"Nooo… but he has an aunt who lives there and he uses her address to register his car there."

"Why?"

"Because insurance isn't required in the state of Vermont."

"You're kidding."

Sandra shook her head. "Not until you get into your first accident."

"Seems like an awful risk to take."

Sandra nodded. "I agree, but…" She shrugged, "Some folks are more comfortable with risk than others, some too comfortable. But… enough of that. C'mon, the trail to the quarry is this way."

As they were walking along Alva noticed that the trees, though tall enough, didn't look all that old. Still, there was shade and even enough of a breeze to rustle the leaves slightly. Things felt just a touch cooler there than back at campus.

"Is this really a park, like with facilities and all?"

"It is, but not here. We came in the back door. The main part of the park is off that way. There's a lake there with bathhouses, a snack bar, and a large picnic area. There's a trail to it, but it's a good mile or so from here. The ranger may pass through here once in a great while just to check on things, but nothing here is maintained or anything. Like this…"

Sandra pointed a few yards ahead of them. Alva saw that they were approaching the end of the trail. A sign was posted there.

NO LIFEGUARD

SWIM AT YOUR OWN RISK

PARK CLOSES AT DUSK

"That's pretty much it in terms of park supervision here."

Just past the sign the path opened up and the trees became fewer. The terrain was pretty much level, consisting of grass and occasional small outcroppings of granite. Up ahead, along the water's edge, Alva could see some people sitting around on the granite or lying on blankets on the grass. Others were diving and swimming. Some were making use of a rope that hung from the limb of a mighty oak to swing out over the water and let go.

Suddenly Alva felt very far away from the university.

"Hey!" Sandra called out.

Startled, Alva turned quickly. Sandra was looking ahead of them. Following her gaze, she saw a young man approaching. He was wearing a pair of wet cut-offs and a shirt that at one time had probably been suitable for weddings and such. The shirt was unbuttoned in the front. Alva saw that his long, black hair was wet, hanging down straight and flat. Alva noted that he too wore a pair of black, high-top sneakers. She saw also that they were untied.

"Well, hello there, Sandra," he said slowly, almost in a drawl as he drew near.

"Hi Steve," Sandra said as the three of them met up. "Alva, this is Steve. Steve, Alva."

"Well, hello there," Steve said, again in that almost drawl. "Alva, huh."

"Yes."

There was, she thought, something unfocused about him, as if his thoughts were somewhat elsewhere.

"Well okay then. Alva it is." He turned to Sandra. "Your crowd is over there," he said turning and pointing off to the right."

"I see them. Are you leaving?"

"Yeah. I have to work tonight."

Sandra reached into her pocket, pulled out her keys, and held them out to him.

"Ah, somebody has somebody boxed in." He reached into his own pocket.

Sandra smiled and shook her head. "No," she said calmly. "How about if you just switch the cars around?"

"Sure," he said smiling and taking Sandra's keys from her. "I can do that."

"And leave those under the front seat?"

"Sure. I can do that too."

"And don't lock the door?"

"Right. Right. You bet. I *cannot* do that too."

"Don't forget."

"Not a problem. Leave the keys and don't forget." He made a slight bow. "By the way. You wouldn't happen to know where Kerry is?"

"No. Sorry."

"S'alright. I'll track him down. Well, ladies, enjoy yourselves. The water is perfect."

With that he headed off. Sandra and Alva stood for a moment watching him go.

"Is he alright?" Alva asked in a whisper.

"Mmm."

"Maybe we should go with him?"

"Probably," Sandra said thoughtfully. Then she turned to Alva and smiled. "Let's be a couple of folks who take a risk this time. Agreed?"

"Agreed."

They started walking towards the quarry.

"He seemed... a little out of it. Like he might be... you know... on something."

Sandra turned to her, shaking her head slowly. "No. I don't think so really. He can come across like that, but it's more like he just doesn't take things as seriously as others do."

"Is he like that with schoolwork?"

"He doesn't go to the university. The last I heard he was taking classes at the community college across town, but there was talk about him heading out to Utah sometime soon."

"How do you know him?"

"He's a good friend of someone that I work with at the dining hall."

"This Kerry?"

Sandra turned to her. "You know him?"

"You and Lily were talking about him that day I first met you."

Sandra nodded. "That's right."

"Does Steve work in the dining hall too?"

"No. At the hospital. He works the night shift in the ICU. He mans the heart monitors."

"Well, he must take that seriously."

"One would hope so."

"So, he's from this area?"

"He has family here," Sandra said. "At least one aunt, and

some cousins."

"It's kind of funny. I always think of people around here being connected in some way with the university."

"It's actually a big city."

"Yes. I guess it is."

"Come on. Let's catch up with the others."

"Hey!" someone ahead of them shouted.

Looking ahead, they saw Lily jump up from where she was sitting with the others from the Cottage and come running towards them.

All smiles, Lily looked at Sandra when she drew near. "So, you managed to shanghai our friend here after all."

"How's the water?" Sandra asked as the three of them drew near the others.

"Perfect." The others nodded. "Hey, where're your towels?"

Sandra and Alva turned, looked at each other. After a brief moment, they smiled and stood there shaking their heads.

"Nice going guys," Lily said. "It doesn't matter though. Not in this heat. You'll dry off soon enough. In fact, I'm ready to head in again. Anybody else?"

With varying responses of agreement, some of the others got up and headed with Lily down to the water. After stripping down to their swimsuits, Sandra and Lily followed, and watched those ahead of them take running jumps into the water.

"Is it deep enough to do that?" Alva asked.

"It's a sheer cliff of granite and drops straight down," Sandra explained. "There's no wading in."

Coming up to the water's edge, they stopped and stood watching the others cavort about in the water.

"So, it's deep enough to dive?" Alva asked.

"It is. But don't go too deep. Like I said, there might be equipment down there on the bottom."

Alva nodded.

"Are you guys coming in or what?" Lily called to them.

Sandra smiled at Alva. "Don't laugh."

"Don't laugh at what?"

"This." Turning, Sandra held her nose, took three quick steps and jumped in. Those already in the water cheered.

"C'mon Alva. C'mon Alva," Lily chanted, and the others joined in.

Alva waited until Sandra surfaced. "How is it?" she asked.

"Like everyone's been saying, perfect," Sandra said as the others continued chanting at Alva.

Stepping forward, Alva brought her feet together and grabbed the edge of the granite with her toes. Raising her arms over her head, she flexed her knees and, with a push, dove in. In contrast to the warmth of the day, the water felt more than just cool, and the deeper she went, the colder it felt. Remembering Sandra's caution about equipment being on the bottom, she only went down a short way before turning and heading back up. Breaking the surface, she wiped the water away from her eyes and commenced to tread water.

The first thing she noticed was that the chanting had stopped. Not only had it stopped, there was now a palpable silence. Looking around she saw that the others were staring at her. This included Sandra, but with a difference in that she was smiling, smiling broadly.

"That was beautiful," Sandra said shaking her head slowly.

"Way to go Alva!" Lily shouted and with that the others started cheering. "And your suit didn't even slip off."

Feeling herself blush, Alva smiled back at them and gave a quick wave. Not being used to this or any kind of acclaim, she felt as if she might get emotional. She lay back and floated with her eyes shut and her arms extended. She continued to do so, luxuriating in the clean, cool feel of the water, the warmth of the sun on her face, and also relishing this nice touch of pride in herself, that and a feeling of acceptance, of feeling that she belonged here with the others. It was a *moment*, and a good one at that.

"That was impressive."

Alva opened her eyes to find Sandra treading water beside her.

"Thanks," she said, righting herself and treading water also.

"A woman of hidden talents."

Alva shrugged. "I can swim. And I can dive."

"Yes. Yes, you certainly can. Want to swim across to the other side?"

"Sure."

The two of them swam side by side, Alva making a point to mirror Sandra's long, clean strokes. They swam slowly. As they did so, Alva, wishing to completely savor the moment, tried to focus on the feel of the water as she moved smoothly through it. The quarry was wide and, even after taking it slowly the entire way, Alva could feel the effort it had taken as she and Sandra climbed out onto the granite on the other side.

There was no tree cover at the water's edge. After the coolness of the water, the granite felt decidedly warm. Finding a spot where they could sit with their feet in the water, they settled in. They sat there quietly, saying nothing, just looking across to the other side where everyone else was.

"This is nice," Alva said finally in a quiet voice.

"Mmm." Sandra nodded. "It is."

"Thank you."

Sandra turned to her. "For what?"

"For this," Alva said, continuing to look out across the water. "For bringing me here. For making this happen." Again, Alva felt that she might be on the verge of getting emotional. She closed her eyes.

The sudden cold feel of a hand on her shoulder caused her to start. Opening her eyes, she turned to find Sandra looking intently at her, looking a little concerned.

"You okay?" Sandra asked.

Alva nodded and smiled. "Yes. Yes, I am. It's just..." She shook her head. "It's just... This is just, just so different. That's all. But it's good. It is."

Sandra smiled. "Then I'm glad." She gave Alva's shoulder a gentle shake before taking her hand away.

"The thing is," Alva said, turning towards her, "I really want things to be different. I want this year to be different. *I* want to be different. I want it so much. But I worry. I don't know how much of what I want is possible."

"Well you know," Sandra said after a moment. "That's one thing about college. It gives a person the opportunity to re-invent themselves. Or maybe it just gives one the chance to be the person that they think they really are. The change of environment is part of it, there's a distance to it, a distance between where you were once and where you are now. You're suddenly away from all those people that you used to know you and you're away from *their* take on who they think you are. In a way, it's a chance to start fresh with folks not connected with your past and all of its baggage."

Alva nodded. "I get that. I get what you're saying. And I've missed that opportunity."

"How so?"

"Here I am a senior and finally getting around to living on campus. Of finally getting away from living with family."

"Why has it been like that?"

"For the first two years I lived with my aunt and uncle. He's a professor here, the head of the religion department. My brother lived there too. Last year, while my uncle was on sabbatical, my brother and I shared an apartment off campus."

"Where's your brother now?"

"He graduated." Alva shook her head and frowned. "And he never had the chance to do like you said, to re-invent himself."

Sandra shrugged. "Maybe he never felt the need to do so. Some people don't. Where is he now?"

"He's in a seminary, back in Kentucky."

"Was that always his intention?"

"I guess so. Yes. At least as far as I know."

"Then I'd say that his self-definition is pretty well set and not open to that much in the way of change. That's just a thought though. Did he seem okay with his status quo?"

Alva considered the question for a moment. "Yes. I would say so. He never complained. He never seemed unhappy."

"Never seemed unhappy," Sandra repeated. "That's not quite the same as feeling happy."

"Oh, I think he was happy. He's just the quiet type."

"And the two of you got along?"

Alva smiled. "We did. I mean, we do. He's always been a good brother."

"Then, and again this is just based on what you're telling me,

I would say that he was fine with his situation, and, hopefully, he still is."

Alva nodded thoughtfully. "I hope... I hope so." Again, she frowned. "I hope that one day he doesn't wake up and suddenly regret the way things have been for him, that he... that he missed out somehow."

"Hopefully not. But people can always move on if they really need to."

"Do you think so? I mean, really?"

"Yes. Yes, I do. That's not to say that circumstances won't make it difficult and that there might be limits, but... But yes. I do think that a person can change and move on. One can always decide to be open to change. That might be the key, being open to it."

"It can be scary though." Alva shook her head. "And sometimes things can seem just so impossible."

"Yes, they can. But, like I said, college is a good place to work on changing. It's a fairly insular environment. And safe. And most everybody is in pretty much the same boat."

Alva nodded. "Yes." And then she turned to Sandra. "I appreciate this, talking with you about all of this."

"Sure. It's good. Good for me too. And...speaking of moving on, by the look of the sky over there, we better head back."

Following Sandra's gaze across the water, Alva saw that the sky over the trees on the other side had taken on an ominous dark shade of gray. She saw that the others on the other side, obviously aware of this development, were gathering up their things. There were only two people in the water.

Suddenly, there was a flash of lightning. Alva turned to Sandra and found her counting on her fingers. When she got to ten, she stopped and turned to Alva and smiled.

"Well, that one was more than two miles away," Sandra said getting to her feet. "And the rain hasn't started yet, so we should be good."

Alva stood up. "Should we hike around?"

Sandra shook her head. "That would take too long. We can swim it faster. C'mon, I'll race you." With that Sandra took two quick steps to the water's edge and, again holding her nose, jumped in.

Chapter 20

Alva dove in after her. By the time she surfaced, Sandra was a few yards ahead and swimming quickly towards the other side. As fast as she was going, Alva soon caught up with her.

Sandra smiled when she saw her. "Keep going."

Alva smiled back and shook her head.

The two of them continued on together, swimming in tandem.

As they approached the other side, Alva saw Lily standing on the shore under a tree with a towel wrapped around her. Beyond her she could see the others already heading back to the parking area. The other two swimmers, both women, were just climbing out of the water. They were both, Alva saw, stocky of build with hair cut short. And they were, Alva was shocked to see, naked, completely naked. By the time Sandra and she reached the water's edge and began to climb out, the two women were standing with Lily under the tree, towels in hand, drying off.

Once on shore, Sandra and Alva gathered their things. Alva made a point not to look over to where Lily and the two women were standing.

"Don't bother to suit up," Sandra said. With that she turned and, to Alva's horror, headed straight to where the others were standing. In a bit of a panic, Alva, with her head down and focusing on the ground between her feet, quickly caught up with her.

"And here are our racing swimmers."

Recognizing the voice, Alva looked up quickly. Bernie smiled at her as she and her friend continued to dry off. Alva saw that it was the same woman that they had seen Bernie with earlier, back at the Cottage.

"What?" Bernie said, looking at Alva and Sandra. "No towels? Here." She held out hers to Alva. Her friend offered hers to Sandra.

Suddenly unable to move or say anything, Alva just stood there staring at the offered towel.

"We're okay," Sandra said quickly, coming to Alva's rescue. "We'll dry off some on the walk back."

"Not if you don't beat the rain."

Dropping their towels, Bernie and her friend picked up their things and started to dress. When Lily dropped her own towel, Alva saw that she too was naked.

"Well we're off," Sandra said.

With that the two of them headed at a quick pace towards the trail back to the parking area. They were about half the way there and moving along at a good pace when Sandra turned to Alva.

"You okay?"

Alva looked at her nervously. To her surprise, she found Sandra giving her a knowing smile. "I... Yes..." She shook her head. "I guess so."

"You don't sound too sure." Sandra said, watching Alva closely, still smiling. "You didn't expect that, did you?" She made a motion with her head back in the direction that they had just come.

"No. No, I didn't."

"Same here."

"Really?

Sandra nodded. "I guess I shouldn't be too surprised though."

"Why?"

"You ever use the pool in the women's building?"

"I do. Once in a while, if I have time between classes or at the end of the day."

"Well, you remember last winter when there was that big to do with a bunch of women protesting their having to wear swimsuits in the pool?"

Alva shook her head.

"Are you serious?"

Alva shrugged.

"Well anyway, it all had to do with the fact that, during regular open hours, the men can swim naked in their pool and women can't do the same in their own."

"The men can swim naked?"

"Actually, they have to. They're not allowed to wear anything except during swim meets."

"Why not?"

"I haven't a clue."

"So, what happened?"

"Well, there was this sort of protest where a group of women went over to the women's building, marched in, took off their clothes and jumped in the pool."

"Naked."

Sandra nodded. "And I'll give you two guesses who organized the whole thing."

"Bernie and that woman she's with?"

Sandra nodded.

"So, what happened?"

"Not much. It's not like they could arrest a whole group of naked women. Bernie was threatened with disciplinary action if it happened again. She could lose her RA position. And her friend was told that she would be arrested for trespassing if she even entered the pool building again."

"Trespassing. Why?"

"She's not a student here. She's just Bernie's... well, friend. Anyway, that's the scoop."

"Seems like a big to do over nothing."

Sandra nodded. "I agree. Except for one thing."

"What's that?"

"When you go to the pool, what color suit do they give you?"

Alva thought for a moment. "Blue."

"Always. Right?"

Alva paused briefly before answering. "Yes."

"Have you ever noticed that other people get suits that are a color other than blue?"

Again, Alva paused. "I guess so. I never really thought about it though."

"There are two other colors. Red and green. You get blue because you're on the thin side. The suits are color coded by size."

Alva shrugged. "Okay. Is that a problem?"

"Think about it. It's okay if, like yourself, you're not carrying any extra poundage, but if you get green, it says that you're kind of... well, let's say full figured. And if you get red, it's telling you and everyone around you that you're fat. And keep in mind, no color draws attention like red."

Alva took a deep breath and let it out slowly. "I... I never thought of that. I never noticed."

"It's subtle. I never noticed it until someone pointed it out to me, but then they always give me a blue suit too. So, in a way, the protest did have a point. It wasn't simply a matter of being able to skinny dip like the men do."

"Why don't they have men's suits that are color coded by size?"

Sandra turned to Alva and gave her a sly smile. "Well, think about it. There's not much to a man's Speedo to begin with. It's certainly not a full body suit. *What* would they be measuring?"

Alva shrugged.

"*What*," Sandra asked again, "would they be measuring?"

"I... I don't know... I..." And then, "Oh!" Alva came to a sudden stop. Standing there she felt herself blush.

"Exactly," Sandra said, nodding her head slowly.

The two of them stood there looking at each other. Then, at exactly the same moment, the two of them broke out into a fit of laughter. And again, and again, for the remainder of the walk back to the parking area, the fits kept coming over them, even when the skies opened up, and the rain came down in a deluge and they were forced to make a run for it.

Chapter 21

"You'll need to get this signed by both the RA where you live and your academic advisor." The woman behind the counter at financial services handed an employment application form to Alva. "We just need to know that they know that you'll have less study time. It's just a formality unless," and here she looked at Alva over the top of her glasses, "unless your grades are atrocious." She pulled her glasses back up the bridge of her nose and smiled. "Which I'm going to assume, they're not."

"No. They're fine."

Then just get that signed and bring it back and we'll get you in touch with the folks over at the library."

"Thank you."

It wasn't quite the job that Alva had in mind. It wasn't, as she had hoped, the dining hall. She felt mildly frustrated by the way things had turned out, mildly frustrated and mildly annoyed, annoyed with herself, knowing that it was *her* fault that things had taken this turn. It was, she knew, because she had let it slip at Sunday brunch with her aunt and uncle the day before that she was going to look for a part time job.

Her Aunt Lillian, of course, took immediate issue with the

idea, saying that it was unnecessary financially for her to do so, that it was bound to be detrimental to her studies, that her parents were not paying good money to send her to the university so that she could go out and earn money she didn't need, and that she was there to study and to get all that she could out of her education.

"And you know very well, Ward," she went on, turning suddenly on Alva's uncle, "that I'm right. So, don't even think of contradicting me."

Alva's uncle put up both hands in a defensive manner and shook his head slowly. "Far be it from me to disagree, dear," he said calmly. "In fact, I couldn't agree with you more."

Alva felt her heart sink. She was not only disappointed by this turn of events, but also surprised by her uncle's lack of support. Right along this semester he had been her champion. His prompt and total acquiescence to her aunt in this matter took her completely by surprise.

Her uncle slowly placed his hands, palms down, on the table. "But what," he asked calmly, "what if she could earn some money at something that is both educational and related to her studies? Not only that," he went on, "but what if it was something important, something well worth the doing from an academic standpoint?"

Aunt Lillian narrowed her eyes at him. "What?" she asked, her tone dubious.

"The university has just received, on loan, portions of the scrolls discovered recently in the Middle East. They're being kept in the Rare Archives Room at the library." He turned to Alva. "Professor Nagy, your adviser, has put together a small team, grad students, to study them and they need someone to coordinate what the team produces. The position will require a considerable amount of typing, but there will be a research aspect to it also in terms of locating related materials that the others can work with." He turned back to Alva's aunt. "How does that sound? I'll defer to your judgment, but do consider how such a job will look on her resume."

For a long moment, Aunt Lillian looked at him, her eyes still narrowed. "Well," she said finally, "I think that might be alright. Certainly, Alva can give it a try. But if it affects her studies…"

"It *will* be her studies," Alva's uncle cut in.

"As I was saying," her aunt said sternly, "but if it affects her studies, she'll have to give it up."

"Of course. But student employment has a cap of twelve hours a week. I have no doubt that she can manage that." Alva's uncle turned to her. "And twelve is not a requirement. You'll have flexibility in terms of when and how long you work. Does that sound reasonable?"

"Yes," Alva said almost in a whisper, not trying to sound too eager in front of her aunt.

"This isn't a funded position. You'll be an employee of the library, but with a twist. You'll have special access to the Rare Archives Room, which means you'll be bonded and fingerprinted."

"Is that necessary?" Aunt Lillian asked. Alva could see that her aunt was genuinely concerned.

"Yes, it is. And they will do a background check on her too. We're talking items of extreme value, irreplaceable items, including," he turned to Alva, "the scrolls that you'll be working with. I cannot overemphasize the responsibility attached to the position. Are you comfortable with that?"

For one brief moment, Alva hesitated. It wasn't that she had any issues with the position. As her uncle had pointed out, it had its merits. And she didn't have any qualms about the responsibility associated with it or about her ability to perform the tasks entailed. If anything, her hesitation had to do with her hopes of getting a job at the dining hall.

"A problem?" her uncle asked. "You don't have to decide now. There's no real hurry. Why don't you think it over and we'll talk about it next Sunday?"

"No," Alva said quickly. "No, it sounds good. It's… it's a real opportunity." She nodded. "I'd like to do it."

"You're sure?"

Alva smiled. "Yes."

"Good. I'll speak with Lorraine, Professor Nagy, this afternoon, and you should head over to the financial services office tomorrow and get a job application."

So here she was – Monday morning, job application in hand, mildly frustrated, mildly annoyed. But, with all of that, she found herself also mildly pleased. She was doing it. She was getting a job. She would be earning money, her money. And in the event that her parents had an issue with this development, she knew that her uncle would be able to smooth things out. She knew that she would not be compelled to give it up. As she walked along, going over everything, she found herself feeling more than just mildly pleased. Things were working out, maybe not exactly as planned, but well enough. The year was continuing to shape up to be a good one.

Chapter 22

Professor Nagy was in her office when Alva stopped in to get her job application signed.

"I'm so glad that your uncle thought of you for this. In fact, I apologize for not thinking of you myself. When he mentioned your name, I immediately thought 'perfect.' You are more than qualified, Alva. And we'll certainly have you doing more than just typing. Much more."

They arranged to meet the following Monday at five at the Rare Archives Room at the library. All Alva needed now was her RA's signature. Deeming it best to get everything squared away as quickly as possible, she headed back to the Cottage, hoping that Bernie would be there. When she arrived, she found Lily sitting outside on the top step of the front stairs reading a magazine and, to Alva's surprise, smoking a cigarette.

"Hey you," Lily said looking up at Alva as she walked up the stairs.

"Hi Lily."

"What do you got there?"

"A job application."

"A job application." Lily tapped her cigarette on the top stair to knock the ash off. "For the dining hall?"

"No. I'm applying for a position at the library. In the Rare Archives Room."

"Really," Lily said with a smile, weighing this piece of information. "You at the library." She nodded. "I can see that. You're a quiet enough mouse. Good for you. I hope you get it."

"Oh, I have the job. I just have to get Bernie to sign this, to give her okay."

"Well, that shouldn't be a problem."

"Do you know if she's in?"

"I don't. I just got back from Market Street." She held up the magazine she was reading. "The latest Cosmo. Couldn't wait to get into this article, 'How To Incite A Man's Lust.' The rag gets some pretty amazing stuff since Ms. Brown took over. You should check it out."

Not knowing quite what to say, Alva just nodded.

"Anyway," Lily went on, "congratulations on the job. It sounds great. Way to go."

Once inside, Alva was disappointed to see that Bernie's door was closed, which usually meant that she probably wasn't in. Still, hoping to keep things rolling, Alva crossed the living room and knocked on the door.

"Come in," a voice bellowed loudly.

Since she didn't recognize the voice as that of Bernie, Alva hesitated. For a moment she just stood there.

"Come in," the summons was repeated, even louder still.

Slowly opening the door, Alva stepped in.

It was a good-sized room, almost as large as the living room. Probably, it at one time served as a dining room. Even with two large bookcases, the roomed seemed spacious. There was also a large roll-top desk and a draftman's table that was even larger. Still, there was nothing cramped about the room. The most impressive item there was the bed, which, if not actually king-size, was definitely a queen.

It wasn't the size of the bed though that caught Alva's attention. It was the woman sitting up in the bed reading. She had the sheets and covers gathered up around her waist. Alva gasped seeing that, from at least the waist up, the woman wasn't wearing anything. Alva recognized the woman as being the same one who was with Bernie at the quarry.

The woman looked up from her book. "What's up?"

"I… I was looking for Bernie."

"Anything I can help you with?" Marking her place with a finger, the woman closed her book and began shifting about among the bedclothes. For a second Alva was afraid that the woman was going to get out of bed.

"No," Alva said as quickly as she could. "No. I just need her signature on something. It can wait."

The woman shrugged. "She just went to the can. She'll be back in a moment. Have a seat." The woman gestured towards a stool near the draftsman's table.

"No, I'll come back later."

"Don't be ridiculous. She'll be right back. Have a seat."

Alva stepped over to the stool and was just sitting down when she happened to glance at a sheet on the draftsman's table. It was, she saw, an etching, one in progress, but completed enough so that she could see that it was of a woman, a woman lounging in bed reading. With a start, she looked at Bernie's companion realizing that the etching was of her.

Alva stood up quickly. "I really can't wait. I'll come back later to get her signature."

"Signature for what?"

Alva started. Turning, she found Bernie standing there next to her. At the sight of her, Alva took a step back, inhaling sharply. All that Bernie had on was a worn t-shirt and a pair of bikini underpants.

"A signature for what?" Bernie repeated.

Alva held out the job application. To her embarrassment she noticed that her hand was trembling. "A job, a job at the library. I just need you to give your okay."

Taking the application, Bernie nodded and smiled. Stepping up to the draftsman's table, she picked up a pen that was lying there, signed the document and then, turning back to Alva, handed it to her.

"A job at the library. Sounds good."

Alva nodded. "In the Rare Archives Room."

"Better still. All the best with it."

"Thank you."

With that Alva turned to go. Crossing the living room at almost a trot, she turned the corner to head up the stairs and almost collided with Sandra.

"Whoa," Sandra said stopping short. "Hey Alva."

"Hi… hi." Alva looked back quickly over her shoulder.

"Something wrong?"

"What?" Alva turned back to Sandra.

"Everything okay? You seem flustered."

"No. Yes." She shook her head. "Everything's fine."

"You headed somewhere?"

"Just… just to financial services." Alva held up the job application. "To drop this off."

"Did you get a job?" Sandra asked, interested.

"Yes. At the library."

Sandra frowned. "Not the dining hall?"

Alva shook her head. "No. It's something my uncle arranged."

"I see. Well, congratulations. Really. It just would have been nice to work together."

"I know."

"Well anyway, I was just going to Market Street to check on something. Why don't I keep you company while you turn that in and then we can go get a coffee or something somewhere. Charlie's should be open."

"Sure. I'd like that." Again, Alva looked back over her shoulder.

"You sure everything's okay?"

Alva turned back to Sandra. For a moment, distracted, she just stood there looking at her. "I..." She shrugged. "Yes. Let's go."

"You sure?"

"Yes," Alva said calming down. "Yes, I am."

Going out the front door they found Lily still sitting there, still reading Cosmo and smoking another cigarette. Alva saw Sandra look at Lily and frown.

"Hey you two," Lily said looking up at them. "What's up?" She looked at Alva. "You find Bernie?"

"Yes."

"So, you're all signed and ready to join the working world." She inhaled on her cigarette. "Way to go," she said, quickly exhaling smoke. "So where are you two off to"

"To drop off the application and then to Market Street for coffee," Sandra said, still frowning. "You want to join us?"

Lily considered the proposition for a moment. "Nah," she said finally. "I was just there. But thanks for asking."

"Another time."

Lily nodded. "Another time. See ya."

They were halfway down the block, passing the dining hall, when Alva turned to Sandra. "I didn't know that she smoked, Lily."

Sandra frowned. "Mmm."

"Why does she do it?"

Sandra shrugged. "Why does anyone smoke? Stupidity."

"Stupidity?"

Sandra shook her head. "Don't get me going."

At the last intersection on the way to the quad the walk light was red. Alva and Sandra stopped at the curb and waited.

Sandra turned to Alva. "Do you want to talk about what's on your mind?"

"What do you mean?"

"When we met up, you seemed... well, distracted."

Alva nodded. "I was."

The light turned green and the walk light went on. They crossed and took the sidewalk that led directly to the quad. A short way up there was a bench that was shaded by a large oak.

"Are you in any real hurry?" Sandra asked.

Alva looked at her watch. "No, the office doesn't close for another hour or so."

"Want to sit?"

"Sure."

Once seated, Sandra turned to Alva. "Well?" she asked quietly.

After a brief moment of hesitation Alva nodded. "I think that... I think Bernie is a lesbian," she blurted out.

Sandra nodded slowly. "Okay. Did something happen?"

Alva took a deep breath. "Just before I ran into you, I stopped in to get her signature on this," she held up the job application, "and she wasn't in but that woman, the one we saw her with at the quarry, she was there and…"

"And?"

Leaning forward, Alva looked down at her feet. "She was in Bernie's bed and she wasn't wearing anything, at least nothing on top. And the bed was all unmade and when Bernie showed up all she was wearing was her underwear. Underpants and a t-shirt, and no bra." Her words came out in a torrent. During all of it Alva continued to stare at her feet.

"Okay," Sandra said tentatively.

Alva looked up at her quickly. "So, do you think that she is, that they both are… lesbians?"

"Do I *think* they are? No."

"Really?" Alva asked, suddenly animated. "So, I was wrong?" she asked hopefully.

Sandra shook her head. "No, Alva. They are lesbians." Sandra shrugged. "They don't hide it. And everyone knows."

Alva sagged visibly with disappointment. "Everyone?"

Sandra laughed lightly. "Well, now that you know, then yes. I would say everyone."

"But how can that be? How can they be lesbians?"

"How?" Sandra repeated. "They just are."

"But how can they go on being like that. It's…it's…"

"An abomination?"

"Yes. Yes, it is," Alva said. "The Bible says exactly that."

"Ah, Leviticus."

"So, you know."

Sandra shrugged. "I do, but…" She shrugged again. "But

what would you have done? Have them stoned?"

"No. Of course not, but…"

"But what?"

Alva looked away. "I don't know. It isn't right. It just isn't right. And I don't feel comfortable knowing that they are and that they are there, there where we live. What will people think?"

Sandra let out a quick laugh.

Alva turned quickly to look at her. "It's not funny."

"Sorry. It's just that people do know. The Cottage is known for it."

"For what?"

"For being… for being open and accepting and…" Sandra looked directly at Alva, her look serious. "It's known for being a gay residence."

"I'm not gay. I'm not a lesbian."

Sandra shrugged. "Okay. I didn't say it was a requirement, but, to be frank, if you're not, you're in the minority."

Sandra could see that Alva was stunned by this piece of news, to the point that she just sat there on the bench unable to say anything. As Sandra looked on, she could see Alva's expression suddenly change as if something had just occurred to her, a thought that troubled her, and one also of sadness.

"Sandra?" she said, almost in a whisper. But she stopped there, as if unable to continue.

Sandra smiled gently. "No, Alva. I'm not."

Alva's expression changed to one of relief.

"But tell me," Sandra went on, calmly, "what if I was? Would it matter? Would it mean we couldn't be friends?"

"No!" Alva blurted out, shocked at the very idea of losing Sandra as a friend.

"What about Leviticus?"

Alva's expression took on a pained and helpless aspect. "I don't know. I…" She shook her head. "I just don't know. And I want to know. I pray… I pray to be…"

"Enlightened?"

"Maybe. Or just to be… to be reconciled in some way to the way that the world is."

"That's a pretty tall order."

"I know."

"Prayer is a good thing."

"Do you pray?" Alva asked earnestly.

"In my own way. I once read something about prayer that kind of hit home. It was in the Bible, one of the gospels, Matthew, I think. Maybe you know it?"

"I should. I've read the gospels, but…"

"It said that when you pray, you should go into your room and close the door. Which I also think goes beyond just praying, but in how one lives one's faith, that it should be a private thing. But…" Sandra smiled and said, "that's just my take on it."

"But what about attending services, keeping the Lord's Day."

"Well, there too, my take might be a little different."

"How?"

"Well, isn't every day His?"

By the change in Alva's expression Sandra could tell that her comment had startled her.

"Yes," Alva said slowly. And then, with a thoughtful smile, "I like that. I can think of people I know that would like to hear that. And wouldn't it be something if people went along that way and…"

"And not just keeping the Lord's morning."

"Yes," Alva said. "There is that."

"It's easy to be a saint on top of a mountain."

"What?"

"That's from a quote. It's from a book, *The Razor's Edge*. It's about a man who, in the First World War, has a brush with death and, because of it, he finds himself unable to settle into the normal kind of life like others expect him to, and he goes off in search for some sort of meaning to everything."

"And he ends up on a mountain top?"

"Just briefly. And he does find a degree of *enlightenment*, but he realizes that even that isn't enough, that it doesn't count for anything away from…from living apart, apart from the world, apart from everything. And that's where the quote comes in."

"*The Razor's Edge*?"

"Yes, it's by Somerset Maugham."

"I'd be interested in reading that."

"I have a copy. I loaned it to someone last spring, but he should be done with it by now. I'll check if you like."

"I would. Thanks."

Sandra glanced at her watch. "Well, we should go. I've been chewing your ear off long enough."

Alva shook her head. "No, you haven't. This has been good. You've given me some things to think about."

"And you're better about…about Bernie and all."

Alva shrugged. "I guess. Yes. I'm better. I just need to think about things some."

"Of course." Sandra stood up. "Shall we?"

Alva got up from the bench. "Yes."

Chapter 23

After turning in the job application, Alva and Sandra left the quad and headed down to Market Street.

While turning the corner, Alva asked. "Where do you need to stop?"

"Right here."

The building directly ahead of them had an outside set of narrow stairs that led to a basement door. At the top of the stairs was a sign in wildly colored letters that read: SOHO BOUTIQUE. Although she had passed it often during her previous three years, Alva had never ventured in.

"What kind of a store is this?" she asked as they started down the stairs.

"Well, they sell a lot of different things, most of it in a hippie slash bohemian sort of vein."

When they reached the bottom of the stairs, Sandra held the door for Alva. "After you."

Alva stepped in and came to an immediate stop. "Oh my."

"Different, huh."

For Alva it was. Completely. She had never seen a shop so cluttered with merchandise and, of the items displayed, there was little, if anything, that she recognized at first glance. Also, the lighting, or rather the almost complete lack of it, had a disorienting effect on her. In the back of the store where the cash register was there was an overhead fluorescent light, but, beyond that, what illumination there was came from half a dozen red and blue bulbs that were strategically placed about the ceiling. Also disorienting was the music playing, music she didn't recognize, music that was unlike anything that she had heard before. Her overall impression of the place was that she had stumbled into some sort of bizarre attic, an attic in a dream, or maybe, even a nightmare.

For a moment she just stood there trying to take it all in. As she did so, she noticed something else. It was a fragrance of some sort, one she did not recognize. Suddenly a thought occurred to her about what it might be.

"No," she said in a hoarse whisper taking a step back and bumping into Sandra.

"What's the matter?"

"That smell," Alva said quickly in a hoarse whisper.

"It's incense. Sandalwood, I think. What'd you think it was? Pot?"

Alva turned quickly towards her. "No," she protested. But then, "Well, yes."

Sandra smiled. "You can relax. It's not."

Alva nodded her head, relieved, and the two of them proceeded on.

"Do you know what this music is?" Alva asked.

"I do. It's early Pink Floyd."

"Pink Floyd? Who is that?"

"It's a group."

"That's a different kind of name."

"From what I've been told it's made up of the names of two blues musicians."

"Pink is somebody's name?"

Sandra shrugged. "Like I said, that's what I was told."

"And this is blues?"

Sandra laughed. "It doesn't sound like it, does it?"

"It's sounds like it could be in a dream. Or from outer space."

Sandra nodded. "You're close actually. This song is called 'Astronomy Domine.' What do think?"

"Well, it's different. And interesting."

"I think so too. Look. I have to go in the back and check on something I ordered. Why don't you poke around, explore, and see what else you find *interesting*."

"Okay."

Wandering around slowly, Alva found that a good portion of the store was given over to the display of clothing, most of which looked as if it came from somewhere exotic: Africa, Asia, or maybe South America. They were all in highly colorful patterns. It struck her as odd that, except for a few items, the hooded anoraks for instance, the fabrics were light, some even sheer, and not exactly practical considering the long, cold months that made up the largest part of the school year. Still, their exoticism interested her. It gave her a slight thrill to think about being daring enough to go out in such attire.

Similar to the clothing, Indian tapestries covered the walls of the shop. They too were highly colorful and patterned and of a light sheer fabric. Thinking of the blank walls of her room back at the Cottage, she wondered how one would look hanging there. It would, she knew, certainly be a departure for her in terms of how she had decorated her rooms in the past. Again, it made her feel that it would be daring to decorate her room in such a way.

In one corner of the store a doorway led into a smaller, second room. Upon entering, Alva once again came to a sudden stop. As *stunned* as she had been on first entering the shop, this room actually took her breath away for a moment. If the rest of the shop had seemed outré, this was something well beyond that. Instead of a bizarre attic, this seemed to her like a wild hallucination.

For illumination there were only ceiling lights. Although fluorescent, instead of a soft white light, they emitted a violet glow. This, in itself, was strange enough for Alva, but what struck her most were the posters that completely covered the walls of the room. Each consisted of figures, objects and words in reds, blues, yellows and greens portrayed on a black background. Not only were the colors bright, but, to Alva's amazement, they actually glowed.

As if drawn in, Alva entered the room, moving about slowly, viewing one poster and then another. At first what was depicted seemed tame enough: celestial and stellar scenes, exotic flowers and jungle animals, lakes and peaked mountains, alpine ranges. But then she came upon a series that pictured amazons, some scantily clad, some totally naked. One particular poster that caught her attention was comprised of twelve squares, three by four. There was a square for each sign of the zodiac. In each square a couple was depicted in silhouette, a man and a woman, each with an Afro, each naked, each portraying a different sexual position. Barely able to breathe let alone move away, Alva stood there staring at the poster.

"And what fresh hell is this?"

Startled, Alva turned quickly to find Sandra standing there smiling.

"Have you seen this?" Alva asked hoarsely, pointing at the zodiac poster, her hand shaking as she did so.

Taking a step closer to it, Sandra regarded the poster for a moment. "Well," she said, stepping back, "it's different."

"Different," Alva repeated. "It's obscene. It's sinful."

Sandra smiled. "More silly, if you ask me."

"But look. Look how the colors almost burn."

"It's the black light effect."

"The what?"

Sandra gestured towards the overhead lights. "Black lights," she said. "Ultraviolet. They make certain paints like these glow. And look at your clothes."

Looking down, Alva saw how the threads and the buttons of her blouse seem unnaturally bright. A feeling as if she had been touched by something evil came over her. Pushing past Sandra, Alva quickly left the room, heading for the entrance to the shop. Reaching the door, she pushed it open. Just as she did so she felt a hand grab her by the arm. Alva tried to wrest her arm away, but the hand's grip held her.

"Alva, hold on," Sandra said.

Alva took a step back, and let the door close. She turned to Sandra.

"You okay?" Sandra asked.

"I'm sorry. I…I don't know what came over me."

"A bit of culture shock?"

"I guess so." She shook her head. "I don't know what's wrong with me. It's like I'm the one from a different planet."

"There's nothing wrong with you. When things are new, they're… well, new, and sometimes they take a bit of getting used to."

Alva nodded.

"You still up for coffee?"

"Sure." Alva smiled with relief. "One thing though."

"What's that?"

"I've never had coffee."

Sandra nodded. "Well," she said, "you are having quite a day, aren't you?"

"I guess I am," Alva said with a quick, shy laugh.

Reaching past Alva, Sandra pushed the door open. "Shall we?"

"Sure."

Chapter 24

Charlie's was located around corner at the other end of the block and down an alley. At one time a pool hall, it was now a small restaurant serving standard fare, sandwiches, burgers, fries and the like, plus pizza. There was also a selection of baked goods and a variety of coffees to choose from.

Except for the barista working that afternoon, the place was empty.

"Hi Nick," Sandra said as she and Alva stepped up to the counter.

A young man with dark curly hair and a Fu Manchu moustache was sitting on a stool by the cash register. He looked up from a paperback that he was reading.

"Hey Sandra. How the hell are ya?"

Sandra nodded. "Good. Real good. How about you?"

"Can't complain."

"Nick, this is my good friend Alva."

"Alva," he said. "Nice to meet you."

Alva smiled and nodded. "Me too."

"What can I get you ladies?"

"I'll have a large coffee," Sandra said.

"Let's see if I remember," Nick said. "French Roast? Black? Large?"

"That's it."

"And you, Alva?"

"I'll have the same. But just a small."

"Two on the French Roast black," Nick said placing his book down on the counter. "One large," he said selecting one cup from a stack on the counter. "And," he continued, as he took another from a different stack, "one small. Coming right up."

As Nick stepped away to get the coffees, Sandra turned to Alva, giving her a questioning look. "Coffee?"

Alva shrugged. "I thought I'd try it."

"You might want to take it with cream or milk, maybe even some sugar."

"I'll try it black first."

"Here we are, ladies," Nick said, returning with their coffees and setting them on the counter. "And... they're on the house as it's good to see you again Sandra, and nice to meet you Alva. Enjoy."

Picking up their coffees, Alva and Sandra thanked him and turned to find a place to sit, deciding on a table in a corner of the room.

"Well," Alva said, "here goes." With that she took a tentative sip of her coffee.

Sandra laughed seeing Alva grimace and make a movement as if she was about to spit it out.

"It's bitter," Alva said after forcing down a swallow. She looked at Sandra. "You actually like this."

"An acquired taste. And, to be honest, it did take me a while to get used to it."

"Why would you persist?"

For a moment, Sandra just sat there staring at Alva. "That," she said finally, "is a very good question. Maybe it had something to do with *my own* redefinition. Why don't you cut yours with some sugar and milk or cream?"

"No... no," Alva said, "I can do this". With that she took a second and longer sip after which she grimaced even more severely. "Then again..."

They both laughed.

Sandra took a sip of her coffee and, placing her cup down, she sat holding it with both hands. "Earlier you asked me about Lily and why she smoked, and I said stupidity. That was unkind, especially since she is a phony smoker."

"What do you mean?"

Sandra smiled. "Watch her sometime. She doesn't inhale. She takes it in, but only just. And she exhales it quickly. I doubt any of it gets to her lungs let alone her throat. And she's a phony drinker too. If she's out with people and they're drinking, she'll have a glass of something. I've seen her with Scotch. She'll fill it with ice, and she'll make it last all evening, just sipping away and adding to the ice as it melts. So, her ounce or two of alcohol is watered down to the max. So, she appears to be drinking, and holding her own all evening. It's actually an old Sinatra trick."

"Why does she go to all that trouble?"

"To feel cool. To appear to *be* cool. To be accepted."

"So... so it too can be seen as a matter of redefinition."

Sandra smiled. "Yes," she said, nodding, "good point."

"Like my struggling with this coffee."

"You don't feel accepted?"

"Right here? Right now? With you? Yes. Yes, I do feel accepted."

"Then why struggle with the coffee?" Sandra teased.

"Because," Alva said with a pompous air, "I want it to be a part of my redefinition. In fact, I want it to be the hallmark of my redefinition, the, how shall I put it, the defining redefinition. And to prove it," she went on, raising her cup, "even as tortuous as this is, I'm going to finish this coffee. Nobody's going to call me a phony coffee drinker."

With that, she put the cup to her lips and, girding herself, took another long sip. Putting the cup down, she hesitated for just a moment before swallowing.

"Oh," she said shaking her head. "It is awful."

They both laughed.

"So," Alva asked, "what did you get at…at that… "

"Head shop?"

"What?"

"Never mind." Sandra reached into her purse and drew out a paper bag from which she removed a box like one playing cards came in, but twice as large. The box was yellow with an image of a young man standing in a garden on it. "This," she said, setting the box on the table and sliding it over to Alva.

Alva reached for it, but then, seeing the words 'The Rider Tarot Deck' printed across the top of the box, she recoiled, quickly drawing her hand back.

"What's wrong?" Sandra asked.

"Those…" Alva whispered, "Those are Tarot cards."

"They are. Is there a problem?"

"Sandra. They…they're the devil's. They're evil."

"What?" Sandra asked, completely taken aback. "Evil?"

"Yes. Yes, they are. The devil uses them to lead us into evil, to make us do things that he wants us to do, things against God.

They do it by making us think that we can predict the future. And nobody can do that, only God. They're the devil's, Sandra, the devil's."

"The devil's," Sandra repeated. "You're serious."

"I am, Sandra. And I'm afraid for you."

For a moment Sandra just sat there staring at Alva. "Well," she said finally, shaking her head. "I...I..." she smiled. "I'm touched by your concern, but I don't think there's any danger here, not with these. They're harmless."

"Sandra. That's what the devil wants you to believe, please," Alva implored. "Just get rid of them. Destroy them."

"Alva," Sandra said calmly, reaching and drawing the box back towards her. "They're just cards, cards with pictures. That's all. And I won't be using them to try to predict the future, or to cast any spells or..."

"You might not intend to, but..."

Sandra shook her head. "Believe me, Alva. Nothing and no one is going to make me use them in any way other than for what I have planned. Not even the devil."

"Then what? What are you going to do with them?"

"They're for the internship that I'm doing over at the Jewish home this semester. Do you know what a Rorschach Test is?"

"Inkblots?"

"Yes."

"And people are supposed to describe what they think they see in them?"

"Where people describe what they *do* see in them," Sandra corrected. "I'll be using these," Sandra tapped the box with her fingertips, "in the same manner, to get people to respond to the images on the cards and talk about how they interpret them which, hopefully, will get them talking about things, things that they are concerned about, maybe issues in their life, or maybe just nice memories."

"But you'll be exposing them to evil images, images that will let the devil into their lives?"

"Have you ever seen these cards? This style deck in particular?"

"No… no I haven't."

Sandra picked up the box of cards.

"Would you like to?"

"No."

"Okay," Sandra said. Noting the finality in Alva's tone, she placed the box back in the paper bag. "I don't want to make you uncomfortable," she said returning the bag to her purse.

Alva smiled meekly. "Thank you."

"Just for the record," Sandra said gently, with a smile, "I don't consider myself to be an agent of the devil, and the cards in this deck, the images, are…well, tame, tame and accessible, simple images in basic colors. I think you would… Well, if you ever change your mind…" Sandra shrugged.

Alva frowned. "I'm sorry. I don't think you're evil. I don't. It's just…"

"It's okay. Next topic? Something less controversial?"

"Yes," Alva said with noticeable relief, but then she hesitated. "When I first met you, you were looking at cards you had spread out on your desk. Were they…?"

Sandra smiled. "Yes. The same. I just needed another deck in a larger format, to use in group situations."

"So, you've been doing this a while?"

"Yes."

"And it works? It gets people to talk?"

"Yes, for the most part. We have a good deal of fun with them. Anyway, I'm about done with my coffee. How about you?"

"Yes…yes, I am."

"Shall we go?"

"Sure."

"And Alva," Sandra said as they stood up to go, "I hope I didn't ruin things today. I've enjoyed spending time with you like this."

"Me too," Alva said quickly and earnestly. "Me too."

Sandra smiled. "We'll have to make a habit of this."

Alva nodded vigorously. "Yes."

Chapter 25

It was early on a Saturday morning a couple weeks later that Alva was sitting up in her bed reading. It was now autumn, or at least it was by the calendar. The days, though mild, still had some warmth to them. The previous night, after arriving home following an evening at the library, Alva had found her room decidedly cool, enough so that, before going to bed, she shut her window. Now though, feeling that she could do with some fresh air, Alva set her book down and got up to open the window a crack.

She had just returned to her chair and picked up her book when Sandra appeared in the doorway.

"You're up," Sandra said quietly, slightly surprised. "You're an early bird for a Saturday morning, especially for this place."

"You're up."

Sandra nodded. "The breakfast shift. I'm subbing for someone. What're you reading?"

Alva turned the book over so that Sandra could see the cover.

"The Nag Hammadi," Sandra said, reading the title. "Sounds serious for a Saturday morning."

"Just getting some background for the job."

"Ah," Sandra said. "Are you going to be around later?"

Alva nodded. "I should be."

"Well, I'll catch up with you when I'm done at the dining hall. Maybe we can go for a walk in the park. It won't be long until old man winter is upon us."

"A walk sounds fine."

"Then I'll see you later. Enjoy the morning."

"You too."

Alva sat there listening to Sandra's footsteps go down the stairs. Then, turning back to her book, she resumed her reading. It didn't go well. With everything so quiet, she couldn't stop her mind from wandering. Again and again she had to bring her attention back to the text, but, again and again, she found her thoughts running to other matters. Even when she forced herself and managed to get through a paragraph, or even just a sentence or two, she realized that her comprehension was nil. For a good hour plus she kept at it, but, finally, frustrated, she closed the book and put it down on the bed beside her.

Although finished with reading at that moment, she still felt out of sorts. She just sat there, a victim of inertia. The morning wore on.

As she sat there, Alva found herself taking in the room as a whole. The bare walls left her with a feeling of emptiness, as if no one lived there. This she found unsettling. Yes, there were articles on the desk and books on the shelves. Those were her clothes in the closet. But nothing in the room said 'Alva,' and this struck her at that moment as wrong, something that had to be corrected. The thought stirred her to action.

Alva suddenly remembered the tapestries that she had seen at the Soho Boutique down on Market Street. She tried to picture the room with a tapestry on each of her two blank walls.

"Yes," she said, deciding that something like that would do. "Yes."

Taken with the idea, Alva got up quickly and got ready to head out. As she did, she found herself feeling slightly agitated. She knew that this was silly, but she didn't let it bother her or even slow her down. She was excited and she was determined to run with that. She was, she felt, *on a mission*. As an afterthought and because she felt slightly guilty about abandoning her reading, she picked up the book from her bed and stuck it inside her bag, thinking that, in the event she couldn't find what she was looking for in the way of tapestries, she might take advantage of the pleasant weather by sitting outside somewhere and continuing with her reading. But, as afterthoughts sometimes go, she did not place much in the way of importance to it. Tapestries were her focus, and focused she was.

The feeling of excitement stayed with her as she made her way to Market Street. Still, she appreciated the quiet of the morning, the emptiness of the streets and the spacious feel to everything. It felt as if the morning was hers and hers alone. She found herself smiling, smiling broadly. Drawing near to the boutique, her sense of excitement increased, and she felt her breathing grow slightly labored. She went down the stairs almost at a trot.

Reaching the shop's door, Alva took hold of the doorknob and pulled. To her disappointment she found the door locked. Looking around she found a sign on the wall next to the door with the shop's hours on it. To her annoyance and further disappointment, she saw that it didn't open until ten. Alva looked at her watch. It was just a little after eight. Annoyed and disappointed, she turned and trudged slowly back up the stairs.

Reaching the street level, she stopped to consider her options. For one brief moment she considered just heading back to the Cottage, but that felt to her like admitting defeat and she dismissed the notion. Remembering the book that she had brought along and with the morning as fair and as quiet as it was, she decided that she would find a place to sit and *try* to read until the shop opened at ten. She saw a bench directly across the street.

"That'll do," she said to herself and started to walk towards it.

She stopped at the curb, and looked both ways before crossing. At that moment she became suddenly aware of the aroma of baked goods. It occurred to her then that she hadn't had breakfast yet, and, taking stock, she found that she was indeed hungry. Looking up Market Street, she wondered what might be open, somewhere that she could get a donut or something. It was then that she remembered Charlie's and she decided to walk over to see if it was open.

When she arrived, Alva was pleased to find an OPEN sign hanging on the door. Once inside she stopped. After the brightness of the morning, Charlie's seemed dark in contrast, and she waited a moment for her eyes to adjust.

Music, something acoustic and instrumental, was playing at a low volume.

"Morning," someone said.

Looking around, Alva found a young woman standing behind the counter looking in her direction.

"Good morning," Alva said walking slowly up to her.

"It takes a minute, doesn't it," said the young woman with a smile.

"Sorry?"

"For the eyes to adjust."

"Oh. Yes, yes it does."

"What can I get you?"

"I'll have a small coffee. The French Roast, black."

The young woman took a cup from one of the stacks on the counter and turned to get the coffee.

Waiting, Alva looked around the room. A group of six young men in army camo were seated at one of the larger tables. One of them had sergeant's stripes. Except for them, the place was empty.

Just as the young woman returned with Alva's coffee, the door which led back into the kitchen, opened and a young man came through carrying a tray of baked goods. Alva saw that it was Nick.

"Well, hello," he said. "You're…"

"Alva. Hello."

"Alva. Right," He set the tray down on the counter. "And I'm…"

"You're Nick."

"Right, and this is Carol. Alva. Carol. Carol. Alva." He turned to Carol. "Alva's a friend of Sandra's." He turned back to Alva. "How about a croissant? They're right out of the oven."

"Sure."

Plucking one from the tray, Nick placed it on a small plate and slid it across the counter to Alva. She was just about to ask for it to-go when Nick spoke up.

"Take an extra napkin." He pointed at the croissant. "They're big time butter."

Realizing the potential messiness, Alva decided to just have it and her coffee there, and, after paying, she took a seat at the same table that she and Sandra had sat at. The group of young men glanced her way once when she sat down and then went back to talking amongst themselves. Settling in with her coffee and croissant, Alva took her book from her bag, opened it and started to read.

She was surprised to find the reading proceed much better than it had back in her room. The low murmur of the young men's voices combined with the music created a backdrop of sorts, one that, to a certain extent, helped against distraction. Sitting there, sipping her coffee and breaking off small bites from the croissant, Alva found herself making good headway through the text; she even became quite engrossed in it. It wasn't until she heard the scuffling sound of chairs that Alva glanced up from her book.

The young men were getting up from their table. For a moment she watched them put on black berets and gather their things before returning to her reading. A moment later the sound, quite close, of someone clearing his throat caused her to look up again. To her surprise, she found one of the young men standing at her table, looming over her and grinning.

"Hello, Sleeping Beauty," he said.

"Sorry?"

"You don't remember me?"

Alva shook her head.

"It's probably the uniform. It's different from my other one."

Alva shrugged. "Sorry?" she said again.

The young man, still grinning, nodded. "It was back at the beginning of the semester, at the library. It was closing time and you were sitting comfortably, sleeping away. I was the security guard, the one that woke you."

Alva nodded her head slowly. "The security guard. Yes, I remember."

"I've seen you there quite a bit. Up in that room where they keep the rare stuff."

"Yes. I work there now, part time."

"So, since we work in close proximity, what do you say if, from here on in, when I see you there, I'll poke my head in and say hello…"

It took her a moment before Alva realized that he was asking for her name.

"Alva," she said somewhat flustered.

"Alva," he repeated. "It sounds southern. But then, so do you a bit." He held out his hand. "I'm…"

"Brian!"

The two of them turned to find the other five young men standing at the door looking their way.

"C'mon," the one with sergeant's stripes barked. "Let's go."

Brian, with a frown, turned back to Alva. "I gotta go," he said hurriedly. "I'll see you around though. Okay?"

"Sure."

With that he turned to go.

"Brian," Alva blurted out.

He stopped and turned to look back at her.

"It was nice to meet you," Alva said quickly. "I'll see you at the library sometime."

Brian smiled. "Sure thing."

"Brian!" the sergeant barked again.

"Coming, mother."

The other young men laughed. A split second later so did the sergeant.

After they were gone, Alva just sat there in a mild state of shock. She couldn't believe that a complete stranger would just come up to her. But more than that, there was something unreal, unreal for her, to the way that she had responded to this, for all intents and purposes, stranger. It was, she felt, as if someone else, some *other* other had stepped in and taken her place during the interchange. It left her feeling unnerved, unnerved but not exactly in a completely unpleasant way. She was, she realized, actually thrilled to find that it wasn't some *other* participating in that moment, but that it was she, she herself that had handled the situation and in a way so out of character for her, but which seemed just right under the circumstances. This pleased her. It pleased her very much.

"More coffee?"

Alva started, drawn out of her reverie, to find Carol standing there with a glass coffee pot in hand. Looking at her watch, she saw that it was almost ten.

"No," Alva said with a smile. "No, thank you."

"You sure? Second cup's free."

Alva smiled and shook her head. "No, no thanks." Closing her book, she tucked it into her bag.

"So," Carol said, "you know Brian."

Alva shook her head, taking one last sip of her coffee. "Not really. I only spoke to him once before, at the library."

"Oh. Well, he's nice. And not your typical *rotsee*."

"I'm sorry?"

"ROTC. Most of them are pretty gung-ho, which, considering the climate here when it comes to 'Nam and all, says something. But Brian..." Carol shrugged. "I don't think he takes it too, too seriously."

"He works at the library."

"Yes, he does." Carol smiled and shook her head. "From one

uniform to another." She shook her head again. "And, on top of all that, he belongs to a fraternity. Talk about unfashionable?"

"Is it?"

Carol gave Alva a questioning look. "One doesn't see much of the Joe College thing here anymore." She shrugged. "Not at the moment at least. 'Going Greek' isn't really *in*, to say nothing of ROTC. But who knows? Maybe it'll all come back some day, panty raids and all. Maybe this stretch is just a brief aberration."

Not sure how to respond to any of this, Alva smiled, stood up, and slung her bag over her shoulder. She started to reach for her cup and plate.

"You can leave those."

"You sure? I don't mind."

"Thanks. Just leave 'em. Things are slow enough this morning, and I have to come back and give the tables a wipe anyway. Enjoy your Saturday."

Alva smiled and nodded. "Thank you. You too."

Alva was still smiling when she left Charlie's. The morning was turning out well. She thought about the possibility of making coffee at Charlie's a regular Saturday morning event, and that maybe Sandra would be interested in joining her. That, she thought, would be great. And she was pleased to remember that Sandra was only subbing today for someone else, that she normally didn't work Saturday mornings.

It was while considering all of this as she walked up Market Street that another thought occurred to her. She wondered if maybe Saturday mornings at Charlie's was a regular thing for Brian and his friends. It was, she thought, possible, and the possibility of it made her smile.

Chapter 26

"What have we here?"

Alva, standing on her bed, her arms raised over her head, held a tapestry up to the wall. Looking back over her shoulder she found Sandra standing there in the doorway. Pleased, Alva lowered her arms, turned and stepped down off her bed.

"I did some shopping."

"I see that." Sandra looked at the tapestry that Alva was holding. "You went back to the boutique?" she asked.

Alva noticed the slight tone of surprise in Sandra's voice. "I did," she said somewhat sheepishly.

Sandra nodded slowly, with a slight smile. "And it was okay?"

"It was."

Sandra pointed at a second tapestry lying folded on Alva's bed. "Two of them?"

"Yes. The pattern is the same. This blue one represents the night. I'm going to hang next to my bed. The orange one, for day, will go directly across from it. What do you think?" she asked eagerly.

Sandra nodded. "I like it."

"Really?"

"Really."

"You don't think it's silly."

"Not at all. How'd you come up with it?"

Alva shrugged. "I don't know. I was in a really good mood and I was taking my time and when I saw this orange one and the pattern with its the big circle… here, let me show you." Dropping the blue tapestry, she picked up the orange one and spread it out on the bed. See, it made me think of the sun and I thought about how it would be to wake up and turn over and see it there." Alva pointed to the opposite wall. "Then when I saw the blue one… well, I figured 'night and day.'"

"Clever. And very good."

"You mean it?"

"I do."

Alva smiled. "I'm glad. I was hoping you'd like them. The woman there told me that they're all the way from India."

"Yes. The Mandala."

"The what?"

"The pattern. It's a Mandala. That's what it's called."

"Oh. The woman said they sell a lot of them."

"I'm sure. Hippie chic."

Alva frowned. "Hippie chic?"

Sandra laughed. "Don't worry. It's not catching, although you might want to resist the any sudden urge to make a skirt or blouse out of them. As a wall covering, they'll do fine. Functional…*and attractive*."

Relieved to hear this, Alva smiled.

"Oh," she said suddenly, dropping the second tapestry on the bed. "I got something else when I was there."

Stepping quickly to her desk, she picked up a white paper bag that was sitting there and turned to Sandra. Reaching into the bag she brought out a pale, white candle about six inches long and with a four-inch diameter. She held it out to Sandra.

"What do think," Alva asked.

"Nice. It's real nice."

"Do you mean it?"

"I do."

"Good. I got it for you. Take it."

"Oh. I can't."

"Yes. Yes, you can. Look." Setting the candle on her desk, Alva reached into the bag and took out a second candle, identical to the first. "One for you and one for me."

"This is very thoughtful of you," Sandra said quietly, taking the candle.

Alva shrugged. "It's been so good for me getting to know you. This is going to sound childish, but I was…I was real worried how things were going to work out this year with everything being so different for me. And I wanted things to be different, but, really, I was scared, which is stupid, I know, like I'm three years behind where I should be. But things…things have been good, real good, and you've been a big part of it and…well, I just wanted to do something to show that I appreciate it all."

"Well, thank you. For this," Sandra said taking up the candle, "and for those kind words. I'm glad things are working out for you. It's been good for me too you know." She looked at the candle, turning it over slowly in her hands. "I do like this. I like its simplicity."

"Me too. That's what I liked about them. As soon as I saw it…them, I knew I had to get them. And with my first paycheck. And there were just these two like this. That made them special.

The others… They were nice in a way. Real colorful, but…" She looked at the candle in her hands. "These just seemed so right."

"There's one thing you should know, Alva."

"What's that?"

"They're not allowed here. Nothing with an open flame is. Not even incense."

"What? No!"

Sandra nodded. "I'm afraid so."

"Why not?"

Sandra shrugged. "Fire safety, I guess. It's the same in all the residence buildings."

"Wait a minute," Alva said. "That incense smell at the boutique, I've smelled that here. And I've seen candles in the other rooms here."

Sandra smiled. "All I said was they're not allowed. I didn't say that people didn't have them."

"But how can they if they're against the rules?"

"Because it's one rule that, apparently, is not enforced."

"But that's wrong. If it's a rule it should be enforced at least until the rule is changed."

Sandra shrugged. "Well, it could be a psychology kind of thing."

"What do you mean?"

"The idea is that people, some people, present company excluded of course, break rules, just for the sake of breaking rules. So certain rules are made just to *accommodate* those people. Rules of no real consequence."

"Do you think that's the case with the candles?"

Sandra shrugged.

"Well," Alva sighed, "I guess I better return these."

"Oh, no. Not mine, you won't."

"Why not?"

"I want it."

"Well, I want mine too."

"Then we'll keep them."

"And besides, no one says we *have* to light them."

"Well," Sandra said with a sly smile, "I have to be honest with you. Let's just say that some evening you may see a bit of candle glow in my room."

"Hmm," Alva said thoughtfully, "and where would you get matches?"

"In my desk. Top drawer."

"Shall we be rule breakers then?"

"Well, I think it would be remiss to not take advantage of this splendid opportunity to be...oh, miscreants. So, let's."

"Let's," Alva said. She motioned to her walls. "Okay, well, back to these tapestries."

"Can you use some help?"

"Sure. I'd appreciate that."

"Do you have anything to hang them with?"

"The woman at the store said that push pins will work." Alva placed her candle on her desk. From the bag she removed a clear plastic container. "Do you think these are enough?" she asked holding it out to Sandra.

"Plenty. The fabric is light, so they should work fine. Let me just get out of these work clothes, and I'll be back."

Sandra was just about through the doorway when she stopped, turned, and held up the candle that Alva had given her. "Thanks again."

Alva smiled. "One thing though. It doesn't make me feel all

that mature, breaking the rules."

"Alva, sometimes maturity can be a bit overrated."

"Hmm. I like that."

"I'll be right back."

Chapter 27

It was on a Saturday several weeks later that Alva woke to the sound of rain pelting against her window. The days had grown shorter. Opening her eyes, Alva found the room dark. Although it was plenty warm there beneath the quilt, it did not leave Alva with that secure, toasty feeling that it should have. With the darkness and with the wind driving the rain against the glass, there was a cold to the small room, one that had a presence that seemed to fill the room. Alva closed her eyes and burrowed deeper under the quilt.

Hoping to fall back to sleep, Alva turned her face to the wall, but sleep did not return. There was something *insistent* to the sound of the rain, as if it was demanding her attention. At times, owing to gusts, the window rattled, causing her to wonder just how much the panes of glass could stand. And so, no, sleep did not return, and there was no indication that it would. Finally admitting this to herself, Alva turned on to her back and lay there looking up at the ceiling. It was while she lay there that something out of the corner of her eye caught her attention. Although too dark to tell for sure, Alva was certain that she had seen something there, some quick movement in her doorway.

Turning her head slowly in that direction, Alva lay there holding her breath and watching intently for any subsequent movement. For several moments nothing happened. Then…

"Alva?" a quiet voice said.

"Yes?" Alva answered, almost in a whisper.

"It's me, Sandra. Did I wake you?"

"No," Alva said rising up on one elbow. "I was just lying here listening to the rain."

"Can I turn a light on?"

"Sure. There's a lamp on the desk."

Alva watched as Sandra's dark form crossed the room. A moment later the small desk lamp came on. Although not exceedingly bright, Alva still raised a hand to shield her eyes. She saw that Sandra was wearing a pair of men's flannel pajamas.

"What time is it?"

"Half past six."

"Are you subbing for someone this morning?" Alva asked.

"No, but I am going in this afternoon."

"It seems like a good morning to sleep in."

"Yeah," Sandra said tentatively, "I tried, but all this raw weather got me to thinking about hot coffee and freshly baked muffins or something along those lines, and I thought about Charlie's and well…I was wondering if you'd like to brave the elements and go there this morning. I know it's a crappy day and all, but…" Sandra shrugged. "What do you think?"

"I think I'd like that a lot." Alva said quickly tossing off her quilt and sitting up in bed.

"Great. They open at seven, which gives us enough time to get ready and hike down there. Shall we?"

"Let's."

"Better dress for the weather."

"I have a big wool sweater and a slicker with a hood."

"Perfect."

Which it turned out to be as, leaving by the front door of the Cottage, they came to a sudden stop at the top of the stairs.

"Is that snow?" Sandra asked.

"It looks like it."

The two of them stood there. There was snow, but just touches of it. They saw that it was mostly a mix of rain and snow that fell.

"And it's not even Halloween yet," Sandra said. "Good thing you mentioned wearing a sweater. It is raw out here."

They started down the stairs, taking them slowly in case they might be slick. There was considerable wind driving the mix of rain and snow at them, causing them both to pull their slicker hoods up and pull the peaks down to eyebrow level. Once down the stairs, they started up the sidewalk and turned at the corner. The wind was now at their backs and pushed them along.

"Are we crazy?" Sandra asked.

Alva laughed. "Definitely."

"But it's okay, right?"

"It's definitely okay."

With the snow being only a small percentage of the precipitation, there was no noticeable accumulation on the sidewalk or pavement, and so they were able to stride along with some confidence.

"An adventure," Sandra said at one point.

"An adventure," Alva echoed.

Since it was early and cold, there was no one else about. It was still dark enough so that the streetlights were on. The surfaces of the sidewalks and streets glistened with their illumination.

Although the wind continued to be at their backs for the better part of the trek, every once in a while a rogue gust pulled at their hoods and lashed the wintry mix at them head on enough so that they had to wipe the wet from their faces and pull their hoods down again.

When they got to Market Street, they found it too was deserted. Although everything was closed, most of the outside lights of the stores were lit, lending a festive feel to the scene.

"It's like Christmas," Alva said as they made their way along.

"That it is."

"Are you sure Charlie's will be open?"

"It better be," Sandra said.

"Well, even if they're not, I'm glad we came out."

Sandra turned to look at her. "You know, so am I," she said. Suddenly, she stopped. "Hey!" she said, placing a hand on Alva's arm. "Smell that?"

"Yes!" Alva said excitedly. "Baking! Somebody's baking!"

"It's got to be Charlie's!"

With that Sandra grabbed Alva's hand and the two of them raced down the sidewalk.

Chapter 28

Coming up to the front door of Charlie's, they were both relieved and thrilled to find it unlocked. Rushing in, they closed the door behind them, and then stood there on the floor mat wiping their boots off. After their walk in the raw weather, the warmth of the interior combined with the aroma of freshly baked goods seemed like something truly wonderful.

"Well, here's two hardy souls," Nick called out to them from behind the counter. "Two hardy souls in desperate need of…of the good French Roast, right? One large and one small?"

"You can make mine a large also," Alva said as she and Sandra stood stamping their feet and trying to wipe some of the moisture from their slickers.

"Don't bother with all that," Nick said. "Just hang your ponchos on the backs of those two chairs by the radiator. That'll dry them off soon enough."

As they did so, Alva looked around the cafe and was mildly disappointed to find that it was empty. Although she had hoped to make these Saturday morning visits a regular thing, with Sandra subbing every Saturday that hadn't happened. Also, since that last time they had talked, she hadn't run into Brian at the library as she had hoped she would.

"You ladies interested in scones this morning?" Nick asked, setting their coffees on the counter. "They're just about to come out of the oven."

"What kind do you have?" Sandra asked.

"Blueberry, apple and…" Nick looked around the room in an exaggerated conspiratorial manner, "something truly decadent. Lemon coconut." He nodded his head slowly. "And I do mean decadent. If they deem pot to be illegal, it should be the same for these."

"Well," Sandra said, "having braved the elements to get here this morning, I'm going to treat myself to a little decadence."

"A fine choice. And you Ms. Alva?"

"I don't know. I…I'm not sure about the lemon coconut."

"Why don't you get one of the others," Sandra suggested, "and then we can share."

"Now there," Nick said, "is a fine piece of wisdom on this raw and beastly morning. Worthy of Solomon. Ms. Alva?"

"I'll have the blueberry."

"And you won't regret it." He leaned over the counter and then, in a whisper, "That's my particular favorite." He stood back up and nodded his head. "They still might need a minute. Why don't you ladies take your coffees and have a seat and I'll bring the scones over when they're ready. You shall be dining in, won't you?"

"Oh yes," Sandra said. "We certainly shall."

"Solomon again. 'Tis not a fit night, *or morning*, out for man nor beast. Or woman nor beast. Or…I think I'll just turn around now and go and see about those scones."

Taking their coffees, Sandra and Alva went to, what Alva now considered, *their* table.

"I need to ask you a question," Alva said as they took their seats.

Sandra looked at her and saw that Alva seemed embarrassed about something. "What's that?"

Alva leaned over in a conspiratorial manner. "What," she whispered, "is a scone?"

"Ah. Okay. How shall I put it? It's sort of like half cake and half biscuit, or maybe I should say it's like a large cookie, but just not as sweet. Trust me, you'll like them, and here they are," Nick stepped up to their table, a plate in each hand, a scone on each plate.

"Yes, and yes," Nick said. "Here they are indeed. One lemon coconut scone for Ms. Sandra," he said, setting a plate in front of Sandra, "and one blueberry," he paused a moment to roll his eyes, "for Ms. Alva. And here's a knife so you can cut them up and mix and match."

"You can keep that, young man," Sandra said as, picking up one scone and breaking it in two, she then proceeded to do the same with the other. She looked up and smiled at Nick.

"How very Biblical of you," Nick said solemnly. "Straight out of the Last Supper or maybe the feeding of the multitude."

Sandra glanced over at Alva and saw her stiffen at Nick's comment. She looked up at Nick again. "Not quite."

"Anything else?"

"We're all set."

"Then enjoy." With that Nick bowed first to Sandra, then to Alva, and then, still bowed over, he backed away a couple steps until he bumped into a neighboring table, at which point he turned and headed back to the counter.

Alva turned to Sandra, her expression serious.

"Is he okay?" Alva asked in a whisper.

"Mmm. I'd say he's more than okay."

"What do you mean?"

Sandra shook her head and smiled. "Nothing."

"Well, he seems different from the last time we were here."

"How so?"

"I don't know. More animated. And his eyes... Did you notice? They're kinda red, and they look strange, like the pupils are too big."

Sandra nodded, still smiling. "That they do."

"Do you think he's been drinking?"

"No," Sandra said, shaking her head. "I can honestly say that I don't think that's it."

"Look at him now."

Sandra turned to look. Nick was standing there at the counter, practically hovering over the tray of scones. He had a scone in each hand. As they watched he proceeded to take a bite from one and then the other. Sandra and Alva watched him repeat the process, eating hungrily, going, over and over, from one scone to the other.

"Maybe," Sandra offered, taking a bite of her scone, "maybe he's doing a taste test."

"A taste test? The way he's devouring them? He's practically inhaling them."

Laughing, Sandra almost choked.

"Are you okay?"

Her eyes moist, Sandra nodded and took a sip from her coffee. "Yes. I'm fine," she said. "Maybe he's just been using an appetite enhancer."

"A what?"

Sandra shook her head again. "Nothing."

"You keep saying that."

Sandra shrugged.

"Hey! Ms. Alva!"

The two of them turned to find Nick still hovering over the tray of scones, but now looking their way. "Blueberry," he said holding up the last bite of one of the scones. "Definitely the blueberry."

Smiling weakly, Alva nodded her head.

Nick popped the last bite of scone into his mouth as well as what was left of the other. With cheeks bulging, he picked up the tray and headed for the door leading back into the kitchen.

Alva turned to find Sandra quietly laughing to herself. "What?" she asked.

Sandra shook her head. "Nothing. Next topic?"

"Okay."

"I've been meaning to tell you that I really like what you did with your room with the tapestries."

"Thanks. I'm pleased with it too. It just feels like the room is more mine now, more *me*."

"Investment."

Alva nodded. "That's it I guess."

"They certainly do something for the room. Any more plans in that line?"

Alva shrugged. "Nothing at the moment, but…but I've been thinking about going to that boutique store again. When I bought the tapestries, I walked around the place a little more."

"Avoiding the black light room."

"Yes," Alva said, frowning, "but not because…" She shook her head. "I was silly that time, wasn't I?"

Sandra shrugged. "Not really. An honest, first time reaction."

"And once again showing how inexperienced I am, and in so, so many ways."

"First experiences."

"Yeah." Alva rolled her eyes. "But it seems to be that way all the time with me."

"That'll change as you go along. Experience, reaction, evaluation, re-evaluation and then...re-definition, that's the process and it goes on over time."

Alva took a deep breath and let it out slowly. "It hasn't been much like that in my case. More inexperience on top of inexperience on top of more inexperience."

"Cut yourself some slack."

"I should, shouldn't I?"

"Of course. Look at you, living in your own place now, decorating it, working *and* going to school and just managing all that. And...well, tell me. How are you doing with sharing a roof with lesbians?"

Alva sat there and contemplated for a moment. "I guess," she said, finally, "I really haven't thought about it much."

"Well, that could certainly be taken as a sign of change, of acceptance."

"I suppose so. That's not saying that I think it's right."

"But it does seem like you're keeping an open mind."

"Maybe."

"'Maybe' is a good point to start from. But we digress. We were talking about your doing more to your room. You said you walked around the boutique some."

"I did. That's how I came upon the candles. And they have all sorts of stuff there. Some of it is pretty weird."

"Like what?" Sandra asked.

"There was this one table that… Well, I have a great uncle back home, Uncle Earl, and he's a smoker, but he doesn't buy cigarettes, he rolls his own from a tin of 'Half And Half.' The thing is, he uses 'Bugler' papers. There're little packets of them all over his house and in his workshop. They have them there at the boutique, and they were on this table with a whole variety of packets of different brands. I mean, more kinds than I ever thought there were. The thing is, there was no tobacco there for sale. Most of the table was taken up with these little pipes made from all sorts of things and then there were these…I don't know what you'd call them. They were clear tubes, open at the top, maybe a foot high, maybe a little shorter. At the base of each, right at the bottom, there was a bowl like on a pipe but real, real small. I was going to ask what they were, but…well, I was too embarrassed to. Do you know what they are?"

"Well…" Before going on, she took a long sip of her coffee, after which she broke off a piece of her scone and popped it in her mouth.

"Well?" Alva asked.

"Sorry," Sandra said swallowing. She looked at Alva and smiled. "Bongs. They're called bongs."

"Bongs," Alva repeated. "What are they for? I mean they look like they're for smoking except…well, except that the bowls are really small. And it's the same with those strange pipes. And if they are for smoking, why don't they sell tobacco there?"

"Yeah," Sandra said taking another sip of coffee and shifting in her seat a bit. "They are for smoking, but for…for something other than tobacco."

"For what-" Alva stopped. A second later her eyes went wide. "No," she said in a whisper.

Sandra nodded. "Yes. 'Fraid so. They're for smoking marijuana. And hash."

"Hash?"

"A distant cousin to pot."

"But that's against the law."

"It is. But the *paraphernalia* is not. At least not yet, not around here."

"Well, that's wrong."

Sandra shrugged. "Be that as it may, there's definitely a market around here for those items." She took another bite of her scone.

"So, there are people around here who actually smoke marijuana?" she asked in a whisper.

This time Sandra did actually choke on her bite of scone. Using her napkin, she spit it out and forced herself to try and breathe deeply.

"Are you okay?" Alva asked, concerned. "Should I get you some water?"

With her napkin to her mouth, Sandra held up her other hand, palm out, and shook her head as she continued to hack and try to breathe.

Alva stood up. "I'll get some water."

"No," Sandra said between hacks. "I'll be okay. Sit."

Sitting down, Alva watched intently as Sandra caught her breath.

"Alva," Sandra said hoarsely when she was finally in the clear. Wiping her eyes with her sleeve, she looked over at Alva and smiled. "You got me that time."

"Sorry."

Finally regaining her composure, Sandra took a sip of her coffee. "Yes," she said, "folks around here smoke pot. Case in point." Sandra gestured towards the counter where Nick, having returned from the kitchen, now stood sorting out another tray of baked goods.

"What do you mean? You mean…you mean him?"

"It's fairly obvious, or it is if you know what to look for. You even mentioned his eyes and that he seemed *different*."

Alva glanced in Nick's direction and frowned. "That's sad."

"What do you mean?" Sandra asked taking a sip from her coffee.

"He must feel…well, pretty alone."

This time, although she did sputter some, Sandra was able to catch herself and not start choking again. "Alva," she said, shaking her head, "he's not alone."

"What…"

"Smoking pot is… It's pretty much accepted as part of the culture here."

"Here? Here at Charlie's?"

"No. Here at the university, and, if not accepted, it's tolerated, and, if not tolerated, well… folks just tend to look the other way."

"But it's illegal. It's a drug. People get hooked on it."

"Hooked on it? Well…maybe. But if they do, it's not like being hooked on heroin. People don't go into any kind of serious withdrawal because of it. Not really. At least not to my knowledge."

"What do you mean by 'part of the culture here'?"

"Its use is fairly widespread. I think it's safe to say that those that don't use it, or haven't at least tried it, make up a small percentage of the university population, a very small percentage."

For a good long moment Alva sat there staring at Sandra. As much as she was shocked and upset by these revelations, she was, once again, also embarrassed by both her apparent *naivete* and her obvious obliviousness in regard to her surroundings, especially since this was her fourth year in college.

"What's the matter?" Sandra asked.

"Nothing," Alva said with a sigh.

"Nothing?"

"It's just that it keeps seeming like nothing is the way it should be, and, even worse, that it's always been like this here and that I've just been unaware, just so unaware as to how things really are."

"I'll say it again, cut yourself some slack. These things weren't an issue, weren't part of the dynamics of where you were and what you were doing. Now they are. And now you're dealing with them."

"Thanks," Alva said quietly.

"And I'll be honest," Sandra went on, "it was 'culture shock' time for me too when I first got here."

"So do most people go through this kind of thing their freshman year?"

"No, I wouldn't say most. To a lot of people, the folks from New York and Jersey and Boston, it was pretty much old hat. And back then I felt pretty intimidated when I was first around them. But then I figured..." Sandra shrugged.

"And you had no problem *accepting* things, like marijuana, and other things?"

"In time. And if not accepting, then at least trying to get to a point where they didn't make me uncomfortable."

"I guess that's what I should try, but...but with some things, like the marijuana...I don't know that I can. It's a crime."

"It is, but it's what some folks call a victimless crime. I don't know of anyone that's been hurt by it, except maybe that their grades suffered because of it. Folks keep a pretty low profile when they use it. Most of the people I know of that smoke pot just sit around quietly, listening to music, or reading, or watching TV."

"Okay."

"As far as enforcement goes, it's kind of like it is with gays. In a lot of places, there are still anti-homosexual laws on the books, but it's real rare that one hears of them ever being enforced. Again, it's probably a 'why bother' kind of thing. And again, if it is a crime, it's a victimless one."

"But what about perverts?"

Sandra frowned. "That's a bogus argument used by anti-gay people," she said abruptly and with enough heat so that Alva noticed. "There's no denying that there are gay perverts, but there is also no denying that there are also straight perverts, and I'd bet that the percentages are higher in the straight world."

"I didn't mean anything by asking that. I didn't mean to offend. I just..." Alva shook her head. "Again, I'm just naïve."

"No offense taken."

"You two are looking mighty serious."

Sandra and Alva looked up to find Nick drawing near them with a full coffee pot in hand.

"We're just discussing life, life in an ever expanding and curved universe," Sandra said.

"Well, that certainly sounds serious. More coffee?"

"Please. But just a drop."

"And you?"

Alva nodded.

"So," Nick went on as he poured the coffee, "have you two come up with the ultimate answer to it all?"

"Close," Sandra said. "We're getting close."

"Fantastic. I think that deserves a round of croissants. On the house."

Sandra held up the remains of her scone. "Thanks Nick, but I'm having trouble finishing this off."

"Same here," said Alva.

"Then let me bag up a couple for you both to take with you."

"Thanks, but that's really not necessary."

"All the more reason to do it. I'll be back."

"Well, that's awful nice of him," Alva said.

"Hmm. He probably thinks we're as hungry as he is."

"What do you mean?"

"That's the appetite enhancer that I mentioned earlier. He probably has what they call the 'the munchies,' one of the side effects of smoking pot."

"Oh," Alva said as she watched Nick walk back to the counter. "You know," she went on, "he is nice. And he is certainly generous."

"Pot can bring that out in a person also." She glanced over in Nick's direction. "Not your typical drug fiend, huh?"

Alva turned to Sandra. "No," she said, nodding her head slowly. "No, I guess not." And then, looking serious, "Can I ask you something?"

"Sure."

Alva hesitated. "Never mind. It's not important."

"No," Sandra said with a sly smile. "Not anymore. But yes, I have tried it."

Embarrassed, Alva nodded.

"Does it matter?" Sandra asked.

Alva frowned. "No," she said. "No, it doesn't. It was wrong of me to ask."

"You didn't. I just figured."

"So, what...what did..."

"It felt good," Sandra cut in. "Pleasant. Peaceful even. I'd say 'quieting.' I could see why it's as *popular* as it is."

"But you don't smoke it now."

"That's just me. It left me feeling less... less *connected*, less *here*. Afterwards things always felt incomplete, like I had missed something. And...well, that just doesn't do it for me."

"So, you're not going to smoke it again?"

Sandra shrugged. "Probably not."

"*Probably* not."

"I'm being honest."

"Honesty," Nick echoed coming up to the table and setting two small paper bags on it. "It is the best policy. And you can quote me on that. I've changed my name you know to 'Anonymous' so I can start collecting the royalties."

Sandra looked up at him. "You might want to change it to Ben, Mr. Franklin."

Nick frowned. "As if everything he said, *and took credit for*, was original."

Sandra leaned across the table towards Alva. "We'll have to take his word for it," she said in a stage whisper, "Nick here being Mr. History Major."

"That's Mr. American History Major," Nick corrected. "Can I take these cups?"

"Yes. And thank you for the croissants."

"Yes. Thank you," Alva said.

"Thank you, ladies, for coming in and bringing your own special sunshine along on this day of drear."

Gathering their things, Sandra and Alva rose and headed over to where their slickers were hanging.

Taking a look at the window, Sandra let out a low groan.

"It doesn't look any better out there," she said.

"At least it's light out now."

"True. True."

Donning their slickers, Alva turned to Sandra.

"So, you're working today?"

"Yes, but later. Right now, I have to get back to the Cottage and go over my notes from my last visit to the Jewish home. It's going to take a while. I've got quite a pile."

"Notes about the Tarot cards?"

Sandra shot Alva a glance. "Yes."

"Maybe some time when you're not busy you can show me what you're doing with them, what it is that you come up with."

"You sure?"

Alva nodded. "Yes."

"I can't today. I'm behind at the moment, but…sure. I'd be pleased to."

"I'd be interested."

"Okay then," Sandra said opening the door. "Ready?"

"I think so."

"Then we're off."

Chapter 29

Back at the Cottage, Alva spent some time at her desk writing letters to her parents and to her brother. After a while, it occurred to her that she wasn't hearing the sound of rain striking the window any longer. Standing up, she leaned over her desk to see how things were outside. The rain and snow mix had stopped, but the sky was still considerably overcast. She could see by the swaying of the old oak near her window that the wind was even more of a factor than it had been. Curious as to how cold it was, she placed the back of her hand on one of the panes. It was, she thought, even colder than it had been earlier.

Sitting down, she returned to her correspondence. When she finished, Alva took out two envelopes and a book of stamps from the top drawer of her desk, and prepared the two letters for mailing. With that done, she glanced at her watch, wondering what time Sandra needed to leave for work. She walked across to Sandra's room and found her at her desk, a pile of papers on her left and a taller one on her right. Between them Alva saw three colorful cards laid out face up as if Sandra were playing some form of solitaire.

"Sandra?"

Sandra turned in her seat. Seeing Alva there, she smiled. "Hi."

"Am I disturbing you?"

"Not at all. Come on in."

"How's it going?" Alva asked gesturing towards the cards and piles of paper on the desk.

"Slow, but I'm getting there."

"Don't you have to go to work at some point?"

Sandra looked at her watch. "Yes. Yes, I do, and shortly. Thanks for reminding me. I can get pretty lost in all of this at times. What do you have there?"

"Letters to my parents and brother."

"They look *substantial*, like you've written a lot."

"Yes. I guess so. I put two stamps on each. Do you think that's enough?"

"Plenty. I can take them out to the mailbox on the corner for you when I leave. There's no sense in you getting wet."

"Thanks, but it's not doing anything outside, at least not at the moment, and I could use some fresh air."

Sandra nodded and then looked at her watch again. "I guess I should get ready." Getting up from her chair, she slid it under her desk. "You going out now?"

"I can."

"I'll walk down with you. You might be in luck. I think the mailbox is one of the postman's last stops on Saturdays."

"That'd be good, but it's not critical."

The pick-up stop at the mailbox did turn out to be a later one. Alva was pleased that her letters would go out that day instead of waiting until the following Monday.

After mailing the letters, Alva walked with Sandra to the dining hall. Reaching the main doors, they stopped.

"Well," Sandra said, "this is where we part. Are you heading back?"

"No, I think I'll go for a walk. I kind of like this weather."

"Yeah, I know what you mean. Mind a suggestion?"

"Not at all."

"Try the park, Horton Park. There's a great view of the city from the hill where the water tower is. With this sky and the clouds scudding by, things should be pretty dynamic. And, what with the weather being what it is, you might have the place to yourself."

"That sounds good, real good. Thanks."

"Enjoy your walk."

With that Sandra turned and headed in.

Proceeding on, Alva went to the next intersection, turned left and headed up the hill to the park, one block away. That stretch of road was steep and Alva felt herself slightly winded when she reached the top of it. Ahead of her, across the street, was the park. Off in the distance she could see the hill with the water tower at the top of it. Unlike the 'tank on stilts' water towers back home, this was a squat, brick structure that looked more like a turret or some kind of fortification.

Although the park was directly ahead of her, the entrance to it, where the drive that wound through the park began, was a block down the road on the right. Being in no hurry, Alva crossed the street and headed down to the entrance, deciding to walk the drive that ran through the park instead of cutting across the lawns and playing fields.

Alva turned at the entrance and saw that the drive was *well-puddled* in places both in terms of numbers and size. Walking along, she found herself meandering to avoid stepping through any wet. Again, she found this far from inconvenient. Also, she was pleased to find, as Sandra had predicted, that there was no one about, that she had the park to herself.

Twice, as she walked along, she came to places where the drive split. Each time the one branch that she took ended at another entrance to the park. Each time, she turned around and went back to the previous intersection in order to take the other branch. And, again, she did not find the detours inconvenient.

Beyond the last intersection, the drive grew decidedly steeper as it led up to the water tower. Owing to the increase in pitch, there were no puddles for her to work her way around. Approaching the summit, Alva quickened her pace. Ten minutes later, to her relief, the drive leveled off. Up ahead she could see where it ended, becoming a circle with the water tower in the center of it. Slackening her pace, Alva made her way slowly along until she came to a point that afforded the best view of the surroundings.

Directly below her was the park. She could see most of it from this vantage point, and she was startled by just how large an area it covered. Noting the way that the drive wound through it, she was able to assess the length of her walk. It left her feeling mildly pleased with herself to have covered so much ground.

Beyond the park she could see several of the university buildings close at hand, including dorms, a three-story parking garage, the dining hall where Sandra worked, and even the Cottage. Farther on, a part of Market Street could be seen as well as many of the houses in the surrounding neighborhood.

After that the terrain dropped off steeply and nothing else could be seen between there and the tall buildings of the downtown center of the city. Finally, beyond all of that was the industrial area way off to the west of the city and the large lake that bordered it. Although Alva had seen all of it before from other vantage points, never was the view as panoramic as where she now stood. She was surprised and impressed by how expansive all of it was.

Standing there she felt well rewarded for having made the trek to the summit. And, as Sandra had remarked, the overcast, the varying grays of the clouds racing along beneath it, all of it added a special dynamic to the scene, one that left Alva with a palpable sense of awe.

As she stood there, Alva felt that there was something else to it all. At first she wasn't quite sure what it was, but then she realized that it had to do with the day, the raw dampness of it and the wind. It pressed against her, buffeting her at times with gusts, and seemingly driving the cold and the damp into her. Alva felt herself in possession of a strength, a stamina, that didn't feel like anything that she had ever known before.

It was at that moment that, well off to the west, a streak of reddish glow suddenly appeared low in the sky above the lake, a thin tear in the fabric of the overcast sky. Startled, Alva stood there holding her breath. The thought suddenly occurred to her that this might be a sign, that it might be a confirmation of this strength that she felt at this moment.

Then, as suddenly as it appeared, the streak of red was gone and there was, as before, just the gray overcast and the racing clouds. Alva felt a calm come over her. It had been, she knew, a moment, just a moment, but, even so, one that was complete in itself, complete to the point that, as special as it was, she was able to let it go.

And with that she turned and started back.

Chapter 30

With the skies laden as they were with gray, the afternoon had already begun its slide into evening. This was very much the case with the park's drive, which was for the greater part lined with tall, full hemlocks and arbor vitae, so much so that the few streetlights that there were had already come on. Recalling the university's warning about avoiding the park at night, Alva quickened her pace and was relieved when, coming around one last curve, she saw the park entrance up ahead.

She left the park and crossed the street intending to turn right to return to the Cottage by the way she had come. Suddenly, from the direction of the street directly ahead she heard what sounded like the ringing of a group of small bells. Curious and in no real hurry to return to the Cottage quite yet, Alva altered course heading in the direction of the ringing. She only walked a few yards before the ringing ceased. Alva stopped and stood where she was considering whether or not to turn back. For no real reason, she continued on in the direction she was going.

Immediately on the right there was the end of a tall wing of an L-shaped dorm, one of a group of dorms on that and the next block. A vehicle that looked like a good-sized camper was parked near the intersection up ahead. The vehicle had a rectangular window on one side with an awning over it. A narrow counter ran the length of the window. Off to the side of the window, in large letters, were the words: 'MR. RALPH'S – SNACKS AND EATS.'

Alva was halfway down the block when the ringing began again. It was, she now realized, coming from this vehicle.

It occurred to Alva that she hadn't had anything to eat since the scone at Charlie's that morning, and she was hungry. She thought about dinner, wondering what they might be serving at the dining hall that evening. Even as hungry as she was, she found the prospect of dinner alone there at the dining hall considerably lacking in appeal. And so, reaching the corner, she turned and walked straight up to the window of the truck and stood there reading the items listed on the menu board.

"Ah, our first customer."

Alva looked over to see a balding, slightly overweight middle-aged man in a short-sleeved shirt with red and white stripes standing at the window.

"And how are you, young lady, on this raw and miserable evening?"

"I'm well, thank you."

"Ooh. Am I hearing just a trace of Dixie?"

Alva shrugged. "Not technically. Kentucky."

"And that's not the South?"

"It's not one of the original eleven that seceded."

"Ah. Okay. So, what can I get for you?"

"I'm not sure." Alva glanced at the board again. "What is a 'Jaw Breaker'?"

At that moment a second man, practically a clone of the first appeared at the window. Seeing Alva, he smiled, nodding once.

The first man turned to him, "A Jaw Breaker."

The second man leaned towards the window. "Two large burgers, top grade beef, on a mini-sub roll fresh from the oven just an hour ago. A meal for a pittance."

Alva glanced at the board again. "And a Cheese Jaw?"

"The same with cheese. Your choice, cheddar, cheddar, or cheddar."

"I'll have one of those."

"And your choice of cheese?" the first man asked teasingly.

"Uhhh," Alva said with a smile, "I think I'll go with the cheddar."

"A sound choice."

The first man turned to the second. "Is the grill ready?"

"It is."

"Then one Cheese Jaw with cheddar, for the young lady."

"Coming right up," the second man said turning and heading back to the grill.

"Anything to go with that?" the first asked. "Something to drink?"

"A Coke, please, and a one of those." Alva pointed to a rack on the counter displaying a half dozen bags of potato chips.

"We have plain, plain, and plain."

Alva smiled. "How about plain?"

"A good choice."

Retrieving a can of Coke from a small refrigerator and plucking a bag of chips from the rack, the first man placed both in a paper bag and set it off to one side on the counter.

"So," he said, "I don't remember seeing you before this. I'm Johnny, and my brother there is Jimmy. And you are?"

"Alva."

"Well, nice to meet you, Alva." Johnny leaned back and turned. "Jimmy, say 'hi' to Alva."

"Hello, Alva," Jimmy called from back in the truck. "Nice to meet you."

"Nice to meet you. Nice to meet you both."

"So," Johnny said leaning forward, resting his arms on the counter and folding his hands, "You must be a freshman"

"No. I'm a senior."

"A senior," Johnny repeated, surprised. "Are you a transfer?"

Alva shook her head. "No. I started here as a freshman."

"Really? Where have you been hiding all this time?"

"I've lived off campus until now."

"Ah. And where do you live now?"

Alva pointed up the street. "At the Cottage."

"The Cottage. Then you must know Bernie."

Alva nodded. "Yes."

"And Julie."

"Julie?"

For a brief moment Johnny stood there giving Alva an appraising look. Then he smiled in a conspiratorial manner. "Bernie's uhh...close friend."

"Oh. Yes. I didn't know her name."

"Ah. Well, they're steady customers of ours. Bernie's a quick one, quick with the wit. Julie keeps to herself pretty much. *The silent partner*, I guess. They're good customers and good people."

Alva nodded.

Just then Jimmy appeared at the window. "Anything on that Cheese Jaw? Ketchup? Mustard? Relish?"

"Just ketchup, please."

"You got it."

Jimmy returned a few moments later with the Cheese Jaw wrapped in white paper. "Where're you from?" he asked as he placed the package along with a handful of napkins in the paper bag.

"The lady is from Kentucky," Johnny said.

"Ah, I knew it had to be from somewhere down that way. You have a nice accent there."

Alva nodded shyly. "Thank you."

"Okay, Jimmy," Johnny cut in, "don't be a nosy parker."

Alva paid and took her change from Johnny, then took the bag.

"Hold on," Johnny said. From a large, flat, Tupperware container on the counter he took a brownie. Wrapping it in a small sheet of wax paper, he leaned over the counter and placed it in Alva's bag.

"A little something extra on a raw and miserable evening. On the house, or should I say, 'on the truck'?"

"Thank you," Alva said, surprised. "Thank you both."

"You're quite welcome. You'll come see us again, right?"

Alva smiled. "Absolutely."

"Good. Now hurry along before your Cheese Jaw gets cold."

Heading back to the Cottage, Alva felt particularly pleased by how this day had turned out, especially with the weather having been so unpromising at the start. Thinking back over it all, waking to the sound of rain on the window, the walk to Market Street in the sleet and rain, coffee and scones with Sandra, her journey through the park – it had all made for a different kind of day, and a special one at that.

And now she had something different and special for her

dinner. She thought of Mr. Ralph's, of Johnny and Jimmy, and she smiled. But then she thought about Johnny being surprised at her being a senior, and she felt, once again, annoyed and disappointed at what she had missed the previous three years by not having a normal living situation here at the university. But then, admitting to herself that she was at least having a more normal experience this year, she let the annoyance and disappointment go, and returned to feeling good about the day.

Walking along now, she also felt hungry, and so, taking note of the aroma of her prospective meal and feeling its warmth, she quickened her pace.

Chapter 31

Alva was drawing near to the Cottage when she happened to look up and see a faint light in the window of her room. Knowing that it wasn't bright enough to be from either the lamp on her desk or from the overhead light of the landing, she figured that its origin must be Sandra's room. The dining hall was still open and serving dinner, so Alva hadn't expected Sandra to be home yet from the extra shift that she was working that day. Apparently, Alva thought, she must have gotten off early, which was just fine with Alva as she was looking forward to telling Sandra about her walk in the park and her stopping at Mr. Ralph's. Also, even as hungry as she was, it occurred to her that she could share her meal with Sandra, and this notion pleased her very much. Excited by the prospect, Alva hurried on, almost at a trot, bounding up the front steps and practically barging through the front door.

"Whoa! Whoa! Whoa!" Lily bellowed stepping back quickly so as not to be run over.

"Sorry."

"What's the big…" Lily stopped and sniffed the air. "Burgers." She looked at the paper bag that Alva held, then reached out and put a finger on it. "Somebody's been to Mr. Ralph's. Let me guess. Cheese Jaw. Chips. And a Coke. Right?"

"Yes," Alva said, both startled and somewhat amazed at Lily's accuracy. "And a brownie," she added.

"And here I was resigned to partake in dining hall food. Well, fuck that shit. I'm with…"

"Lily!"

"What?"

Frowning and glaring, Alva shook her head vigorously. "Please. Please don't talk like that around me again. You should never… you…" Looking away, Alva shook her head.

"I'm sorry," Lily said in a whisper. "Hey. I really am. I'm…I just have this real potty mouth. And…I'm sorry."

"No," Alva said, still shaking her head, her eyes still averted. She looked back up. "No, Lily," she said quietly. "No. I'm sorry. That kind of anger… There's no excuse for it. Bad anger is worse than profanity. Much worse."

"If you say so, but I'm still sorry."

"Is Sandra here?" Alva asked, mostly as a diversion just to get past the moment.

"I don't know. I thought she was working for someone today."

"She was, or maybe she still is, but coming up the road I noticed a light on upstairs."

"You know, I did hear footsteps a little while ago. But I wasn't really paying attention."

"It must be her then. Maybe she got off early."

"I s'pose so. Well, smelling those burgers there is making me real hungry. So, I'll see ya."

"Sure."

Alva held the door open and let Lily pass. Stepping in and closing it after her, she started quickly up the stairs.

Reaching the last set of stairs to the third floor, Alva, suddenly feeling a need to be as quiet as possible, slowed her pace as she started up. When she reached that point where she was eye level with the landing floor, she stopped and looked in the direction of Sandra's room. As she had guessed, there was a light on there. Pleased that Sandra was home, she quickly climbed the remaining steps and crossed the landing to Sandra's room. She was just about to let her presence be known, when she stopped short.

Someone was standing at Sandra's desk, and it wasn't Sandra. It was someone tall, male, with long hair, and wearing a wool coat that came down to mid-calf. His collar was up. His hands were buried in the coat's pockets. An old canvas backpack, olive drab, hung from his left shoulder. With his head bowed slightly, he stood there examining the three-card Tarot spread on Sandra's desk. Moments passed as Alva just stood there staring at the back of this *intruder*.

"So," the person at the desk asked calmly without looking up, "just how long are you planning to stand there without saying anything?"

Recognizing his voice, Alva almost blurted out the name Kerry.

"Can I ask what you're doing here?" she asked, surprised at the hoarseness in her voice.

"I don't know," Kerry said without looking up from the cards. "*Can* you?"

"Alright," Alva said, annoyed with his impertinence, "*may* I ask what you're doing here?"

"You most certainly may," Kerry said calmly as he continued to look at the cards.

Alva stood there waiting for his answer, and she continued to stand there and wait for it until it finally dawned on her just how particular he was being in terms of her grammar.

"Right," she said, her nervousness now gone, but not her annoyance. "What are you doing here?"

"There you go," he said, still surveying the cards. "Grammar and concision, Alva. The hallmarks of any good writing." He turned his head to look back over his shoulder at Alva. "Even poetry." He looked back at the cards. "I was looking for Sandra," he said calmly.

"She's at work," Alva said. "At the dining hall."

"Is she?" he said, still looking at the cards.

Reaching for the deck, Kerry selected the one on top and turned it over to look at it.

"What are you doing?" Alva asked, indignant that he would take such a liberty with Sandra's property.

Without bothering to respond, Kerry held the card up over one shoulder, turning it so that she could see it.

"The Nine of Swords. Now that's ominous."

He set card down in line with the spread, and selected another from the top of the deck.

"Oh dear," he said, his tone still calm. "The Tower."

Again, he held up the card for Alva to see.

"This isn't good," he said, placing the card next to the Nine of Swords. "You might want to give Sandra a heads up that…"

"She doesn't use the cards that way," Alva said quickly and with considerable heat. "They're just cards. She uses them with the work that she does with the old folks."

Surprised by Alva's vehemence, Kerry turned to her.

"I'm sorry. Strike a nerve, did I? Actually, Sandra is the last person that I can see ever dabbling in alchemy or the dark arts."

"You still haven't answered my question," Alva said with asperity.

"No, Alva," he said, turning back to the cards, picking up the two that he had selected and returning them to the deck in their proper order. "You're right," he said. "I haven't. And it is Alva, right?" he asked, his attention still on the cards.

"Yes," Alva said. "Yes, it is. And you're Kerry."

He turned to her and bowed slightly.

"English 221. Creative Poetry. Spring semester. Sophomore year. Right?"

Alva nodded. "I didn't think you'd remember me."

"And why not?"

Alva shrugged. "I don't know. I just didn't."

"Well, you were on the quiet side."

"And you were on the absent side a lot, even more in Religion and Ethics."

"You were in that one also?"

Alva nodded.

"Yeah," he said. "Attendance hasn't exactly been my strong suit here." For a moment he stood there looking at Alva. "You've let your bangs grow out some, right?"

Alva could feel herself blush. "Yes."

"Very becoming." Kerry set his backpack on Sandra's desk chair. "Any way," he said opening it, "you asked what I was doing here." Reaching into the backpack he pulled out a narrow book of some vintage with a black cover. "I finally remembered that she asked me a while ago if I was done with this yet." He held up the book. "She said she wanted to lend it to someone."

"Is it *The Razor's Edge*?"

"That it is."

"Then it's for me," Alva said.

For a moment Kerry just stood there looking at her with an expression that Alva thought was a mix of mild surprise and curiosity.

"Well," Kerry said finally, holding out the book to her. "Here you go."

Alva took it. "Thank you."

"And," Kerry said, reaching into his backpack again, "I brought this for Sandra." He pulled out a thin paperback that looked as if it had had many readers. "She'll know what it is," he said placing it on Sandra's desk. Turning back to Alva, he pointed at the paper bag that she was holding.

"You've been to Mr. Ralph's."

Alva nodded. "Yes."

"And I'm keeping you from your dinner. My apologies."

Alva shrugged. "It's okay."

"Well," he said picking up his pack and slinging it over one shoulder, "I'll be off." With that he and Alva stepped out of Sandra's room and crossed over to the stairs. Just as he was about to descend, Kerry stopped and turned to Alva.

"You know, your name came up the other day. Remember that poem of yours, the one about your grandmother, about her sitting on her porch, her old wicker chair, and the empty veins of the *now hollowed hills?*"

For a moment Alva stood there stunned that he would remember any poem of hers, stunned but also pleased.

"Well," Kerry went on, "I'm in Edmund Phillips's poetry workshop this semester and last week we were discussing voice in poetry, and he read your poem. He called it a good and subtle example of voice."

Again, stunned, Alva just stood there.

"It went over well. Especially that one line, *and all that wasn't anymore*." Kerry nodded. "That's good. Real good. Grammatically wrong, but...poetically right."

"Thank you. I guess."

"So, you still writing?"

Alva shrugged. "Some. But not much."

"Some is still good," Kerry said nodding his head slowly. "You?"

"Not so some," Kerry said with a mildly guilty smile. "Not some enough, but... anyway..." he pointed at the bag that Alva held. "Your dinner's getting cold. Go." With that he started down the stairs.

When he reached the next landing, he turned and chanced to stop and glance up. Seeing Alva still there, he pointed a finger at her. "Dinner," he whispered. "Go."

Hurriedly, Alva waved and then retreated quickly into her room. Once inside she just stood there for a moment trying to assess this unexpected encounter. Something about it made her feel good and excitedly so. There was, of course, the matter of her poem being referenced and discussed. Even if it didn't compare with actually being in the creative writing program, it was still something, a definite plus. To a certain extent, she felt validated. But mostly it was something to do with Kerry, with interacting with him, the give and take involved. Standing there, going over what had occurred, she found that, try as she might, she couldn't quite put her finger on what about it made her feel so good. But it did feel good, and she let it go at that.

Chapter 32

Finishing her Cheese Jaw, Coke and chips, Alva reached into the bag and took out the brownie. She was just about to take a bite when, glancing towards her door, she saw that the light was still on across the way in Sandra's room. Brownie in hand, she got up and went to turn it off.

She was reaching across Sandra's desk for the lamp when she noticed the three Tarot cards laid out on it. Besides their bright primary colors, what caught her eye was that, in each card, an angel was depicted. This surprised her; she expected them to deal more with things Satanic than Biblical, or at least something more in line with the two cards that Kerry had selected earlier. The cards in this spread didn't seem to have anything even vaguely sinister about them.

The scene in one, titled 'The Lovers,' was obviously, she thought, of Adam and Eve and the Garden of Eden. 'Temperance' had an angel pouring water from one chalice to another. And 'Judgment,' with figures rising from the dead to the call of an angel's horn, was, she was sure, about the Resurrection. Again, she could find nothing Satanic or sinister in them. If anything, they struck her as being quite religious in nature. Standing there, looking at them, she felt a twinge of embarrassment remembering that morning at Charlie's when she had made such a fuss about them.

Alva noticed the box that they came in and reached over and picked it up. When she did, a small booklet fell out it. She picked it up, reading the words imprinted on the side.

The Rider-Waite Tarot Deck.

Thumbing through it, she discovered that it contained a brief introduction to the Tarot followed by general write-ups about each card. Although curious, Alva, after the long and busy day, didn't feel up to getting into all of that just right then and there. She returned the booklet to the box and set both aside. She sat at the desk, picked up the deck, and started going through it, card by card, taking the time to look at each. She was about halfway through it when...

"Well, hello."

Startled, Alva nearly dropped the deck. She turned and found Sandra standing there in the doorway.

"Sorry," Sandra said. "I wasn't trying to sneak up on you." She noticed the deck in Alva's hands and smiled. "What...what are you doing?"

"I'm sorry," Alva said, flustered and getting to her feet. "I had no right to... I just came in to shut off your light and...and I saw the cards and... I'm sorry. I..."

"It's okay," Sandra said calmly. She shrugged. "I'm just surprised that you...well, you know, *the cards.*"

Alva bowed her head slightly. "I know."

"So...what do you think?"

"They're interesting."

"And not so evil?"

Alva shook her head. "No. I guess not."

"Well, good. Feel free to check them out whenever the mood strikes."

Sandra glanced around the room. "You said my light was on?"

"Oh. Yes. Kerry was here."

"You know him?"

Alva nodded. "Yes. I mean I *kind* of know of him. We were in a couple classes together sophomore year. He was returning your book, *The Razor's Edge*, and," Alva picked up the other book Kerry had dropped off and continued, "he left this for you."

Sandra took it from her and read the title. "*The Way of a Pilgrim*," she said quietly. "I've heard of this." She held it up for Alva to see. "Ever run across it?"

Alva shook her head.

"You ever read any Salinger?"

"*Catcher in the Rye*. 'A Perfect Day for Banana Fish' and the other short stories."

"*Franny And Zooey*?"

Alva shook her head.

"You ever hear of the Jesus Prayer? It comes from St. Paul and his instruction to pray without ceasing?"

Again, Alva shook her head.

"Well, it's referenced in *Franny And Zooey*, another piece by Salinger. This book is mentioned in it too." Opening the book, Sandra started to page through it slowly. Then, quite suddenly, she stopped and shut the book. "But not tonight. I'm beat."

Setting the book down on her desk, Sandra took off her coat and tossed it on her bed. She walked over to her easy chair, and flopped down into it, then sat there, slouched, with her legs extended in front of her.

"It's been a long day," she said wearily.

Alva held up her brownie. "Want to share?"

"Is that from Mr. Ralph's?"

"It is."

Sandra smiled and nodded. "Yes," she said, sitting up straight. "Yes, I certainly would."

Breaking the brownie in two, Alva gave half to Sandra. "Here's to one long day," she said, holding her half up as if making a toast.

Sandra nodded. "To one long day."

They were each just about to take a bite when suddenly the sound of rain slapping against Sandra's window caught their attention.

"Looks like we've come full circle," Sandra said.

"Yes," Alva said, "yes, it does."

"A good circle," Sandra said taking a bite of her brownie.

Alva nodded. "Yes. Yes, indeed."

Chapter 33

During the night the rain changed over to snow. There was about an inch of it when Alva left for church that morning. Snow squalls, continuing throughout the day, added little, if anything, to what had already accumulated. There were touches of snow the next two days, but when Wednesday came around, the temperature rose, and the world of white melted away.

"Good thing," Lily said.

She and Alva were walking towards campus.

"I don't know," Alva said. "I like the snow. It makes the world seem a little cleaner."

"It's just a cover-up. All the ugliness is still there underneath."

"So, then the snow *is* a good thing."

Lily looked at Alva and smiled. "Well, aren't you just Little Miss Sunshine today?"

Alva shrugged. "I guess."

"Well, hang on to it. Winters here are plenty long enough as you well know, and this one damn well...*darn well* better not kick in until after Friday."

"Why? What's Friday?"

Lily frowned. "Halloween, of course."

"Oh."

Lily shot Alva a glance. "Don't tell me. Let me guess. You don't celebrate Halloween."

"Not really."

"A religious thing, right? Well, we won't go into all of that today if you don't mind."

Alva smiled and nodded. "Yes. Let's not."

"So, then you haven't done Halloween here."

"No."

"Well, you've been missing out. Parties everywhere. The biggest, the best, is at the cemetery. The frat boys throw a big one there with a couple kegs of beer. That's where I'll be heading."

"The cemetery?"

"Yeah. The one at the other end of campus."

"The one that runs along Oneida Street?" Alva asked, thinking of the straight lines of standard granite tombstones that could be seen from the road and not thinking that it made much of a place to celebrate anything.

"Yeah. But that's not where the party is. There's this cool older part in a far corner where the drive winds around these hills and there are old trees and mausoleums. There's even a pyramid. It's creepy, even in the daytime. And just...so...cool."

"And people dress up and go there and do what?"

"Well, not everybody dresses up. People run around scaring people, jumping out from behind tombstones, going 'boo' or blasting them with air horns. Mostly though people just hang out by the kegs. The frat boys will be blasting scary sound effects and music. You should go. You really should. Hell! This'll be your last chance."

"We'll see."

Lily frowned. "My father says that a lot."

"What?"

"'We'll see.' It's parent code for 'no.'"

Alva laughed. "That's funny. It's the same with my father. It must be a generational thing. Like 'let's not and say we did.'"

"Oh God, you're right. I forgot about that one, but really, you just gotta go. You don't have to dress up or do anything else that might offend your religious scruples. Think of it as just a party. You're okay with parties, right?"

"Sure."

"Then you'll come," Lily said with some finality.

"We'll see."

"Arrrrgghh."

"No, really," Alva said quickly. "It sounds like fun."

"Then it's a yes. Don't say another word. You're going. Even if I have to drag you there."

"Oh. Wait." Alva frowned. "I have to work Friday afternoon at three."

"Til when?"

"Five. Five thirty."

"Perfect. I think sunset is right around six. So, you're going, and that's that."

"Okay."

It was going on three that next Friday, and Alva was preparing to leave for the library when Lily showed up at her doorway in a get-up that made Alva blink with some astonishment.

"So, what do you think?" Lily asked.

She was wearing a too long, gray raincoat that had probably belonged to someone's great, great, grandfather way back when. On her head was a faded gray fedora that had lost a good deal of its shape, and which probably shared the same original owner as the raincoat. Both items were far too large for Lily, the raincoat reaching almost to her ankles, and the hat large enough for her to tuck the tops of her ears into. Lily stood there smiling, proud of her attire, holding the front of the raincoat closed with two hands.

"Is this your costume?" Alva asked.

"It is, and all this from Goodwill for only five bucks. Talk about a deal."

"And what are you supposed to be?"

"A flasher."

"A flasher," Alva repeated. "What's that."

With a flourish, Lily whipped open the front of the raincoat.

Alva saw that, beneath the raincoat, Lily wore a pair of shorts and a t-shirt with the image of a smiling Richard Nixon on it.

"Get it?" Lily asked expectantly.

Alva shook her head. "No."

Lily rolled her eyes. "It's Richard Nixon."

"I see that."

"Get it? Dick Nixon. Dick…Nixon. Dick?"

Alva shook her head.

"Really?" Lily asked, her tone one of disbelief.

Alva shrugged.

"You don't know what a flasher is, do you?"

"No. What is it?"

"It's somebody who goes around…"

"Hello," Sandra said, appearing in the doorway. "Happy Halloween." Turning to look at Lily, she slowly examined her attire. "Is this your costume?"

"It is," Lily said, quickly closing up the front of the raincoat.

"And you're supposed to be a…" Sandra paused, waiting for Lily's response.

"A flasher!" Lily crowed, flinging open the front of the raincoat.

Sandra gave Lily's costume a slow look-over. "Richard Nixon?"

"Yes," Lily said. "A…K…A…Dick."

"Oh," Sandra said with a slow, knowing nod of her head. "I see. I see. Clever."

Lily frowned. "So much for an enthusiastic response."

"It is something of a stretch. But I get it."

"Well, you watch. I bet it goes over big tonight."

"I have no doubt it will."

"Anyway," Lily went on, "either of you two have any artist's charcoal. I gotta dirty up my face some. Get that real seedy effect."

Both Sandra and Alva shook their heads in response.

"You might ask Bernie," Sandra suggested. "She sketches."

"Oh, yeah, right. Good idea."

Lily started to leave, but stopped in the doorway. "See you guys tonight. Right? At the cemetery." Then looking pointedly at Alva. "Right?"

Alva nodded. "Sure."

"Don't chicken out."

With that Lily left them.

Sandra turned to Alva.

"Are you really going?" Sandra asked seeming both surprised and pleased.

Alva shrugged. "I told her I would. But…are you going?"

Sandra nodded. "For a while. It is fun. You want to go over together?"

"Oh, that would be great. Can…" Alva stopped and frowned. "I have to work until five or so. I was just heading over to the library now."

"Well, why don't we plan to meet up there at the cemetery? I'll hang around by where they have the kegs. They'll be easy to find. Just follow the noise."

"Okay. Are you going to dress up at all?"

Sandra smiled and shook her head.

Relieved, Alva smiled. "Me neither." She looked at her watch. "I have to go."

"See you by the kegs."

"By the kegs."

Downstairs, just about to go out the front door, Alva glanced into Bernie's room. With a charcoal stick in hand, Bernie was dirtying up Lily's cheeks.

"A flasher," Alva said to herself. She would have to remind herself to ask Sandra about that when they met up later.

Chapter 34

Alva was in the middle of making copies of documents recently sent from the Middle East when Professor Nagy came into the Rare Archives Room at the library.

"Still at it?" she asked, coming up to the copier where Alva stood. "And this a Friday night and Halloween no less."

Alva looked at her watch and saw that it was already half past five.

"I just wanted to finish making these copies before heading out."

Professor Nagy took a page from the pile of those items that Alva had already made copies of.

"Anything of particular interest here?"

"Some old maps of the area where the caves are. Some old photographs too, some of them going back to the late eighteen-hundreds."

"And this?" Professor Nagy held the sheet up.

"Yes. It's an extract from a diary. Someone on an archaeological dig back in the late forties."

"Detailed?"

"Some. Mostly though it's a description, day by day, of what it was like being in the area, the weather, the landscape, the locals that they encountered, and some politics. Would we be interested in that kind of thing?"

Professor Nagy nodded, placing the sheet back on the pile. "Maybe not from a technical standpoint, but it may offer clues, maybe insights about what we're dealing with, and maybe, more importantly, how we're dealing with what we have. It is certainly worth processing."

"I found it interesting. What I read."

Professor Nagy looked at Alva. "Did you?" She gestured to the diary page. "Would you care to take charge of it?"

"I was going to process it in its own notebook like I've been doing with everything else, and put it with the others."

"No. I mean take responsibility for it. Go through it and report on your findings like the other team members are doing with their work. You certainly know how we process things by now. Also, with the exposure you've had in terms of what everyone else is working on, you're the obvious choice to handle something like this. You know," she went on, "you've certainly proven yourself capable, and then some. It's time that we moved you beyond the strictly clerical side of things. What do you think?"

This was something that Alva hadn't expected, and for a moment she just stood there.

"Alva?"

"Yes. Yes, I would like that. I would like that very much, if you think I can do it."

"*Think* you can. I *know* you can."

"But what if things get backed up, if I can't keep up with everything else, the typing and the filing and everything."

"I think we've reached a point where that will taper off. And folks can start taking care of their own needs when it comes to that. I would still like them to funnel everything through you, just to keep everything together and in sync. That way, you will also still have the big picture about everything."

Alva made a gesture towards the pile of documents she was copying. "But what about when more of this comes in."

"Then everyone will be responsible for those items that concern them, including me. And besides, we've received most everything that will be coming in for a while, possibly until the end of the semester. It's time, Alva. You are as capable and as qualified as anyone on the team."

Again, this wasn't something Alva had expected, and, again, she just stood there.

"Alva. Say, 'yes.'"

Alva nodded her head, smiling broadly. "Yes."

"Good."

"And...and thank you, Professor Nagy. I really appreciate this."

"It's me who should thank you. You've been a real asset to the team. We're much further along than I ever expected we would be at this point, and you've been a big part of that."

A sudden knocking caused the two of them to turn in the direction of the room's glass door. Sandra, standing there beyond the glass, smiled and waved. Alva waved back.

"Company?" Professor Nagy asked.

"A friend. We're going out this evening. For Halloween."

"To the cemetery?"

"Yes," Alva said, surprised.

"A school tradition. Give me those." Professor Nagy gestured for what remained to be copied. "I'll finish them up."

"I can do it."

"So can I. It's time I did. Now give them to me and go."

Alva handed the remaining pages over. "Thank you."

"One more thing, Alva. I know you'll be graduating in the spring. How far along are you in regard to requirements for your major?"

"I've finished. I'm just doing electives."

"I see," Professor Nagy said thoughtfully. "Good. That's good."

"Why?"

"I'm just thinking about next semester. But we'll talk about that later. Right now, go. And Happy Halloween."

Chapter 35

"I hope I wasn't interrupting," Sandra said when Alva came out from the Rare Archives Room."

"No," Alva said. "We were just finishing up."

They started off.

"Alva?"

"What?"

"You seem…you seem extremely pleased about something."

Alva smiled shyly. "I am."

As they walked along, Alva filled Sandra in on what had just transpired with her and Professor Nagy.

"That's really great," Sandra said when Alva had finished. "It shows she thinks a lot of you, which is not surprising. And it sounds like you'll be kept on for next semester."

The sun was well off to the west as they made their way across the quad.

"So, do we go down Oneida Street?" Alva asked.

"We can, but it's a bit longer that way. There's a path," Sandra said pointing to the other side of the quad, "behind the old library that goes over the hill to the old part of the cemetery."

"Okay."

"Would you rather go down Oneida? It is a nice walk that way."

"Whatever you think."

"Well, let's go that way. We're in no hurry. Also, it'll take us by my favorite spot in the cemetery."

By the time they reached the cemetery entrance on Oneida Street, the sun was just about to drop behind the bare trees on the top of the hill that marked the border of the university campus.

"Still plenty of light though," Sandra said as they entered. "Have you been here before?"

"No. I've only ever driven by."

"Well, you're in for a treat. The design is what's known as 'rural cemetery,' a form of landscape architecture that was in vogue in the second half of the nineteenth century. Put simply, the idea was to create a peaceful environment that would draw people to it, something more like a park than a graveyard. Henry Daniels and Frederick Law Olmsted were major proponents of it. You might have heard of Olmsted."

Alva shook her head. "No, I don't think so."

"You've heard of Central Park in New York."

"Yes."

"That's what he's most famous for."

They had only gone a short way when Alva turned to Sandra.

"This is beautiful," she said in a hushed tone. "And not at all creepy like I was expecting."

"Why were you expecting that?"

"Lily. Lily said that it was creepy even in the daytime."

"Well, that's Lily. How would you describe it? What's your first impression?"

"I don't know," Alva said, looking around as they strolled

slowly along. "Romantic, I guess. And, at the same time, it's somber, especially now with the sun going down. It's these old trees, the way they're empty of leaves now. And it's the way this drive winds its way through everything so that you can only see just so far ahead. For some reason it makes me think of George Eliot."

Feeling suddenly self-conscious, Alva turned and was surprised to find Sandra looking intently at her. When moments passed without Sandra saying anything, Alva grew even more self-conscious, even embarrassed.

"I'm sorry," she said turning away. "I'm being silly."

"No, you're not, not at all," Sandra said quietly. "Pardon my using a trite expression, but I think what you said was right on the money.

Alva looked up at her quickly. "Really?"

Sandra nodded. "George Eliot. Yes. *Middlemarch*."

"Yes."

"You know, I'm glad that we came over here together instead of meeting up where the festivities are. And," she said wistfully, looking about, "I'm almost inclined to forego all of that and just hang out somewhere over here for a while."

"I could be talked into… Oh. Look at that," Alva said coming to a sudden stop.

They had just come around one of the curves in the drive and were at a point where the terrain rose up slightly steeper. In front of them stood a semi-circle of Corinthian columns that encompassed the back portion of a wide slab of granite. A set of steps led up to the slab from the drive.

"Yes," Sandra said. "It's something, isn't it?"

"It sure is. What is it?"

"A burial plot."

"Well, I've never seen the like of it before. It looks like something out of classic Greek, like there should be women dressed in diaphanous gowns, chitons, sleeveless, seated or strolling about languidly, all of them somber and solemn, and… and here I go again."

Sandra laughed. "Well, c'mon. Take a closer look."

"You sure it's okay?"

"Of course. See the benches. I think it's obvious that they were put here intentionally to draw people in and have them sit."

The benches, of which there were two, stood on either side of the slab facing towards its center. They were made of granite and carved in a way as to fit in with the columns.

"C'mon," Sandra said as she started up the steps.

Alva fell in behind her.

Reaching the top step, they stopped. In the center of the slab, raised an inch or so above its surface, were two rectangular slabs, side by side, that had not been visible from the drive.

Raising a hand, Sandra waved in the direction of the two slabs. "Good evening, Celia. Good evening, James. This is my friend, Alva."

Alva waved.

Sandra walked over to the bench that was on her right and sat down. Alva came over and sat with her.

"So, you've come here before," Alva said sitting down next to Sandra.

Sandra nodded. "It's my favorite place here, the one that I was telling you about. I like the idea of it, a place where people can come and spend some time, not just to drop off some flowers and say a few words, but actually sit for a while." She gave the bench a pat. "Of course, all of this," she made a sweeping gesture encompassing their immediate surroundings and went on, "is a bit much. A simple granite bench with maybe a plaque flush with the ground would have been sufficient."

"Do you think cemeteries are a waste of space?" Alva asked.

"Maybe, on one level. But they are a good way of preserving land, especially when they create something park-like like this. This is all pretty much static. It's not like they can dig up everybody here and move them out to make room for another high-rise dorm or a dining hall."

Alva nodded. "You know," she said, "back home, on certain days, we drive my Grandma to the cemetery where her folks are, and it's nice to see the quiet way she smiles when we're there. It's a little sad, but in a good way. Do you know what I mean?"

Sandra nodded. "I think so."

"It does something for her. And, even though I don't remember anything about them, it makes me smile too and I'm always glad when we go there with her. The one thing that is sad, when you think about it, is that, once I'm gone and my parents and Grandma are gone, there'll be no one left who remembers the people buried there, no one left to go there and spend a little time with them."

"Not unless someone comes along and adopts them."

"Is that what you've done?" Alva asked very much pleased by the notion.

Sandra shrugged. "In a way. This will seem weird, but I do talk to them. Nothing serious. Just 'hello,' something about the weather, and maybe just things that I've been thinking about or that pop into my head when I get here."

Alva laughed. "I guess it would seem weird if I didn't know

you, and I happened along and saw you sitting alone here and talking with no one else about."

"Maybe that's the way it is with *weird*, you know, how maybe it has to do with not having the complete picture or enough of one."

"Good point. Sort of like the character Larry in *The Razor's Edge*, where people can't figure out why he's doing what he's doing, or, even more to the point, why he's not doing what everyone expects him to do."

"So, you've started in on it."

"I have.

"And?"

"It makes me want to go to Paris."

"Yes," Sandra said with some enthusiasm. "Doesn't it."

"One thing that I'm afraid is that the story will...will take some sort of wrong turn and that the ending will somehow be unsatisfactory, even dishonest."

"It doesn't. I guess you could say that it doesn't really end at all so much as wind down. It's more like a final divergence of the different paths that everyone in it is traveling. There's nothing really special about the ending, except that it is honest."

"Well," Alva said, "that's pretty special."

"Indeed, it is, and..." Sandra stopped suddenly. "Do you hear that?" she asked looking down the drive back in the direction of Oneida Street.

Alva turned to look in that direction and listened. "Bagpipes?"

"Bagpipes."

Though not completely, it had grown dark enough so that they could only just make out the figure slowly coming along the drive in their direction. As he drew near they could see that the bagpiper was dressed in full bagpipe attire including kilt, high socks with garters and a caubeen.

"Is this really happening?" Alva asked in a whisper.

In response, Sandra gave her leg a pinch.

Alva laughed. "I guess it is," she said, continuing to whisper, "but…but isn't this something more than just real?"

"Yes," Sandra said, also in a whisper. "Yes, it is."

They sat there watching as the bagpiper continued to approach. When he reached that point in the drive closest to where they sat, Alva held her breath hoping that he wouldn't see the two of them sitting there. It wasn't that she felt guilty, that they were spying on him. It was more that she didn't want what felt like a spell to be broken. Her relief was palpable when he passed by without noticing their presence.

Sitting there, Alva and Sandra listened as the bagpiper continued moving slowly away until, reaching the point where the road curved away, he seemed to just vanish, as if swallowed up by the evening. But even out of sight, they could still hear his music, which now seemed to have a presence of its own, one that seemed to belong there, to belong to that moment.

"Such a sad melody," Alva said quietly. "Sad, but beautiful."

"Mmm. Yes. 'Flowers in the Forest.'"

"Is that the name of it?"

"Yes. It's one that bagpipers often play at funerals."

"Well, I guess that's kind of fitting, considering where we are."

"Yes, but not exactly in keeping with the Halloween festivities. Speaking of which, things must be well underway by this time. Are you up for it?"

Alva hesitated. "I guess so," she said tentatively.

"C'mon. We should at least make an appearance."

Alva nodded. "Sure," she said with a smile. "You're right. Let's go."

Getting up, they made their way down to the drive.

"Which way?" Alva asked.

"Follow the bagpiper."

Chapter 36

A short way on, the pavement gave way to gravel. The drive itself became narrower and more winding, the terrain even more hilly. The trees were older here, the nearest ones leaning out over the drive and making things darker still. The deeper Alva and Sandra went, the less they saw of individual gravestones. Mostly there were mausoleums now tucked in, some almost hidden, among the trees.

Alva looked about nervously. "Are you sure this is the way? I feel like I'm lost in one of Grimm's fairy tales."

Sandra laughed. "I know what you mean, but you can't get lost in here. It's not that big a place. It's just the dark that gives it a feel of vastness. And…hey." She came to a sudden stop. "Hear that?"

Alva listened. "Voices."

"We're almost there. C'mon."

After a couple more turns the drive ran up a long hill. Reaching the top, they stopped. The drive ran straight down from where they stood into a glade where groups of people were gathered. From where they stood, they could see all of it. Most everyone there was dressed up in keeping with Halloween. A half dozen camping lanterns, spread out strategically and usually set atop an above ground grave, provided what illumination there was. Alva noticed that there were several of these *sarcophagi* about and that most of them were in use either as a table or as a place to sit. The entire scene reminded Alva of paintings by Bosch.

"There's Brian," Sandra said, pointing across the grade to where a large group was gathered.

"Brian?"

"The bagpiper."

"Oh. You didn't say that you knew him."

Sandra gave Alva a sly smile. "I didn't want to detract from the mystique. Anyway, I see there's a keg there too. I imagine that's where we'll find Lily. Shall we?"

Alva nodded. "Sure."

They were about halfway down the drive heading into the glade when there was a sudden burst of loud, strident music. At the sound of it a mighty cheer went up throughout the glade.

"Sounds like someone brought along a sound system."

"It's awfully loud," said Alva.

"Wagner lends itself to this kind of thing."

"You know this?"

"'The Ride of the Valkyries.'"

As they made their way down into the glade, passing various groups, Alva noticed that most everyone held the same type of plastic cup.

"People are drinking," she said at one point.

"That they are."

"*Drinking* drinking?"

Sandra shrugged. "Just beer I would expect." She turned to Alva. "I'm guessing you don't *drink* drink."

"No. I mean sometimes, on Thanksgiving or Christmas or something I'll have a glass of wine with the dinner. Special occasions."

"Beer?"

Alva shook her head. "No." And then, "You?"

Sandra smiled. "On special occasions."

"Hey, you two," someone said behind them.

Alva and Sandra stopped and turned. Kerry approached them beer in hand.

"I thought it was you two. Happy Halloween." He said and raised his cup. "What?" he said. "No libation? On Halloween? For shame."

"We just arrived," Sandra said.

"Well, step this way. We've got a pony keg right over here. C'mon."

Kerry led them to an above ground grave where a small group was gathered. A pony keg, tapped, sat on the ground next to the grave. An open and almost depleted package of plastic cups rested on the grave. Sitting next to it was someone that Alva was sure she had met before.

"Hey folks," Kerry said as the three of them approached the group, "we've got company. You all know Sandra." Greetings were exchanged. "And *this*..." he said, turning to Alva, "is Alva." Again, greetings were exchanged. "Hey Steve," Kerry said, "two beers for the late arrivals."

"Two beers each?" Steve asked, reaching for the package of cups.

"Sure. They need to make up for lost time."

"Just one each," Sandra said. Alva was just about to protest, when she felt Sandra's hand on her arm. "And make those halves."

Alva turned to her. "I really don't..."

"Just take it," Sandra said quickly under her breath. "I'll take care of it if you don't want it." She turned to Kerry. "Have you seen Lily?"

"You mean the flasher? Last I saw her, she was headed yonder." He gestured with his cup of beer to where the largest group in the glade was assembled. "Up there with the frat boys."

"Yeah. She was following the guy in the skirt," Steve said approaching them with a cup in each hand. "Here you are, ladies." Alva and Sandra each took one and said thanks. "Don't take too long with those. Stocks are running low." He turned to Alva. "We've met, right?"

Alva nodded. "I think so. At the quarry. Back at the beginning of the semester."

"Right. That's right. Well ladies, enjoy. I've got a keg to mind."

Sandra turned to Kerry. "So, Lily's with Brian?"

"She is. Or at least she was. You know Lily, she can be…"

"So Lily?"

"Just so," Kerry said raising his cup. "Just so."

"I didn't know they knew each other," Sandra said taking a sip of her beer.

"Small world and all that."

"Like Brian and Steve." She turned to Alva. "They're cousins."

"Though you wouldn't know it," Kerry said turning to Alva and cutting in. "Except when a party is involved. Then all the Irish in both of them comes out."

"They're locals," Sandra said before taking another sip of her beer.

"Home grown. True west side boys." Kerry turned to Alva. "You okay with that?" he asked gesturing towards the cup she held.

"Alva's not really a beer drinker," Sandra said quickly.

Kerry shrugged. "That's okay. You can pour it out if you want. Just do it when Steve isn't looking."

"Or you can add it to mine," Sandra suggested holding out her cup.

"No," Alva said. "I should at least try it."

"You sure?"

Alva nodded. Lifting her cup to her lips she took one tentative sip and held it briefly in her mouth before swallowing. "It's bitter," she said with a frown, "but…but it's not actually bad." Feeling a little brave, she took a longer sip, again holding it briefly in her mouth before swallowing.

"Careful there, young lady," Kerry teased. "We don't want to be carrying anybody home tonight."

"Stop it," Sandra said quickly seeing the look of alarm on Alva's face. "Don't pay any attention," she said to Alva. "Half a cup isn't going to do anything."

"But it's a start," Kerry said with a sly smile.

"Stop it," Sandra said with enough vehemence to startle both Alva and Kerry.

"Sorry," Kerry said backing off. He turned to Alva. "Just teasing." He pointed to the cup that she was holding. "There's not enough there to cause a problem. And, like I said, you can just pour it out if you want."

Alva smiled. "No, that's okay. Besides, the nuns back home ingrained it into us not to waste anything."

"The penguins?"

"The what?"

"Penguins. Black habits. Head to toe. Full wimple."

"Penguins," Alva said with a laugh. "I never thought of that.

Penguins."

"The infamous and dreaded Sisters of *Mercy*. Mercy," he scoffed. "I never saw much of that from them. More like the Sisters of no mercy." He turned away. "Hey Steve!"

In the middle of drawing off some beer from the keg, Steve looked over in their direction. "What's up?"

"The Sisters of Mercy."

Instinctively, Steve ducked. "Where? Where?"

"False alarm." Kerry turned back to Alva and Sandra. "A penguin. Now that would have made a great costume for this evening. Talk about scary."

"Speaking of costumes," Sandra said glancing over at Alva, "why don't we track down *the flasher*." She turned to Kerry. "Care to join us?"

"In a bit." He lifted his cup. "I'm gonna refresh this first and check on Steve's...*status*. He's supposed to work tonight. I'll catch up with you."

Turning, Sandra and Alva headed towards where the larger group was.

"Sandra," Alva said, "Lily's costume. I don't quite get it."

Sandra smiled. By her expression, Alva could tell Sandra was amused by her comment, like the way older folks looked at a child who just said something precocious and unintentionally funny.

"It has to do with the long, seedy coat and the shirt that she's wearing underneath. You saw it, right?"

"Nixon."

Sandra nodded. "Also known as...?"

"As...President Nixon."

"Right, but first name?"

"Richard."

"Or…?"

Alva paused. And then, "Oh. Dick?" she asked tentatively.

"You got it."

"I got what?"

Sandra stopped and stood for a moment looking at Alva. "You're not making this easy. Okay," she said taking a deep breath and letting it out slowly, "you're going to be offended. Do you really want to know?"

Alva paused for just a moment. "I guess not."

Sandra nodded and the two of them proceeded on. But they had only gone half a dozen steps when Alva stopped and turned to Sandra.

"Yes, I do. I want to know."

"Okay," Sandra said, "remember, you asked for it. Think crude. Think Nixon's first name, which we've already determined."

"Dick."

"Right, which can also refer to…?"

Alva thought for a moment, but then just shrugged and shook her head.

"Which can also refer to a certain part of the male anatomy."

For a brief moment Alva just stood there thinking. Then her eyes went wide. "His penis?" she whispered, embarrassed and hoping that she was wrong.

"You got it."

"So, a flasher…?"

"The seedy get up is a stereotype. A flasher is a type of pervert, someone who startles others by coming up to them and exposing his penis."

For a moment Alva stood there holding her breath. "That's

disgusting," she said finally, in a whisper.

Sandra shrugged. "Yes…yes, it is."

"It's awful. I've never heard of such a thing, I…" Alva suddenly felt disappointed with herself. "Here I go again. God, there's so much I don't know."

"Well, don't obsess about it this time. Not when it comes to something like this. Consider yourself lucky for getting this far along without being, pardon the pun, *exposed* to such things. C'mon."

"So why," Alva asked as they walked along, "would Lily want to portray such a person?"

"Actually," Sandra said, "if you think about it, she's not representing a real flasher, and it is kind of clever, flashing people with 'Dick' Nixon, instead of…well, you know."

Considering this, Alva nodded. "I suppose so. Still…"

"And there she is," Sandra said pointing up ahead.

Looking to where Sandra pointed, Alva saw Lily with a plastic cup in hand. She was talking to the bagpiper whose back was to Sandra and her. She was talking to him rapidly and gesticulating with considerable abandon, enough so that, at least once, Alva saw a portion of the contents of Lily's cup spill out.

"Oh dear," Sandra said. "It looks like Lily is fairly well along tonight."

It was at that moment that Lily, glancing up, saw Sandra and Alva approaching.

"*There* you are!" she called out with more volume than necessary, loud enough so that several people in the crowd turned to look, including the bagpiper.

Seeing him, Alva found to her surprise that Brian the bagpiper was also Brian the library security guard and Brian the ROTC recruit. She was so startled to discover this that she came to a dead stop right where she was.

Sandra turned to her. "What's up?"

"The bagpiper," she whispered. "I know him."

"Brian?"

Alva nodded.

"Really," Sandra said smiling, both surprised and pleased. "How so?"

"Back at the beginning of the semester, remember when I said that I fell asleep in the library?"

Sandra nodded.

"He was the security guard who woke me. He called me Sleeping Beauty."

"So," Sandra said in a teasing tone, "you've already met your Prince Charming."

"Go on," Alva said giving Sandra a slight push. "I also ran into him at Charlie's that morning I bought the tapestries. He was in an army uniform."

"ROTC," Sandra said. "He *is* one for the uniforms. ROTC. Security guard." With one hand she gestured in his direction. "AOH bagpiper."

"What kind of bagpiper?"

"AOH. Ancient Order of Hibernians. I'll fill you in later."

Detaching herself from Brian, Lily came running towards them. Drawing within a dozen feet of them, she came to a sudden stop. She pulled the front of her raincoat in her free hand, and whipped it open.

"Waaahhhhh," she yelled swaying slightly. "Happy Halloween from Tricky Dick."

"You look as if you're enjoying yourself," Sandra said.

"Oh yes. Oh, very yes. Halloween is just the absolute best holiday ever. I mean ever. Better than Christmas and St. Patrick's…" She stopped. "Well, better than Christmas."

Alva noticed the slight slur in Lily's speech. There was also, she thought, something in her expression that seemed to say that things weren't as great as she was making them out to be.

"Lily," Sandra said, her tone becoming quiet and serious. "Are you okay?"

"Okay?" Lily asked. "Never better. Or do you mean have I reached my limit?"

"Have you?"

Lily took a deep breath and let it out slowly. Doing so her shoulders sagged. To Alva it looked as if she were deflating. She also saw that Lily's eyes were moist as if she were on the verge of crying.

"Honestly," Lily said, "I think I'm a little past." She took a step towards Sandra and Alva, leaning her head towards them she whispered, "I think…I think I've scared him off."

"Brian?" Sandra asked quietly.

Lily nodded solemnly.

"I doubt it. Just try and relax and you'll be fine," Sandra said in a reassuring tone. "Do you want to head home?"

"No," Lily whined. "Everybody's going over to a party on Fraternity Row and I want to go too."

"Okay," Sandra said calmly. "We can do that. Why don't we head that way now? The walk will probably make you feel better."

"You think so?"

"It can't hurt. C'mon."

"Hello ladies." The three of them turned to find Brian approaching them. Tucked under one arm was his bagpipes.

"You," he said with some surprise seeing Alva. "You're…"

"Alva."

"Right. Alva. Good to see you." Alva saw Lily give first her and then Brian a sharp look. "So," he went on, "how do you know Sandra and…and Lily here?"

"Alva lives at the Cottage with us," Sandra said.

"Ah. Nice. So, c'mon," he said gesturing back towards where the crowd was. "Join the party."

"Actually," Sandra said, "we're heading out."

Brian gave Alva a quick glance. "Already?" he asked, disappointed. Alva saw that this did not go unnoticed by Lily.

"We were just going to walk over to check out the party on Fraternity Row."

"Oh good." Again, he glanced at Alva, and again Sandra saw Lily give them both sharp looks. "I'll catch up with you there. I just have to make sure that Steve rounds up the kegs and taps when things finish up here. *Stocks* are getting low, so it shouldn't be too much longer."

"Well," Sandra said, "we'll see you there."

"Great."

With that they parted company.

"We should check in with Kerry before we go," Sandra said as they started off.

"Hope you ladies aren't looking for anything more in the way of libations," Steve said when they got there. "The well, alas," he said holding up the tap, "has run dry."

Kerry was picking up empty cups that were lying around and stashing them into a large plastic bag.

"Those empty?" he asked.

"This one is," Sandra said handing him hers.

"Same here," Alva said doing the same.

"Well done, Alva," Kerry said with a smile, one that didn't go unnoticed by Lily. "And hello Lily," he said. "You done with that?" He gestured towards the cup she was holding.

With undisguised sullenness, Lily tipped her cup bottom up, the remainder of its contents pouring out at her feet. Rearing back, she threw it at Kerry. Lunging for it quickly, he caught it one handed, but only just.

"What's the matter, kiddo?" he asked. "Some raging Republicans take issue with your get-up?"

"Just a long night," Sandra said quickly. "We're heading over to the party on Fraternity…"

"I'm not," Lily cut in, her tone unmistakably petulant. "I'm going home."

"Okay," Sandra said giving Lily a concerned look before turning back to Kerry. "I guess we're not."

"You two can go," Lily said. "I don't need no one to walk me home. Just go to your stupid party." With that she turned and strode off.

"What was that all about?" Kerry asked.

Sandra shrugged. "I'm not sure."

"Is she alright? She doesn't look too steady there."

Sandra smiled and turned to Alva. "We'll follow her."

Alva nodded.

"I'm going to pass on the party too," Kerry said. "I've got to get the kegs and taps and all back to the AOH tonight, *and* I also have to get Steve to work too."

"Well," Sandra said turning to Alva, "we should get a move on before we lose sight of Lily." She turned to Kerry. "See ya."

"Good luck with Lily, and Happy Halloween."

Chapter 37

It took them a while to get back to the Cottage. Three times Lily had to stop to vomit. Each time Sandra and Alva kept their distance, waiting to see if she needed assistance. But the third time, when Lily fell to her knees, they ran up to her.

"Lily," Sandra said quietly, kneeling down beside her and taking one of her arms.

"Oh, thank God," Lily said hoarsely, her chin on her chest.

"Can you get up?"

"I don't know. I don't think so. Not without help."

Sandra looked up at Alva. "Give us a hand."

Each taking an arm, they got Lily to her feet.

"This way," Sandra said, turning Lily around.

Alva saw that they were near where she and Sandra had sat earlier talking. Slowly they walked Lily over to one of the benches where they had her sit with one of them on each side of her. Turning her head to one side, Lily looked up at Alva.

"You," she said as if surprised to find Alva there. Looking down at her feet, she shook her head.

The three of them sat there silently for a good long while. Finally, Lily sat up straight and closed her eyes.

"Can either of you stop the spinning?"

"Are you any better?" Sandra asked.

Lily shrugged. "Maybe."

"Do you want to try standing up?"

"I guess."

Each taking an arm, Sandra and Alva helped Lily to her feet. For a brief moment she stood there swaying slightly.

"You might do better if you opened your eyes."

Lily laughed. "I'm afraid to but, okay." She took a deep breath. "Here goes." For a moment she stood there looking about.

"You okay?" Sandra asked.

"Yeah," Lily said, nodding, "so far so good." Then, seeing Alva, she smiled, "You again. You. You. You." And then she laughed. "You're something else. You really are, you know. You really are." Then, letting her chin droop, she closed her eyes again.

Alva looked across to Sandra and gave her a questioning look, to which Sandra just shrugged.

"I'm going to try something," Lily said, her head still down, her eyes still closed. "Let go of my arms."

Sandra and Alva did as she said.

"Here goes," Lily said. Quickly she lifted her head and opened her eyes. "Whoa! Whoa! Whoa!"

Seeing her sway, Sandra and Alva quickly took hold of her arms again.

Lily laughed. "If I wasn't so nauseous, I'd really be enjoying this." She looked around. "We're still here?" She turned to Alva. "And you're still here." She shook her head. "This won't do. This won't do at all." She took a deep breath. "We should go."

Slowly Sandra released Lily's arm. Seeing her do so, Alva did the same.

"You good?" Sandra asked.

Lily nodded. "Let's get out of here."

Chapter 38

The rest of the trip back to the Cottage was slow, quiet, and, thankfully, uneventful. They were just about to the front steps when a white car pulled up at the curb and stopped. Alva saw that it was the same white car, the Studebaker, Stu, from the quarry.

"Hello ladies," Kerry said, leaning out of the driver's side window.

Sandra and Alva stopped and turned, but Lily kept going, starting up the steps when she reached them.

"Is she going to make it?" Kerry asked.

The three of them watched as Lily took each step slowly and with a touch of swaying. When she reached the top, she stopped and just stood there for a moment. Then, almost with a single lunge, she made her way to the front door, opened it and disappeared inside, the door slamming shut behind her.

"Well, that's a relief," Kerry said.

"That it is," Sandra said. "You checking up on us?"

"Yeah, I thought I would. I just dropped Steve off at the hospital and Brian at his frat."

"You're back already? From the west side?"

"No." With a nod of his head, Kerry gestured towards the back seat. "I still have to drop everything off. Anyone care to go for a ride?"

"I should make sure Lily gets squared away and tucked in," Sandra said. Then she turned to Alva. "Why don't you go," she suggested.

Alva shrugged. "I don't know. It's late and…"

"I'd really appreciate some company," Kerry cut in. "C'mon. I don't bite."

Sandra smiled at Alva. "Go."

"Okay."

"Great," Kerry said, "climb in."

Sandra looked at Alva. "Stop in when you get back."

Alva nodded, and she and Kerry started off.

"So, we're going to an AOH?" Alva asked.

"Close," Kerry said. "They won't be open this late, but there's a place, Ryan's, across the way, where we can leave everything."

"Ryan's?"

"A bar, or, if you're one of those people who see the world through emerald colored glasses, a *pub*."

"And they'll still be open?"

"Oh yes. It's still early, at least for Ryan's it is." Glancing over at her, Kerry gave her an amused smile. "So anyway," he asked, "you brought up the AOH. You're familiar with this Hibernian madness?"

Alva shook her head. "No."

"Well, I'd be surprised if you were. I take you for being from a more Baptist background. But then…" He glanced at her, his expression one of curiosity. "From what you said earlier, I gathered that you went to parochial school."

Alva nodded. "My parents thought I would get a more disciplined education from the sisters."

"Disciplined," Kerry repeated. "Yeah. There would definitely be that, and in spades. But then, I wouldn't think that discipline, even self-discipline, would be an issue with you. Anyway, the Hibernians, want some background?"

Alva nodded. "Okay."

"AOH. The Ancient Order of Hibernians, an Irish fraternal organization. They have a chapter on the west side, over where the famous, or should I say infamous, Tipperary Hill is. Have you heard of it?"

Alva shook her head.

"Well," Kerry continued, "we're talking *tres* Irish. Get this, there's an intersection there that, when they put up the traffic light there, they put the green on the top and the red on the bottom."

"Seriously?"

"I kid you not."

"That can't be right," Alva protested. "What about drivers who are color blind? That would be dangerous."

"And so, the authorities said, and they set it right, but…it was *hooliganized* and the authorities were notified that it would continue to be so until the green was put back on top. Well… the authorities relented, and the green went back on top."

Alva shook her head. "It's still dangerous."

Kerry nodded. "Yeah, it is. One thing though, it is an aspect of the neighborhood's identity, which *is* very much Irish, an ethnic identity, like the North End in Boston, and the South End there too, like Harlem back in the twenties. So…having one traffic light not quite right…" Kerry shrugged.

"It's still dangerous."

"Well, a lot of things are."

For a while they drove without talking. A light rain started to fall at one point. Alva sat looking out the window, taking in all the lights, their number, their variety, and the way they glistened and reflected in the wet pavement. Being unfamiliar with the city anywhere beyond campus, it occurred to Alva at one point that she didn't have a clue where they were, and that, if something happened, she would probably not be able to get back to the university on her own. Considering this, she was surprised to find that she wasn't all that concerned about it, just surprised and, even strangely enough to her, pleased.

"This is nice," she said continuing to look out the window, but then she started, immediately regretting having said aloud what was really just a thought.

"It is," Kerry said glancing briefly her way. "I appreciate your coming along. Thanks."

Alva laughed.

"What's so funny?"

Alva shook her head and then sat there looking ahead. "I just thought of my parents, or my Aunt Lillian. They would be... well, in the very least, upset, more shocked though, or even scandalized."

"About what?"

"About this, about being out this late, driving around in the rain with someone I don't really even know." Alva turned to him quickly, smiling broadly. "And going to a *bar*."

"Ah," Kerry said. "Sandra mentioned that you've led something of a quiet life."

"I have." Alva nodded. Then she turned to him. "Do you

really talk about me?"

"All the time."

"What!"

Kerry glanced over and smiled. "Just kidding. But yes, you've come up in conversation from time to time, usually at the dining hall when I'm scraping plates and she's loading them into the dish machine."

"She probably tells you about all the naïve things I say and do."

"Mmm," Kerry shrugged. "Some, but mostly she talks about your being a breath of fresh air. She *likes* having you for a friend." Kerry turned for a moment to look at her. By his expression she could tell that he was thinking about something serious. "Have you heard of Margaret Clark?"

Alva shook her head. "No."

"Sandra's never mentioned her?"

"No."

"I guess that's not *too* surprising. It's not my place to go into too much detail, but Margaret was Sandra's roommate the past three years. The first two years they shared a double over in Stradler, but last year Margaret insisted that they get away from dorm living. Sandra wasn't all that keen on the idea."

"Was there a problem?"

"Yeah. Yeah, there was. Margaret needed crutches, those metal kind with the forearm clasps to get around. That's why they were on the first floor at Stradler." Kerry gave Alva a quick glance. "Margaret had MS and pretty bad. They lived on the first floor there at the Cottage, in the big room beyond the living room. That was the best that they could come up with, but it was still a struggle for Margaret what with the crutches and all. But she had something. Grit, I guess."

"You keep referring to her in the past tense."

Kerry looked at her again. "Margaret passed away last May, just before the end of the school year."

"Oh my God," Alva said quietly.

"Mmm. Not that I know for sure, but I'm thinking that Margaret knew that she didn't have much time left and that's why she insisted on moving off campus."

"The Cottage isn't really off campus."

"No. No, it's not, but because she needed crutches the university wouldn't let her live somewhere other than in university housing, so the Cottage was the closest they could get to living some place more like a home."

"And that was what Margaret wanted."

"That was what she wanted for the two of them. She wanted to have a home with Sandra before…" Kerry shrugged. "They were close. Real close. I don't mean in an intimate way, at least not that I know of, and not that it would have mattered if they were."

"So, Sandra took care of Margaret."

"Well, yeah…but that door swung both ways. Margaret took care of Sandra too."

"What do you mean?"

For a moment Kerry just drove on looking at the road ahead.

"Has Sandra ever mentioned her mother?"

"No."

Kerry nodded. "That doesn't surprise me. But that's not to say that it would have surprised me if she did. If I can see her telling anyone, it would be you. Hands down. Again, it's not my place to go into any detail, but Sandra's mom died freshman year."

"No." Alva felt her throat tighten and her eyes tear up. "Why? I mean, how?"

Kerry shrugged. "I never got the full story. I think Margaret was the only one that did. And..." Kerry took a deep breath and let it out slowly. "It's not important. Suffice it to say that Margaret was there for Sandra, right up to last May."

For a short while the two of them rode along in silence. At one point the rain picked up enough so that Kerry switched the wipers on to continuous.

"You know," he said. "Thinking about it, it may well be that you came along at just the right moment when you did, you know that, with Margaret gone, you were meant to be here for Sandra, to, you know, be here for her."

Alva was so startled by this that for a moment she just sat there saying nothing, just letting things sink in. As they did, Alva grew more and more pleased and more and more excited by the idea of it. The prospect of truly *being there* for Sandra, of being *that* person, made her feel special in a way that she had never felt before in terms of anybody else. In a way it felt as if it were defining her. Then something else occurred to her. She turned to Kerry.

"You know," she said quietly, "that door swings both ways too."

"Yes," Kerry said after a moment, "I suppose it does, seeing as...well, from what Sandra has said about you and, more to the point, the way that she's said it, it's obvious that she thinks you're pretty special, maybe," he glanced at Alva, "more than you give yourself credit for. And now..."

Putting on the directional, Kerry turned the wheel and pulled into a parking spot in front of a two-story brick building.

Turning off the engine, he turned to Alva. "We're here."

The building was designed for a commercial enterprise at the street level, with living quarters above it. There were two doors, one off to the far right that provided access to the second story, and another mid-building for the first floor. Above this middle door was a sign that read, in plain letters, "Ryan's". There was a small rectangular window above eye level on either side of this door. In each window there was a neon sign, one read 'Guinness,' the other 'Harp.'

"Ready?" Kerry asked reaching for the door handle.

"Not really. I'll just wait here."

"'Fraid not, milady," Kerry said with a smile. "You're my alibi, or, I should say, my excuse."

"I'm your what?"

"You're my excuse to get in and out quickly and avoid a lot of…nonsense." Opening his door, Kerry climbed out. Before shutting it he leaned into the car. "Seriously. Please come in with me."

Alva took a deep breath and let it out slowly. "Okay," she said grimly.

"Move quick. It's really coming down."

Alva reached for the door handle. For a brief moment she hesitated. "Go," she told herself. "Just go." With that she opened the door and climbed out.

Kerry was standing at the front door waiting. When she drew near, he opened the door and held it to allow Alva to enter first.

Chapter 39

"Close that feckin' door, ya moron," someone yelled from inside the bar just as Alva reached where Kerry stood. Alva hesitated. Kerry quickly took her arm and led her through the door, closing it behind them.

"Oh, I'm sorry missy," a middle-aged man sitting at the bar called to her. "Really I am. A thousand pardons."

"That'll teach ya, Jimmy. That'll teachya," said an almost identical middle-aged man sitting next to the first. Both men were wearing sweater vests over their button-down collar shirts. Both men wore cloth caps and corduroy slacks. Alva noticed that both of them even wore the same dark brogues. Both pairs were well polished.

Looking around, Alva saw that there were only two other people in the bar, two men who were shooting pool. One of them, who wore a short apron wrapped around his waist, was in the process of taking a shot. He looked up once as she and Kerry walked in. Then, sighting up, he took his shot sinking the eight ball. "Game," he said quietly, placing his cue on the table and standing up. Turning, he looked at Kerry. "You want something?"

"I'm dropping stuff off for the AOH." Hearing this, the two

men at the bar turned their heads and looked Kerry over. "A couple empty kegs and taps," Kerry went on. "I was told to drop them off here."

"And who told you that?"

"Steve, Steve Walsh."

The bartender nodded. "Right. You've been here before... with him. Where you parked?"

"Right out front."

"Pull around the back." With his head he gestured towards the person he had just been playing pool with. "Joey will meet you at the door." Without saying anything, Joey placed his cue on the table and headed towards the back exit. Wiping his hands on his apron, the man with the apron went back behind the bar.

Alva noticed that the two men at the bar were watching her and Kerry as they headed back towards the front door. She and Kerry were just a few feet passed them when Kerry stopped and took her arm.

"You stay here," he said in a low voice. "No sense both of us getting drenched."

Alva shook her head emphatically.

"Stay here," Kerry said with noticeable emphasis. "I'll just be a minute."

"Stay here, missy," said the one the other called Jimmy, "give 'im a chance to play the gentleman. He could use it."

Kerry nudged Alva over to the nearest stool. "I'll be right back." With that he turned, made his way quickly to the front door and went out.

"No sense standing, missy, when you can sit," Jimmy said pushing a bar stool a few inches closer to her.

"Thank you anyway," Alva said quietly, "but I think I'll stand."

"Hear that Mike?" Jimmy said, "'tis a southern belle we have here."

At that moment the bartender came up to them. "You two having another?"

Jimmy and Mike looked at each other. "Well, Mike?" Jimmy asked.

Mike looked at his watch. "I got time for one more."

"Can I get you anything?" Mike asked, turning to Alva.

"I could use a glass of water."

Alva saw Jimmy and Mike smile at each other.

"I'm guessing, missy, that you're not quite old enough to, shall we say, *partake*."

"Leave the young lady be," Mike said.

"But," Jimmy went on, ignoring him, "I've seen your boyfriend in here before partaking and needing some assistance to make the door when time was called."

As uncomfortable as she had been feeling up to that point, her discomfort gave way to one of anger. A sudden urge came over her to tell this Jimmy off, and she was on the verge of doing just that when the bartender came up to them.

"Here you are," he said quietly setting a glass of water on the bar near where Alva stood.

"Thank you," Alva said quickly picking up the glass.

"Not much call for one of those here," Jimmy said. "Is there, Jack? Ah, this could be the start of terrible things." He leaned close to Alva. "Terrible things."

"Jimmy," Mike said quietly, but also, Alva thought, with a definite intensity.

"Yes. Terrible things," Jimmy went on still leaning towards Alva.

With a sudden lunge, Jack reached across the bar, planted a hand on Jimmy's shoulder and, with a good degree of force, pulled him away from Alva, almost on top of the bar.

"You're done Jimmy."

"What's this?" Jimmy protested giving Jack a vicious look. "Take your paw off me," he said twisting his shoulder free, and turning to Alva. "She should know. She should know the things about her boyfriend, about the drunk he is, and that she's not the first *child* that he's brought in here. That…"

With a sudden twist of her wrist, Alva threw the contents of her glass in Jimmy's face.

"You're one to talk about someone else's drinking," she hissed disgustedly. "You sitting there with your face all fat and red. You sitting there, all big and brave, maligning someone else, someone who isn't here to defend himself and maybe even take a swing at you. And it just so happens that I am old enough to be here and to drink a drink if I want to. But I'll tell you something, if I was thinking of having *something* when I came through the door, I would have lost that desire the moment you opened that big mouth of yours. And one more thing, just to set the record straight, as far as me being his girlfriend goes, I'm not, but that's just because…because I'm not and not because I wouldn't be. And…"

Feeling a hand on her shoulder, Alva turned to find Kerry standing there, his look both concerned and curious. It was then that she noticed that she was trembling.

"Trouble in paradise?" Kerry asked. When no one said anything, he nodded his head slowly. He turned to Alva. "I'm sorry I left you here. C'mon," he said quietly. "Let's go."

Chapter 40

It was still raining when they left the bar. Kerry trotted ahead to the passenger side door and opened it for her. Once she was in, he closed the door behind her, trotted around to the driver's side, and climbed in. Leaning slightly forward, Kerry put the key in the ignition, but instead of turning the engine on he just sat back.

"So," he said looking straight ahead. "You have any idea where Alva disappeared to?"

Alva turned to him. "What?"

Kerry shook his head and smiled. Then he turned to her. "You look an awful lot like the attractive woman I showed up here with tonight, but…" He shrugged. "You're certainly a different number altogether."

Folding her hands in her lap, Alva looked down at them. A moment later she started sobbing quietly.

"Hey, hey, hey," Kerry said reaching over and laying a hand gently on her shoulder. "What's this?"

Still looking down at her hands, Alva sat there shaking her head. "I'm sorry," she said. "I just…I'm sorry."

"Sorry? For what? For giving that bastard what he deserved?"

Kerry laughed. "And that was one hell of a shot with the water. Impressive. I don't think a drop missed him. Really. *Im-pressive.* And then some."

Alva looked at him quickly. "No," she said shaking her head. "Why would I do something like that, and say the things I said? Why would I even go into a place like…like that? What am I even doing here with you?" Letting her head drop, she looked at her hands again. "What's happened to me? You're right. Where did I go?"

For a moment they just sat there. Noticing his hand on her, Alva drew away from him.

"Alva," Kerry said quietly, "I'm the one who's sorry. I shouldn't have brought you here. And I certainly shouldn't have made you come inside with me. I just… You're just… I…I wasn't thinking." He turned his head to look straight ahead again. "The thing is…" He took a deep breath and let it out slowly. "The thing is, I'm just not that good when it comes to paying attention. Certainly, that was the case tonight, here, with you. And…" he went on with a sigh, "and I'm sorry." He turned to look at her again. "I really am."

Looking over at him, Alva nodded her head.

"And," Kerry said, starting the car, "I'll make a point to do better next time. I promise."

"Next time?" Alva asked, surprised.

"Yeah," Kerry said putting the car in reverse and backing out. "It was good hanging out with you. It was good. At least it was until this." Putting the car in drive, he started off. Glancing over at her, he smiled. "It was, wasn't it? I mean, the cemetery, and driving over here and talking."

Alva smiled, nodding her head. "Yes, yes it was."

"And now we can just enjoy this drive back, right?"

Alva nodded. "Right."

"Well, there you go."

When they arrived at the Cottage, Kerry pulled up to the front steps and put the car in park. For a brief moment Alva felt a slight sense of panic, the thought suddenly occurring to her that he might lean over and try to kiss her goodnight.

"And here we are *m' lady*, safe, sound, and...without further mishap. You'll excuse me if I don't escort you to the front door as, *sans parapluie*, it would only result in us both getting wet."

"Some gentleman you are."

Although she had only meant to tease him, Alva was shocked at actually having said what she did, and she was just about to apologize when, looking over at Kerry, she saw that her remark had not only taken him by surprise, but that it also left him smiling. Reaching over, she placed a hand on his arm.

"Just kidding."

Kerry nodded. "Good one. Real good."

Pleased with herself, Alva released his arm, turned and opened her door a crack. She was just about to climb out when she stopped and turned back to him.

"We forgot something."

"What's that?"

"You forgot to show me the traffic light, the one with the green over the red."

Kerry frowned. "You're right. I guess we got distracted. Sorry."

"Another time?" Alva asked. For a moment Kerry just sat there looking at her. Again, Alva saw, there was the look of surprise and the smile. "And," she went on, "maybe you can show me how to play pool."

"Yeah," Kerry said, nodding his head. "Of course. You bet."

"Goodnight," Alva said, and with that she pushed her door open and climbed out.

When Alva got to the front door, she cracked it open, but, before going in, she stopped and turned to look back. Seeing the car still there, she waved. With the rain and in the dark, she couldn't tell if Kerry waved back, but with the car pulling away only after she waved, she was just pleased that he waited, that he had sat there watching her go. With that she turned and went in closing the door behind her.

Chapter 41

The rain on Halloween night proved to be the cold front that marked the onset of winter weather for the school year. From that point on the thermometer wouldn't wander much above the high forties until late February at best. By the middle of the following week there was snow on the ground, snow that had come to stay *for the duration*.

In what almost seemed connected to the cold weather, Lily's attitude towards Alva after that Halloween night took on a cold feel, one that Alva found both unsettling and difficult to account for. More curt than uncivil, Lily would give Alva little more than a glance when their paths crossed and would only speak after Alva spoke first and then only in single syllable responses. Certainly, Alva saw nothing of the *exuberance* that she always associated with Lily's manner and that, more than anything else, troubled Alva, making her feel even sad. She wondered why she was obviously the cause of this change in Lily's spirit.

Alva considered speaking to Sandra about the matter to see if she knew what she might have done to cause this change in Lily's attitude towards her, but, at first, she refrained from doing so. She didn't want to sound whiny and possibly childish. She hoped that, if she just gave her time, Lily would come around, but when a week had gone by without any change in Lily's treatment of her, Alva felt compelled to talk to Sandra about it.

"Yeah," Sandra said with a sigh. "I've noticed her sullenness around you."

It was late on a Sunday afternoon. There had been a low, gray sky all day and the snow flurries that had punctuated things since early morning had turned to a light, but steady snowfall with evening approaching.

"Do you have any idea what I did to bring this on? I feel bad, and I'd like to apologize but..." Alva shrugged.

Concerned, Sandra frowned. "You have nothing to apologize for," she said after a moment. "You didn't do anything, except maybe..."

"Except what?"

Sandra smiled. "Except maybe charm someone."

"What? What do you mean?"

"Well, on Halloween, when we met up with Lily and Brian, it was fairly obvious that Brian was, let's say, *interested* in you. Lily definitely took notice of it. You see she's had a thing for Brian for some time. And later, when Kerry also paid, again noticeably, attention to you...well, that didn't make things any better."

"Are they...have they dated or anything? Lily and Brian?"

"No, at least not that I know of. Not just the two of them. We've all done things together at times. The thing is, Lily... well, you know Lily. Subtlety is not one of her strong points. To say that she's gone out of her way to let Brian know that she's interested is putting it mildly. And Brian...Brian is kind of on the conservative side. I think he's somewhat daunted by the way she comes off at times." Sandra smiled and shook her head.

"Maybe even scared."

"I feel bad for Lily."

"Tell me. What's *your* take on Brian? Are you…interested?"

"I…I don't know." Alva could feel herself blush. "Not…I don't know. Not really. No."

"Hmm," Sandra said. "Methinks she doth protest too much."

Alva frowned. "I don't know if I'm interested in him. I don't really know…I don't really have any experience when it comes to that kind of thing."

"Methinks…"

"Alright…I could be. Maybe. But I don't know. I don't really know him, and I don't know how to go about getting to know him."

Sandra shook her head. "You're like the opposite of Lily. Hmm. Maybe that's part of what interests him about you."

"What do you think I should do?"

"You could ask *him* out."

Shocked by such a notion, Alva just stared at Sandra.

"Seriously," Sandra said, "see if he'd like to meet you for coffee or something sometime, or to go for a walk. Here's an idea, steal a couple of trays from the cafeteria and invite him to go sledding in the park."

"I couldn't do that," Alva protested.

"Why not?"

"Women don't ask men out."

"What?" Sandra laughed. "Maybe back in Kentucky they don't, but here they do."

"Well, I can't. And I can't do that to Lily."

Sandra shook her head. "If Lily has a problem with that," Sandra said seriously, "it's really Lily's problem. Not yours."

"Maybe. But I still can't."

Sandra nodded and smiled. "Okay. But what if Brian were to ask you out? Would you go?"

Alva shook her head. "No. I guess I wouldn't."

"Because of Lily."

Alva nodded.

"Even if he has no intention of ever asking Lily out, or *succumbing to her feminine charms.*"

Alva shook her head. "No. I could never feel good about doing that."

Sandra shrugged. "Okay."

"You think I'm stupid."

"No, not at all. I think you're a person of principles, of your own principles." Sandra smiled. "No, you're not at all stupid."

Alva frowned. "But where does that leave me in regard to Lily? Should I tell her I have no interest in Brian?"

"I wouldn't. Again, it's her problem, not yours. Just go on being you. Eventually...hopefully...she'll come around, especially if it becomes obvious that anything to do with you and Brian is going nowhere. And if she doesn't..." Sandra shrugged. "Then it's her loss."

"Okay. Can I ask you one more thing?"

"Of course."

"Does she also have an *attachment* thing for Kerry?"

"No, at least not that I know of. Why?"

Alva could feel herself blush. "It's just that...well, the other night, Halloween, when I went with him to take the kegs back, we sort of made a date to drive over to the west side again sometime, so he could show me that traffic light, the one with the green over the red."

Sandra nodded. "Okay," she said slowly and tentatively.

"He said he would also teach me how to play pool."

Again, Sandra nodded. And again... "Okay."

"Do you think that would be alright?"

"Sure, I guess," Sandra said quietly. "Of course."

Even though Sandra said so with a smile, Alva detected something reserved in her manner.

"Are you sure?" Alva asked hesitantly.

As if snapping out of a quiet reverie, Sandra shook her head and smiled. "Sorry," she said. "It's just that... Kerry... You should know that Kerry has a way about him, a way of keeping people at arm's length and..."

"Yes?"

Sandra shook her head. "Nothing. He's a good person, really, and good to be with. Go. Definitely go. You'll have fun. You will."

For a moment, Alva just looked at Sandra, curious about this response of hers. "Methinks..."

Sandra smiled. "Right. But seriously, you should go. One thing though, he's not always that reliable on the follow-through. Sometimes he needs a bit of a reminder. You might have to keep after him about this...date."

"Okay. And...you're sure about this, about my doing this, honestly?"

"Alva," Sandra said patiently.

"What?"

"I'm sure. Just go."

Alva nodded, pleased. "Okay."

Chapter 42

As November wore on, the weather grew colder and snowier. To Alva it seemed like each day started with some amount of snowfall. Stomping one's feet to get the snow off boots became a ritual of sorts on entering any building. Salt stains on footwear and the lower leg bottoms of jeans had almost a fashionable element to them. With possibly only one exception the newer campus buildings were as excessively heated as the older ones were cold, that one exception being the Rare Archives Room where Alva worked, which was climatically controlled.

One day the week before Thanksgiving, Alva was in the room typing up her notes when Professor Nagy came in. Picking up the previous sheet that Alva had typed up, she stood there reading it. Although she knew there was no basis for feeling so, Alva grew uneasy as she sat there continuing to type. The longer Professor Nagy stood there reading, the more Alva's unease increased.

"Alva," Professor Nagy said quietly holding up the sheet when she finished, "this is one you wrote, right?"

"Yes, yes, it is."

"It's good. It's very good." She placed the sheet of paper on the pile.

"Thank you."

"I know that exams will be starting up soon after the holiday, so if you'd like to take a break, we can wrap things up for the semester."

"That won't be necessary," Alva said quickly. "I've completed all my course work and all I have to do is review my notes before taking the exams. And I only have to take two."

"Sounds like you're right on top of things." Professor Nagy smiled. "As usual. Of course, we can certainly use you around here, but if at any point you feel the need to take time off, please feel free to do so."

"Thank you."

"By the way, have you spoken to your uncle recently?"

Alva nodded. "Last Sunday. After church."

"Not since then?"

"No."

Professor Nagy nodded. "Will you see him again before the holiday? I know that many students, *and faculty*, leave early to make a week of it."

"I'll see him Thanksgiving. My folks are coming out here and we're having dinner with my aunt and uncle."

"Well, that sounds nice. Anyway...I'm keeping you from your work. If I don't see you before then, have a good Thanksgiving."

"Thank you. And you too."

Alva went back to her typing, but, as she went along, she found it difficult to stay focused as she kept going back to Professor Nagy having asked if she had spoken to her uncle, as it seemed like she had something on her mind.

Eventually she got through her work and after putting it all into a notebook and labeling it appropriately, she gathered her things to leave. Looking around she found, to her surprise, that she was the only one left. With that being the case, on leaving the room she shut off all the lights and checked to make sure that the door was locked.

As she made her way through the library, she found it much emptier than usual. This reminded her of Professor Nagy's comment about folks leaving early to make a longer holiday of it. This she found unsettling. At first, she didn't know why she would feel this way, but then it occurred to her that it had something to do with being there at the university when everyone else was gone, that it almost felt like being left behind. Once again, she felt outside the mainstream.

Try as she might, she couldn't shake the feeling, and grew more and more obsessed about it. The worst was when she passed through the reading area, a large open area of tables, which was, except for two young men in a far corner playing chess, empty. Somewhat paradoxically, their presence, to Alva, only served to accent the emptiness of the room.

Quickening her pace, she headed for the elevator and was just about to hit the down button when she heard her name called out. Turning she found the two young men looking her way, one of whom she recognized.

"Hey Alva," Steve called rising up from his chair, "come on over."

Alva's first reaction was one of embarrassment at being part of a commotion in the library, but, realizing that there was no one else about, she let it go, smiled and started back in their direction. As she drew near, Steve's companion rose from his seat and smiled. He was taller than Steve and with noticeably wider shoulders. Although as long and as straight as Steve's hair, his was lighter in color, with a tint of something like copper to it. What struck her mostly about him were his dark brown eyes and high cheekbones. There was, she thought, something Native American about him.

"Hawk, meet Alva," Steve said. "Alva, meet Hawk, the Bobby Fischer of the reservation."

"Aw," Hawk said sheepishly and smiling shyly, "Howdy Alva."

"Hello."

"Alva," Steve said, "is a good friend of Sandra's. They are, in fact, roomies."

Hawk smiled again, this time more broadly. He also nodded his head vigorously. "That's great. That's really great. Sandra. She's great."

Steve turned to Alva. "And you work here at the library, right?"

Alva nodded. "I do."

"At the library," Hawk repeated. "You work here at the library. That's great too. Really great."

Surprised as she was by his exuberance over such simple matters, she was also taken by how genuine it appeared to be.

"Oh!" Steve said to Hawk, "And *she's* the one at Ryan's that threw the glass of water in my Uncle Jimmy's face."

Horrified at being reminded of that night, Alva instinctively took a step back. Worse was the realization that if Steve and Hawk knew about the episode, then, in all probability, others did too. And then, on top of all that, was finding out that it was Steve's uncle that she had dowsed.

"Kerry told you."

Steve shook his head. "Didn't have to. You're the talk of Ryan's. Hell, you're the talk of Tipperary Hill. Your glass has been enshrined on the shelf of honor behind the bar. You're a hero, you know, the new hero of Tipperary Hill. You are legend."

"You sure are," Hawk said. "You certainly sure are. Except," he turned to Steve, "isn't that 'heroine' and not 'hero.'"

"Oh, yeah. Right you are. Heroine." Steve turned to Alva. "Heroine. The heroine of Tipperary Hill."

"I'm sorry," Alva said nervously. "I didn't know it was your uncle. And I shouldn't have done it anyway. Not to anyone."

"Au contraire, mademoiselle. If anyone had it coming, it was old Uncle Jimmy, and a long time coming it was. Ask anybody." He turned to Hawk. "Ain't that right?" Hawk nodded, his expression serious. "Hell," Steve went on, turning back to Alva, "ask my Aunt Peg. She says now she'll know just what to do when he starts in again with any his nonsense. And…just so you know, from now on your money's no good at Ryan's. As far as Mike the barkeep there is concerned, for you, drinks are on the house."

"Whose drinks are on the house?" a voice behind Alva asked.

Turning, Alva was startled to find her uncle standing there.

"Hers," Steve said.

"Yours," Uncle Ward said looking at Alva and smiling. "Really. And why would that be?"

Alva shook her head. "It was nothing. It was just a misunderstanding."

Uncle Ward nodded. "Okay, Still, we best not let your Aunt Lillian catch wind of it." He glanced in Steve and Hawk's direction. "Aren't you going to introduce me to your friends?"

Alva made the introductions, and everyone smiled and shook hands.

"Nice to meet you both," Uncle Ward said.

"Same here," said Steve. Hawk nodded.

"Now, if you two don't mind, I'm going to *spirit* this young lady away from you as I need to speak with her about *matters of consequence.*"

"Spirit away. Catch you later, Alva."

Alva and Uncle Ward were just about to leave when her uncle noticed the chess game in progress. After studying it for a moment he looked at Hawk.

"Are you black?"

Hawk nodded.

"And it's your move."

"It is. Yes, yes, it is."

"Then king's rook to queen's bishop three".

Hawk looked down and studied the board for one brief moment. "Right," he said excitedly. "Right. Right. Right."

Steve frowned. "Like he ever needs extra help."

"Sorry," Uncle Ward said with little in the way of conviction. With that he and Alva took their leave.

"You were looking for me?"

"Yes. Lorraine said you were working today. She wanted me to talk to you about something, something to do with next semester."

"What is that?"

"Let's find a quiet place to sit. Or would you like to go somewhere for coffee? I know a place down near Market Street that's good."

"Sure."

"Wait, you don't drink coffee."

"I do."

"Since when?"

Alva shrugged. "Since this semester."

Uncle Ward nodded. "So…there have been some changes,

huh. I mean besides your bangs being longer."

Alva smiled. "Some."

"Good, very good. Well, let's go."

Chapter 43

Alva was surprised and pleased when she found that the coffee place that Uncle Ward had in mind turned out to be Charlie's. On entering she saw that Nick was working the counter. As they approached, Nick looked up and smiled.

"Hello Alva," he said. "How're you?"

"Good, Nick. I'm good."

"And who's this?" Nick asked, looking at Alva's companion.

"This is my uncle, Uncle Ward."

"Well, hello Uncle Ward. You've been in here before."

"I have."

"I knew it. So, what can I get you two?" He looked at Alva. "The usual?"

Alva nodded. "Just a small."

"And you sir?"

"I'll have the same, whatever it is."

"Two French Roast black it is. Small."

When they were seated with their coffees, Uncle Ward gave Alva a questioning look. "The usual?"

Alva shrugged.

"So," Uncle Ward went on, "another change. I'm getting the

impression that there have been many others."

"Yes, I guess so," Alva said with a shy smile.

Uncle Ward nodded. "I take it that, in many ways, it has been a good semester."

Alva nodded. "Yes. It really has."

"I'm glad. Not that I had any doubts. I didn't. Still, I, for one, am pleased, pleased that you're so obviously pleased."

"Thank you. You made it possible."

Uncle Ward shrugged. "Maybe I helped. But you made it happen. Anyway, I have something, something concerning about next semester, something that I need to run by you. It has to do with Lorraine, Professor Nagy. First of all, she is something more than just pleased with how things have worked out with you on board there at the library. Way more. And she wants you to stay on board as part of the team next semester."

Alva smiled. "That would be great. I was hoping that the work would continue."

"Good. The thing is, there's a slight glitch."

"What's that?" Alva asked, curious, and also somewhat concerned.

"Lorraine, as well as other members of the team, will be on a sabbatical of sorts next semester."

"Oh. So, they won't be here?"

Uncle Ward shook his head. "No. They'll be in the Middle East. Most of the time in Israel, but also in Egypt."

Alva frowned. "I see."

"Is that a problem?"

Alva shrugged. "No, but, it's just that the reason why I wanted to get a job this semester, besides earning some money that is, was to be with people."

"And?"

"Well, I like the work, I really like the work, but the idea of staying behind and working alone…it's not what I had in mind. I wouldn't feel like I was part of things anymore. Not really."

Uncle Ward grinned. "Who said anything about staying behind?"

For a moment Alva just sat there not quite getting what her uncle was driving at. But then it dawned on her.

"She wants me to go too, to go with them?"

Uncle Ward nodded. "That's the idea."

"But, but what about my schoolwork…and graduation?"

"What about it? You already have enough credits to graduate, and you've fulfilled all of your requirements in your major. You can graduate come this January. Also, Lorraine has recommended you for acceptance in the graduate program here at the university, so this work in the Middle East would be part of your working on your masters." Uncle Ward paused. "And…there you have it. So, what do you think?"

For a moment Alva just sat there stunned. "I…I don't know really what to say. I mean… yes, yes, I want to do it, but, but I…I don't know. I don't know what to say."

"That's fine. I think you should take some time to really think about it, think about what it involves, and talk to Lorraine, and just…and just try and determine what you, what Alva wants because the decision is yours, all yours."

Alva nodded. "Yes. Right."

"It would be best, if possible, to come to some decision before Thanksgiving, before your folks get here, so that they can be filled in on everything."

"Do you think they might not let me go?"

"It's not their decision. It's yours. You're twenty-one. And as far as finances are concerned, as a grad student you'll be working *for* the university, so that end of things is covered. And, beyond all of that, it's a pretty special opportunity for the right person, and, as far as Lorraine is concerned, you are that person, and I couldn't agree with her more. Still, it's up to you and you should do what you feel is right for you. One last thing, no matter what you decide, things will work out for you. There is no wrong decision here. Make sure to keep that in mind too."

"Okay," Alva said with a smile. "I'll think about it, but...but, right now, I want to say yes."

"Well, I think that's the good position to start the decision process from, better than an outright 'no.' So, again, think about it, and if your final decision is yes, then we'll discuss how we'll handle things with your folks *and your Aunt Lillian* on Thanksgiving. Now, with that out of the way, there's one last matter to attend to here."

"What's that?"

Uncle Ward smiled. "Back at the library, what was all that about drinks on the house?"

Chapter 44

By the time Alva and her uncle had finished their coffee and left Charlie's, the afternoon was well on the way down its slide into evening. The streetlights were on and the air, colder now, had the feel of impending night to it.

"Beastly weather," Uncle Ward said turning up the collar of his long wool coat and readjusting his scarf as they stood there just outside the door. "And it's not even Thanksgiving yet. The Middle East should be a nice break for you weather-wise."

Not getting a response, he turned to look in Alva's direction and found her looking straight ahead and smiling, her attention obviously far elsewhere.

"Alva?" he said, gently laying a hand on her arm.

Mildly startled, she turned quickly to him. "I'm sorry. I guess my mind wandered off a bit."

Uncle Ward smiled. "That's understandable considering. Everything still alright?"

Alva nodded. "Yes. Very much so."

"Good. And now I hope you don't mind if I don't walk you home. It's getting late and I have to go back to campus to tie up some loose ends before the holiday."

"No, not at all. I have all sorts of thoughts to keep me company."

"Good thoughts?"

"Good thoughts."

"Then," Uncle Ward said giving her a quick hug, "I'll see you later."

Alva's thoughts, which were many and wide-ranging, did keep her company, to the point that she barely noticed the cold at all. In fact, on turning the corner by the dining hall and seeing the Cottage just up ahead, she stopped short, amazed to find herself there already and not able to recall barely anything of the walk after parting from her uncle. Realizing that this had to be some sort of manifestation of just how excited she was about her prospects, she just stood there feeling more than pleased.

It was then though, standing there, seeing the Cottage, that, for the first time since being apprised of this opportunity to study and work in the Middle East, she sensed there was more to her decision than just whether she would take it or not. It was now, seeing the dormer of her room, that it began to hit home that this *sojourn* to the Middle East entailed giving up some things, things which, over the course of that semester, had become important to her.

There was her room, her room with the bed and desk that she had placed *just so* when she moved in, her room with the tapestries on the walls, tapestries that she had selected herself and purchased with her own money, money she had earned, money that she had *worked* for. She had made the room just what she had wanted it to be and in doing so the room had given her a sense of place. It was a place that was hers and hers alone, a place where she truly belonged, a place that had become an important aspect of her self-identity.

Standing there, looking up at the dormer, she reminded herself that deciding against going to the Middle East would only serve as a postponement in terms of giving up the room. The spring semester would end. She would graduate and, with that, she would have to vacate the room and leave it, leave it empty save for those items that were there when she first arrived, empty of all that she had brought to it. She would be gone. She would be *not there*, just as Sandra would, come graduation, be *not there* across the landing.

This last thought caught Alva by surprise, causing her to inhale sharply. Yes, Sandra would be *not there* come the end of next semester whether Alva went to the Middle East or not. By not going there, all she was buying was one more semester, another five months, tops, with Sandra. Alva felt a profound sense of impending loss come over her. Standing there, her overriding feeling was that she wanted those five months, that she did not want to give them up, she did not want to lose them, that she did not want to lose them no matter what.

"What's the matter? Lose your way?"

Startled, Alva jumped ahead a step. Turning quickly, she found Lily standing there looking at her sullenly.

"Oh Lily," Alva said with a mix of relief and sadness. "I'm so glad to see you."

"What's your problem, girl? Can't find your way home?"

"It's..."

Lily raised a hand dismissively. "Yeah," she said sarcastically, "like I want to hear it." With that, she stepped past Alva and headed for the Cottage.

Alva grabbed Lily's arm and held it tightly before she got past.

"Lily, please."

Lily turned quickly. Glaring at Alva, she wrenched her arm away. "What's wrong with you?" she hissed.

Unnerved by Lily's hostility, Alva took a step back, quickly getting out of her way. "Sorry," she said, almost in a whisper. "I'm sorry."

"Moron," Lily said under her breath, turning and proceeding on.

Alva watched Lily reach the front steps of the Cottage and start up the stairs. She was surprised when Lily, once she reached the top, stopped and turned back to look her way. For a moment the two of them stood there looking at each other. As they did so, Alva felt a slight glimmer of hope. But then, shaking her head, Lily turned away, crossed the porch to the front door and went inside.

Alva continued to stand where she was, trying to compose herself. It was then that she realized that she was shivering. Suddenly feeling the cold, it dawned on her that it was the first time since she and Uncle Ward parted that she even noticed how cold it was. She also realized that, for the first time since she turned the corner and saw the Cottage up ahead, she wasn't either wrapped up with thoughts of the Middle East or envisioning this present *life* of hers coming to an end, that she was, at this moment, in this moment, this cold winter moment.

It was almost in a sleepwalk that Alva started towards The Cottage. Even so, her focus, instead of being on any one thing, instead embraced everything – the cold, each step she took, the hard, unforgiving surface of the sidewalk, the snow along its edges, what cars there were passing by, the street-lights, the cold, clean taste of the winter evening air. She felt that she could even sense the presence of stars that were, as yet, unseen. And yet, even with all that *stimulus*, there were no accompanying thoughts. Even as she mounted the front steps, it was more on impulse than a conscious climb, and it was the same as she opened the door and went in and then climbed the stairs to her room where, without bothering to take off her coat or mittens, she sat down on her bed. And she remained there, sitting like that until…

"Hey."

Turning her head, Alva found Lily leaning against the doorjamb.

"You okay?"

Alva nodded. And then, with a hint of a smile, she shook her head. "No. No, actually. I'm not."

"Well…what's wrong?"

Alva shrugged. "Nothing really."

Lily rolled her eyes. "Nothing really," she repeated. "Then why all the fuss?"

"I…I just got wrapped up in a bunch of thoughts thinking about…thinking about things."

"Like what?"

"Like this being senior year and all," Alva said quietly.

"Yeah? So?"

"Well…this is it, really. Things are going to end. This," she made a gesture encompassing the room. "This is all going to go away, at least it is as far as we're concerned."

"Alva," Lily said with a touch of exasperation, "pardon my French, but…no shit, Sherlock. That's the way it works, kiddo. Like the man said, this too shall pass."

"Right. I know but…it just all seems like so short a time that we're here."

"For you maybe."

"What do you mean?"

"Well, c'mon. You've been here taking classes for four years, well, almost four years, with the rest of us, but you weren't *really* here in terms of *being here*. Not really. I can see why you might be feeling short changed, but that's just how your hand played out. At least you got this year in under your belt. Right?"

"I guess so. Least-wise this part of it."

"What do you mean this part?"

"Nothing."

"What nothing?"

"Just next semester…things might be different."

"In what way?"

"I…I don't know yet, not definitely. There's something I've got to decide about during the next week."

"What?"

"I really can't talk about it. Not right yet. Not until I make a decision about it."

"Oooo," Lily said, her eyes wide. "Big mystery."

Alva frowned. "I'm sorry. I really am. I only just realized that it's not going to be an easy decision to make and…and I just need to think about it more before telling anyone."

Lily shrugged. "Okay. Have it your way." With that she turned to leave.

"Lily," Alva said quickly.

"Yeah?"

"It would help me a lot if we could go back to being friends again, like we were before, you know. It really would. Can we?"

For a moment Lily just stood there looking down at her feet. "Yeah," she said finally, looking up. "I guess so. It was really about me, all this nonsense, not you. I just sort of took it out on you. It's tough, you know," she went on, shaking her head, "trying to be a certain way, trying to make someone take an interest in you." She laughed to herself. "I *can* come on kinda strong sometimes." She gave Alva a knowing look. "You might have noticed."

"Well," Alva said with a slight shrug, "I've missed your being you these last couple of weeks. You're a good you. And your being you has been a good part of this semester for me. That's why it would mean a lot to me if we could be friends again."

Lily nodded. "Yeah. Sure. Let's do that. But part of me being me is being nosy, especially when it comes to my friends. So…"

Alva nodded. "I'll tell you as soon as I can."

"Okay. But don't dawdle about it."

"I won't."

"So…you're okay now? I mean, not like you were earlier?"

Alva nodded. "Yes. This has helped, this talking with you. It's really helped."

"Good. See what a good friend I can be. Now if only some guy would notice."

"Someone will. I'm sure of it."

"Yeah right," Lily said doubtfully.

After Lily left, Alva sat there on her bed for a while thinking again about this *ending* of things. But she also started thinking again about being in the Middle East, about being a graduate student and with those thoughts she started feeling excited all over again about all of that actually happening, but it was different now. It was, she realized, a serious decision that she had to make, one to be made with a balanced and sober perspective.

Leaning forward, Alva took off her mittens and, undoing the laces of her boots, she took them off and slid them under her bed. Slowly, she got to her feet and tucked her mittens into the pockets of her coat. Walking across the room to the closet, she removed her coat, hung it up and closed the door. She leaned back against the closet door and stood there taking in her room.

"Yes," she said to herself, "this too shall pass."

Chapter 45

With the Middle East decision needing to be made in relatively short order, Alva thought of little else. More than anything, she wanted to discuss the matter with Sandra. The difficulty here, to some extent, was Lily. After being reluctant to discuss the matter with her, pretty much insisting that she needed to work on the issue alone, she felt that, should Lily catch wind of her having no problem talking the matter over with Sandra, it would not go down well.

Two days after speaking with Lily, Alva was still wrestling with the decision and feeling that she was making no progress at all. Each time she met up with Sandra she had to fight the impulse to unburden herself about everything. It got to the point where, if she were in her room, a sense of something like dread would come over her any time she heard Sandra's steps coming up the stairs.

It was the evening of the second day of her dilemma that, sitting at her desk and hearing Sandra start up the stairs, she actually got up with the intention of shutting the door and turning out the light. However, in her haste, she tripped over her own feet and fell with a resonating thud to the floor. Before she could get up Sandra was at the door.

"Alva! Are you okay?"

"Yes…yes I am. I'm fine," she said struggling to her feet and then sitting on the edge of her bed. "It's just clumsy old me."

"You sure?"

Alva nodded.

"So, what's this big secret of yours?"

For a moment, startled by the question, Alva just sat there. "What do you mean?" she asked finally.

Sandra gave her a wry smile. "Don't be disingenuous. You've been going around like a nervous mouse the last couple of days."

Alva frowned. Again, in Sandra's presence, she felt the urge to tell all, and once again, thinking of Lily, she fought it off. "It's nothing. Really, it's nothing."

Sandra nodded her head slowly. "Okay. If that's the case, why has Lily been on my case to corner you and drag it out of you?"

Stunned at hearing this, Alva just sat there. What she felt most was a huge wave of relief. With a sigh and a smile, she nodded her head slowly.

Crossing the room, Sandra pulled Alva's desk chair near to Alva's bed, turned it to face her, and sat down. With a mild look of concern, she leaned forward. "It's nothing bad, is it?"

Alva shook her head. "No. No, it's not."

"Something serious?"

Alva shrugged. "Not really. Just… Well, I found out the other day that Professor Nagy, whom I work for over at the library, is going on sabbatical next semester, to the Middle East."

"Well, that tends to happen here. Didn't your uncle go on one last year?"

Alva nodded. "Yes, yes, he did."

"Well, I'm sorry to hear about this. I know that you really like your job. But hey," Sandra brightened. "Maybe now you can see about a job at the dining hall and we can work together. That's if you still want to."

Alva frowned.

"Or," Sandra continued quickly, misinterpreting Alva's reaction, "I'm sure you'll find something else."

Alva took a deep breath and let it out slowly. "The thing is... the thing is, Professor Nagy's staff is going too."

"And...?"

"She wants me to go with them."

Slowly, Sandra sat back in the chair. For a moment she just sat there, expressionless. "To the Middle East? For the semester?"

Alva nodded. "Yes."

"Well," Sandra said shaking her head slightly as if waking up, "that's certainly one out of left field." She smiled. "And, of course, it's something pretty wonderful too. They must think the world of you, which, I mean really comes as no surprise. Wow. The Middle East. That'll be a change for you."

"I know. But...that's if I go."

"What do you mean *if* you go?"

"Well, it's up to me. I have to decide whether to go or not. I might not."

For a moment Sandra sat there looking at Alva as if she couldn't quite understand what she was saying. "But you have to if they offered it to you."

"Why? Why do I have to?"

"Well, you don't. I guess. But really, you do."

"Why?"

Sandra shrugged. "I just think..." She stopped. "Alva," she

said pulling her chair closer, "when I was in the eighth grade, my teachers and the counselor and the principal told my parents that I should apply to this private school that was about an hour from where we lived."

"And did you?"

Sandra nodded. "Yes, yes, I did. But I really didn't want to."

"Did you tell them that?"

"I did. But they told me that I should apply, even if I didn't end up going, just for the experience. So, anyway…I did."

"And did you get accepted?"

"Well, as part of the process to get in, there was an interview with a couple members of the faculty and the staff there at the school. My father drove me to it. On the way over he must have sensed that I wasn't too keen on the whole thing because he told me that I shouldn't be all shy and quiet at the interview, that I should be open and positive." Shaking her head, Sandra smiled to herself. "He said that I should just be me. You know how parents can be."

Alva nodded.

"But then he said something else. He said that I should try to do my best at the interview because, if I didn't, if I didn't make the effort to be honest with the folks who were going to interview me, that, later, later and always, I wouldn't feel good about it. Not that it would actually haunt me, but that I wouldn't forget it. And then he said something else. He said that, if I was accepted, it didn't mean that I had to go, that it was my decision entirely and that he and my mother would not try and influence me one way or the other. He said that what I decided should only depend on what *I* wanted, what *I* felt was right for me, that I shouldn't be swayed by what he or anyone else said."

"So, how did things turn out?"

"I was accepted."

"And?"

"I went. How could I not?"

"But it was your choice."

Sandra shrugged. "It was and it wasn't."

"What do mean?"

"It was an opportunity, a real special one, one of those that, if you don't take it, you end up *wondering*, wondering 'what if' and 'why didn't I' and…well, it just goes beyond being a matter of what you want."

"And now?"

Sandra shrugged. "I have no regrets. It was the best choice. And it was the right choice. It was, really, the only choice. And I'm glad that I was at least smart enough at the time to realize that. But…" Again, she shrugged.

Alva smiled. "But at the time you really *wanted* something else."

Sandra nodded. "Yes, I did."

Alva nodded. "I see. So, I'm going to the Middle East. Even though I want to spend my last semester here with…" She shrugged.

"Well," Sandra said, "if we're talking about what one wants, in all honesty, *I* want you to spend your last semester here too, but… it is that kind of special opportunity, isn't it?"

"I guess it is. I guess we'll just have to make the most of this next month together, won't we?"

"I wouldn't obsess about that. I think we've been doing well in that department right along."

Alva nodded. "True."

"And now," Sandra said getting up from her chair, "you ought to track down Lily and confess all this before her curiosity does someone, namely her, some damage."

Alva stood up. "Right. Right away. And Sandra…thanks. I feel a whole lot better about all this now."

Sandra nodded. "You bet. One thing. Is all this still hush-hush?"

"No. Not now."

"Good. It *is* exciting."

Alva nodded. "Yes. Yes, it sure is."

Chapter 46

With the decision made, Alva lost no time in informing both Professor Nagy and her uncle that she was going to accept the position offered. Both of them, she was glad to see, were genuinely pleased. Professor Nagy said that she would take care of updating her status to graduate level and all that it entailed. Her uncle said that he would see to informing Alva's parents of both the opportunity that had been offered to her and her acceptance of it, making sure to emphasize that the decision to take it was Alva's and that it was, as he would put it, a done deal. As it turned out, the day before Thanksgiving, when Alva's parents and her brother arrived at her aunt and uncle's, Professor Nagy was on hand, a strategy on her uncle's part to, as he put it later, *double team the opposition*. When Alva arrived there that evening before dinner, the six of them were seated in the living room. Although apprehensive when she came through the door, this was dispelled by both the warm reception and the congratulations she received from everyone. If her parents' smiles had an element of strain to them, they were still smiling nevertheless, and as the evening progressed Alva could see them both relax and even get caught up in the excitement of her prospects.

From the start, her brother Arvel had no qualms or reservations, and his congratulations were the heartiest of anyone's.

"I have to be honest," he said as he walked Alva back to the Cottage after dinner that evening. "I am jealous. I am big time jealous. But I couldn't be happier for you. It is a wonderful thing and you deserve it. You've earned it. I couldn't be prouder of my little sister."

Taking his arm, Alva leaned against him as they walked. "Thank you," she said with a quiet earnestness. "That means a lot to me coming from you," she said turning her face up to him and smiling, "big brother."

A little further on Arvel turned to her. Glancing up at him, she waited as it looked to her as if he were about to say something, but then she could tell that he had changed his mind.

"What?" she asked looking up at him and smiling.

Arvel shrugged. "Nothing," he said. "It's just that…well, you've changed."

"What do you mean?"

"I'm not sure. Your hair's different for one. And the 'no bangs' look suits you. But…but it's something else beyond the way you look. It's more…it's more that you seemed pleased, pleased and comfortable about…about how things are for you. I don't mean just this Middle East thing. It's like you are truly in the life that you are living. You know, for the first month or so all I heard from the folks was about how you were turning away from everything and everyone. Seriously, by the way that they talked, one would have thought that you had dropped out and joined some cult or something." Arvel frowned. "And Aunt Lillian didn't help matters much." He shook his head. "Not that she actually said something against you," he said quickly. "It was more that she pointed out certain shortcomings in campus life, pointed them out again and again."

Alva smiled. "That doesn't surprise me. She is who she is."

Arvel nodded. "True. And it's nice to see you take all of that well."

Alva shrugged. "One thing that really helped was having Uncle Ward on my side."

"I'm sure. It's good one of them was in touch with reality here."

"Anyway," Alva said as they came to the front steps of the Cottage, "here we are."

"This is where you live?" Arvel asked with some surprise.

Alva nodded. "Home sweet home."

"I thought…" Arvel paused and then, smiling to himself, he shook his head.

"What?"

"Never mind."

"What?" Alva insisted

"Nothing."

"C'mon. You were going to say something. What is it?"

"What I always heard was that lesbians lived here."

"They do. Some."

For a moment Arvel just stood there looking at her. Seeing that he looked uncomfortable and that his expression was one of concern, she smiled. "No," she said, shaking her head, "I'm not."

"Well, that's a relief."

"Why?" Alva asked. "Why is that a relief? You mean because of the whole Leviticus thing?"

"No. I'm not about to throw that in anyone's face."

"Then what?"

"Just…I don't know. Just because it would make things difficult, wouldn't it, if you were? I mean in the way that a lot of people are about homosexuality. I'd just… Well, I just don't like the idea of your having to deal with all of that all your life."

Alva shrugged. "The thing is, from what I understand, it's not a matter of choice. If you're gay, you're gay."

Arvel nodded. "I suppose…I suppose you're right. You are." He smiled. "And you don't have a problem with…with you know…" He gestured towards the Cottage. "You haven't felt…I don't know, uncomfortable?"

"No," she said. "Well, maybe at first, but that passed. The people here are great. *All of them.*"

"Well," Arvel said with a smile, "that's even more of a relief. They're good people?"

"They are."

"Good. But tell me, do the folks know?"

Alva shook her head and laughed. "Oh my no. I'm sure if they did there would have been all sorts of wailing and gnashing of teeth."

"Yeah. You got that right. But what about Uncle Ward? He must know."

"I don't know. Not for sure. But yes, he must know. I mean, he's the one that arranged my getting in here."

"Right."

"You know, that never occurred to me. It makes me wonder."

"What?"

"That it might have even been intentional on his part. That," she smiled thoughtfully and continued, "that he thought it would do me good to be exposed to it."

Arvel nodded. "I can see Uncle Ward doing that. I guess he

has been on your side."

Alva nodded.

"So," Arvel said looking up at the Cottage, "seems pretty quiet."

"Just about everyone is gone for the Thanksgiving weekend. Because it's a grad student residence mostly, it stays open. It's one of only a couple that do."

"I see. So, can you give me a tour?"

"Sure. I can show you my room at least. C'mon."

Chapter 47

"Wow," Arvel said as they climbed the last flight of stairs. "Talk about being stuck in the attic."

"I prefer to think of it as a garret?" Alva said as she opened the door to her room and they stepped inside. "And I haven't been *stuck* here."

"Sorry," Arvel said somewhat distractedly as he looked around the room. "A bad choice of words. Really. This is...this is just so good. I said I was jealous before. Now I'm doubly so. I can see this," he said continuing to look around. "I can see you here. It's you. Definitely you."

"Thank you. I like to think so."

Arvel nodded. "It is. I can see you here, sitting at your desk there, working on your poetry. And how's that going?" he asked walking over to her desk and leaning across it to look out the dormer window.

Alva frowned. "I haven't kept up with it as much as I intended to."

"Well, don't beat yourself up over it. Some things just go in cycles. Hey," he said suddenly, "that's fraternity row over there."

"It is."

Arvel turned to her. "Where're your curtains? What do you do at night when…"

"You're talking about telescopes."

"Uh huh."

Alva frowned. "I thought that might just be a rumor."

Arvel shrugged. "Maybe it is. I don't know for sure. But…but that is what they say. Anyway," he said straightening up, "I like this. I like this a lot. Too bad there's a gender issue."

"What do you mean?"

"I'd move in here while you're in the Middle East."

"What about the seminary?"

"Oh that," Arvel said continuing to look around the room, "therein hangs a tale."

"What do you mean?"

Arvel looked at her. "I'm not going back."

Stunned by this revelation, Alva just stood there.

"My, my," Arvel said smiling, "now there's a reaction for you."

"Sorry, but…why?"

"It's just not working out."

"Why? Why not?"

"I don't know exactly. I just…I think I've just moved beyond all that Old Testament stuff and that's all the place seems to be about."

"Do the folks know?"

"Oh no." Arvel laughed. "I'm not going down that road. Not right now."

"Then what?"

"Considering everything, I think it better to hand them a fait accompli."

"And what, just stay at home and not return?"

"Oh no, that would never work. Can you imagine what kind of drama would ensue and for how long? Oh, no."

"So…?"

Arvel smiled. "I've signed on with the Peace Corps."

"Oh," Alva said, somewhat startled. "Well, that's…" She shrugged. "That's commendable. Is this something that you really *want* to do?"

"It is. I think it's worth the doing."

Alva nodded. "Certainly."

"And…" Arvel went on, "since I can't come up with any long-term plans as far as what I *want* to do with my life, I think it's a viable option at this point. And it should look good on my resumé further down the road. Last of all, if I'm sure of anything, the seminary is not the place for me. I gave it a shot and it's just not *it*."

"So," Alva said, "what now?"

"Now, after the first of the year, I go in for three months of training."

"And then?"

"And then I'll be assigned somewhere for up to two years."

"Somewhere like…?"

Arvel shrugged. "I won't know that for a while. Somewhere. Africa. South America. Asia maybe. Somewhere. It doesn't really matter to me where, so I left the preference item blank."

"And what about the folks? When do you plan to tell them?"

"Well, certainly not now," Arvel said with a laugh. "They've got plenty to come to grips with at the moment thanks to you. I'll finish out the semester at the seminary and then spring the Peace Corps thing on them *after* Christmas. I figure let's just get through the holidays."

Alva nodded. "That sounds best. And…"

"Hey!" a voice called from downstairs. "Who's up there?"

Alva smiled at Arvel. "Hold on a second."

Stepping out of the room she made her way over to the top of the stairs. "It's just me, Lily," she called down.

"You got company? I hear voices."

"Just my brother."

"*Just* your brother?" Arvel whispered teasingly coming up behind her.

Alva looked back over her shoulder at him and smiled. "Brace yourself."

"Your brother!" Lily called. "Hold on. Don't anybody move."

Standing there, Alva and Arvel heard Lily's steps come quickly and loudly up the stairs. When she reached the top, they took a step back.

"Well," Lily said looking Arvel over from head to toe, "look at you. Are you engaged, married, got a girlfriend or what? "

"Lily," Alva said in a tone of great tolerance, "easy. This is Arvel. Arvel…Lily."

"Easy?" Lily said as she and Arvel shook hands. "This is one you can't steal from me." Still holding his hand, she looked at him. "So how about it? You attached, or what?"

"Not that I know of."

"What kind of answer is that?"

"Lily," Alva cut in, "don't you have a bus to catch?"

Releasing Arvel's hand, Lily frowned. "Your sister can be a real killjoy at times." She looked at her watch. "*Yes*," she said with exasperation. "Guess I better call for a taxi."

"I can take you to the bus station if you like," Arvel offered. "My car is at our Uncle's, just a few blocks from here."

"Oh," Lily said taking hold of his upper arm and moving up close on him. "My gallant." She turned quickly to Alva. "And don't you dare try and talk him out of it."

Alva smiled and shook her head. "I wouldn't dream of it."

"Damn right," Lily said turning back to Arvel.

Seeing her brother's eyes widen, Alva smiled. "Good luck, brother of mine."

Chapter 48

It was late in the evening on the Sunday after Thanksgiving. Alva was sitting on her bed leaning against the wall, her back supported with a pillow. She was looking over a list of items that Professor Nagy said she would need for the trip to the Middle East, making notes about what she needed to do, when Sandra came in.

"So, I take it things went well with your parents?" Sandra asked as she sat down on the edge of Alva's bed.

Sandra had just returned from spending the holiday with her father. The drive back to the university had taken twice as long as usual owing to the snowstorm that had started just after six that morning. Although never heavy, there was considerable wind that made travel hazardous owing to white outs. It had also turned bitterly cold, just barely getting into the double digits. Having heard the forecast on Friday, Alva's brother and parents left early on Saturday morning.

"Yes," Alva said. "They took it well. That's not to say that they were anywhere near being ecstatic, but they were really very good about it."

"Well, that's good."

"It is."

"So, what's your game plan for the next couple of weeks?"

"Just getting things together, like my passport and clothes and all, and all the work-related items that I'll need."

"When will you be leaving'?"

"Sometime in January."

"Is that enough time to get a passport?"

"It should be. Professor Nagy said that the university should be able to expedite the process. If it takes a little longer, I'll just catch up with everybody later."

"Well, I hope things go smoothly."

"Me too. I don't need to be any more nervous than I already am."

"Are you nervous?" Sandra asked, concerned.

Alva laughed. "Some. I was doing all right until the holiday. It's funny. I thought that once I was past the hurdle with my parents, I would be okay, but I guess the whole thing didn't sink in until after all that."

"Well, I'm sure you'll be fine, and there's still these last few weeks here with exams and all to provide some distraction. And…speaking of distractions, can you keep next Saturday evening open?"

"Sure. What's up?"

Well, Food Service throws a Christmas party for all the student workers on the Saturday evening before exams start. It's held up at Skyline, at the university's lodge there, and we're allowed to bring a guest or two, so I was wondering if you'd like to go."

"Skyline," Alva said. "That's the new place, right? The student apartment complex?"

Sandra nodded. "It is. The lodge is just past that, where the ski jump is. I was thinking of inviting Lily too, that's if things are good between you two."

"Yes. Yes, they are. That would be fine."

"Speaking of Lily, do you know if she's back yet?"

"I don't. The last I saw of her was last Wednesday. She was heading out with my brother. He was giving her a ride to the bus station."

Sandra laughed. "My, he's a brave young man."

"I saw him the next day, at Thanksgiving dinner, and he seemed alright."

"Well, I'm sure she'll show up shortly. Anyway, I'm beat. The drive back here was torture. So, I'm going to brush my teeth and turn in. I'll talk to you in the morning."

"Good night."

Alva returned to looking over Professor Nagy's list, but she didn't stay with it long as her thoughts kept turning to the food service Christmas party, especially when it occurred to her that it was likely that Kerry would be there. She wondered what type of entertainment there might be, specifically if there might be dancing, which led again to Kerry. She imagined dancing with him, and then, afterwards, sitting a dance or two out, sitting together and talking, getting to know each other better and...

"Stop," she quietly reprimanded herself. A wave of embarrassment came over her, but she wasn't too troubled by it, feeling that, yes, she was being silly, but then... "Why not," she thought. "Why not."

Chapter 49

Alva heard Sandra pad across the landing from the bathroom to her room and looked over at her alarm clock. Although not late, she saw that it certainly wasn't too early to turn in. Taking stock, she decided that she was not all that tired, and she started in again on Professor Nagy's list, picking up where she had left off.

It was an hour later when she finished up. By then she was more than ready to turn in. Sitting up, she swung her legs over the edge of the bed and was just about to rise when she heard the faint sound of footsteps coming up the stairs. Knowing that Sandra was already in bed and asleep, Alva sat there waiting. A moment later, Lily appeared in the doorway.

"Hi," Lily whispered after glancing back at Sandra's room.

"Hi," Alva said, "come in. You made it back."

Lily rolled her eyes. "Yeah. The bus ride from hell," she said stepping into Alva's room. "It took forever." After glancing back at Sandra's room again, Lily quietly shut Alva's door. "I want to talk to you," she said, stepping quickly to where Alva sat and sitting down on the bed next to her.

"What about?" Alva asked.

"Your brother. Arvel," she said anxiously. "Is he still around?"

Alva shook her head. "He and my folks headed back to Kentucky yesterday ahead of the storm."

"Damn," Lily said to herself. "Did you see much of him while he was here?"

Alva nodded. "Yes. We spent a good deal of time together."

Lily took a deep breath. "Did he mention me at all?"

Taken off-guard by the question, it was a moment before Alva responded. "Yes, a couple times."

This wasn't exactly a lie. When asked if he had delivered Lily to the bus terminal without any problem, he said 'yes,' only commenting that he found Lily...*different*. And that was pretty much it.

"Really?" Lily asked, brightening. "Like what?"

Alva shrugged. "Just normal stuff."

"Like what?" Lily repeated, this time with an insistent tone.

"Well...he thought you were different."

"Different?" Lily stiffened. "Different *how?*"

"Just...just that you had a lively manner," Alva lied. "That you seemed interested in things, and that you were interesting to be with."

For a moment Lily just sat there staring at Alva. Alva began to worry that Lily suspected that she wasn't being told the truth. But then Lily sat back in a relaxed manner and smiled.

"So, he does like me," she said wistfully. "I knew it. I could tell. He kept shaking his head and smiling at me. He even laughed a couple times. Oh," she said, falling back onto Alva's bed, "this is just so great. Just...so...great."

Feeling that Lily was making way more of the situation than it merited, Alva tried to back-pedal.

"You know," she said hastily, "my brother is just a really nice person, very outgoing and friendly with everyone. And generous, generous in spirit."

Lily sat back up quickly. "Oh, I'm sure. And that's the kind of guy that I've been hoping to meet. And I bet he's real spiritual."

"Well," Alva said, "he is in a seminary."

As if she had received a shock, Lily started and then just sat there, a blank expression on her face. "No, he's not," she protested. "He's in the Peace Corps."

"Not yet. But he is joining."

Lily frowned. "Okay," she said after a moment. "He didn't say anything about a seminary. Does that mean he's into the whole celibate thing?"

For a moment, all Alva could do was stare at Lily. "It's not a Roman Catholic seminary," she said.

"Well, that's a relief. I mean, Christ…uh, sorry, I mean for crying out loud, this is my senior year. As the spirit said, 'my time grows short.'"

This whole exchange made Alva think of that Sunday back at the beginning of the semester when her Aunt Lillian made the claim that there were women who only went on to college in order to find a husband, to earn their MRS. Remembering it, Alva had to laugh thinking that Lily was not exactly the type of woman that her aunt was thinking of.

"What's so funny?" Lily asked.

Alva smiled and shook her head. "Nothing. I was just thinking about a comment someone made about women here at the university."

"Well, stay on topic."

Alva nodded. "Will do."

"I meant it when I said that Arvel was the kind of guy I was hoping to meet up with. Yeah, yeah, yeah. I could tell that he was on the conservative side, you know, reserved and all that. And that certainly isn't me at all. But someone like me might be good for someone like him, you know, liven him up some and round him out. You know what I mean?"

Alva shrugged. "I guess so."

"And you know," Lily went on, "he could be good for me too. You know, rein me in a little. Not totally. But some. A little."

"And you're willing to have someone have that kind of effect on you?"

"As much as I would have some kind of effect on him."

"Well, that seems fair enough, I guess."

"Sure it is. People, couples, are supposed to complete each other, right?"

Alva smiled and nodded. One, she thought, couldn't doubt Lily's earnestness, and she couldn't argue with what she said about couples completing each other. If anything, it sounded both wise and like common sense. Alva was impressed.

"So," Lily went on, "do you think you can give me Arvel's address so that I can write to him and…" Seeing Alva's eyes go wide she stopped, and then, "What's the matter? Don't worry. I'm not going to throw myself at him. I just want to get in touch with him and…and connect."

"Sorry."

"Sorry you won't give it to me?"

"No, no," Alva said quickly. "Sorry for that knee-jerk reaction. Sure, I'll give you his address. Of course. I bet he could use a letter."

"Why?"

"Well, there's going to be stormy weather at home when he

lets my folks know that he's leaving the seminary and joining the Peace Corps."

"Oh. Yeah. Well, I'll write him a nice friendly letter. I'll thank him for that ride to the bus station." Lily leaned towards Alva. "That'll be the excuse for writing to him," she said in a conspiratorial manner.

Alva laughed. "He'll have his hands full if he tries to change you too much."

"I guess so. I guess so."

And with that they both laughed.

Later, after Lily left with a scrap of paper in hand with Arvel's address on it, Alva sat down on the bed and thought about what had just transpired. Considering what both Lily and Arvel were like, she felt like there was something unreal to it all, even surreal. But going over what Lily had said about couples changing each other some, it did make sense to her, it did sound right.

"People can change," she said quietly, nodding her head. "Yes, they can." She smiled. "Yes, we can. And now…time for bed."

Chapter 50

"Better dress real warm," Sandra said. "Like *real warm*. I was just outside, and it feels like it's down below zero already."

Sitting on her bed, Alva looked up and smiled meekly. "I've put on just about every warm piece of clothing I own."

"Just about?"

"If I put on anything else, I won't be able to move my arms and shoulders."

"The thing is, it'll probably be as hot as anything in the lodge, especially by the fire. There's a huge fireplace. Ducking a little, it's almost big enough to walk into and they'll probably have a roaring fire going in it."

"Oh boy," Alva said pulling on one boot and then another.

It was the night of the food service Christmas party. When they were both ready, they headed down the stairs with Alva leading the way. Reaching the bottom, Alva headed for the front door.

"Hold on," Sandra called after her. Alva turned. "This way." Sandra turned and started down the hall towards the rear of the house. Alva followed. Reaching the rear door, Sandra paused to let Alva catch up. "Ready?"

Putting on her knit hat and pulling it down until it reached her eyebrows Alva nodded. "I am now."

"Here goes." Sandra pushed the door open letting in a blast of cold air. "You go first," she said extending one arm to hold the door open, "and be careful on the steps. They haven't been shoveled."

Stepping past Sandra, Alva started slowly down the stairs keeping a death grip on the banister and carefully watching where she put her feet with each step down. Even while concentrating hard on each step she took, she was still more than aware of how bitterly cold it was. Reaching the last step, she looked up and saw that Sandra's car was there parked in front of the dining hall's loading dock. Its parking lights were on and the engine was running. Stepping to one side, she let Sandra go by.

"Get in. Get in," Sandra said taking Alva's arm and urging her towards the car.

Being backed in, the passenger side door was right there for Alva. Doing as she was told, Alva opened the door and climbed in. To both her surprise and delight, the interior was toasty warm.

"How's this?" Sandra asked climbing in on the driver's side. "Warm enough?"

"Oh yes. You have got to be the most considerate person on the face of the planet."

Sandra smiled. "You ready?"

"I am."

The drive to the university's lodge was uneventful. There had been snow that morning, but the roads were clear now. Even so, there was next to nothing in the way of traffic. Obviously, the brutal cold was deterrent enough for most folks in terms of venturing out that evening.

"Do you think there will be many people at the party?" Alva asked.

"I don't know. It is mighty cold, but the party is always a good one, well attended. Free food, beer and wine can be an effective inducement, even when it's as cold as this."

As it turned out the parking lot at the lodge was practically full. In one corner there was a mountain of snow of some height where the plowed snow had been piled. Seeing a space next to it, Sandra pulled in and parked. Headlights came up quickly behind them; she glanced up at the rearview mirror.

"We've got company."

The car pulled up so closely behind them that the headlights vanished behind the rear of Sandra's car.

"They're kind of close," Alva said after turning her head to look out the rear window. "Are you going to be able to get out later?"

When Sandra didn't answer right away, Alva turned to look at her and found Sandra just sitting there smiling.

"Sandra?"

"What?" Sandra asked coming out of her reverie. "Oh. No. I mean, yes. We're fine. Recognize the car?"

Alva looked back over her shoulder. "No."

"It's Stu, Steve's car. Remember?"

"Oh yes. But he doesn't work for food service."

"Kerry must have invited him, and," Sandra said, looking into the rearview mirror, "by the looks of it, part of their west side gang has tagged along."

Both cars emptied at the same time. Of the five that emerged from Stu, Alva was pleased to see that Kerry was one of them. Besides him she recognized Steve and Hawk, but the other two she did not know.

"King of the mountain!" one of the two *unknowns* shouted and, racing to the mound of piled snow, he started up. He was on the short side with shoulder length blonde hair. Alva was surprised to see that, for warmth, all he had on was a short coat, no gloves, no hat, and his coat wasn't even closed.

"King of the mountain!" three of the remaining four shouted as they started up in pursuit of the first, and, Alva noted, none of them were any better clothed for the brutally cold weather.

Turning her attention to the one straggler, Alva was pleased to see that it was Kerry and also pleased to see that he was wearing his long, wool coat, scarf and mittens, lacking only a warm hat.

Sandra and Alva walked over to where Kerry stood. Standing there, he didn't notice their approach until they came up to him. Turning, Kerry looked at them with a questioning look, as if he didn't know who they were.

"Hi Kerry," Sandra said.

For a moment Kerry just stared at the two of them. Then, after blinking once, he smiled, "Oh. It's you two. Evening ladies."

It was then that Alva noticed that he was shivering some, his shoulders hunched up. She also saw that he was swaying slightly. Sandra, obviously noticing this too, walked up to him and took his arm.

"Shall we head in?" she asked.

"Yeah. Yeah," he said in a distracted manner. "That's a good idea, but first," he turned to look at his cohorts climbing the pile of snow, "but first this…this is going to be good. You got to watch this. Joey's almost to the top, and Sammy's right behind him."

Sandra and Alva turned to watch just as Joey reached the

summit.

"I'm king of the mountain!" he crowed.

He was, but his reign was short lived as, just moments later, Sammy was upon him. They struggled, ending up wrestling, and when Hawk and Steve reached them it turned into a free-for-all.

"Hey guys!" Kerry called to them after a few minutes. "I'm freezing my ass off out here! Let's go in!"

"Wuss!" Steve called back to him as the four of them continued to wrestle.

"Suit yourselves, but me and these lovely lasses are heading in for the comestibles and libations. Maybe we'll save some for you all."

At that the melee ground to a halt and the four participants struggled to their feet.

"Now comes the good part," Kerry said, as if he were just talking to himself.

Sandra and Alva watched as Joey stepped away from the others and walked to the edge of the summit. He stood there for a moment, taking a deep breath, and then, to Alva's total amazement he took three quick steps and flung himself into a forward flip, landing on his back a few feet down the side of the pile. Getting up, which, after that, seemed like a miracle to Alva, he proceeded to do it again. One by one, the remaining three stepped up to the edge of the pile and proceeded to follow suit. The four of them continued to do so until each one of them reached the base of the pile. Standing up, they dusted the snow off themselves and off each other's backs.

It was then that, putting an arm around Sandra and one around Alva, Kerry smiled. "Come one and all. Let us go forth to the festivities."

"To the festivities!" the other four chimed in.

With that the seven of them started across the parking lot towards the lodge, Kerry still with his arms around Sandra and Alva, Steve and Hawk next to Sandra, and Joey and Sammy on Alva's right. Alva turned to Joey who was closest.

"I'm Alva."

"Well good for you," he said with a big grin and in a tone of exaggerated congratulations.

Alva, somewhat taken aback, saw Sammy laugh, turn and punch Joey on the upper arm.

"Hey!" Steve called over to them. "Enough of that. These aren't the wenches that you usually accost. These are ladies. Treat them accordingly."

"And," Kerry cut in, "this is *the Alva* from Ryan's, the heroine of Tipperary Hill."

Joey turned to look at Alva. "That was you?" he asked, this time genuinely impressed. "Good to meet you. Like really good."

"Same here," Sammy chimed in.

Alva smiled. "Good to meet you. Good to meet you both."

"Alright," Steve said. "Enough with the pleasantries. Let's pick up the pace. In case you haven't noticed, it's colder than a witch's…something or other."

It was indeed cold Alva thought, but at that moment she mostly felt good, good about herself, and good about feeling like she was a part of things, a part of this group, a group going to a party.

Entering the lodge there was a young woman seated at a table by the door. She glanced up when they came in. Recognizing both Sandra and Kerry, she nodded once and waved the seven of them through.

As Sandra had predicted, it was warm in the lodge, and there was a fire blazing away in the fireplace. There was also a good turnout, and they had to snake their way through the crowd to the other side of the room where the tables and chairs had been pushed aside, where they could leave their coats and things.

"Now where did he go to?" Steve asked.

"Who?" Hawk asked.

"Kerry."

Looking around, Alva saw that Kerry wasn't with them.

"There he is over there," Joey said, pointing across to where the refreshment area was located. "And look, he's got a beer already." Pulling off his coat he threw it on to one of the tables and started off in Kerry's direction. Steve, Hawk, and Sammy did likewise.

Sandra turned to Alva. "Shall we?"

"Kerry is headed back this way. Maybe we should wait for him."

"Sure."

When Kerry reached them, he held up his cup of beer. "Here's to all of us. God bless us everyone."

Alva noticed that his speech was slurred some, and that his sway of earlier was more pronounced. Sandra must have seen this also as she stepped towards him quickly.

"Okay Tiny Tim," she said reaching for his cup of beer. "Let me hold that for you while you take your coat and things off."

"Oh, that's a splendid idea," he said, relinquishing the cup and leaning towards her, "my ever wonderful Sandra." He turned to Alva. "She is wonderful, isn't she? The most wonderful. And patient. And tolerant." He leaned close to Alva. "I even asked her to marry me once. Did you know that? I did. I asked her to marry me." He turned back to Sandra. "Ain't that right, right?"

Sandra nodded. "Was it just the once?"

"Just the once," Sandra said, glancing at Alva and rolling her eyes. "Give him a hand with his coat."

After first taking his scarf and setting it down, Alva helped Kerry out of his coat, folded it over once and placed it with his scarf on one of the tables.

Kerry turned to her. "Thank you, Alva. You're wonderful too you know. You are. And you are a mighty fine poet. No, poetess. A mighty fine poetess." He turned to Sandra. "Did you know that?"

"I knew she wrote poems."

"She does. That she does. Mighty fine poems. That's what makes her a mighty fine poetess." Kerry sighed. "God, sometimes I am just so lucid. It's scary."

"Maybe you should sit down for a moment," Sandra suggested.

"Now there's an idea. Yes." He looked around. "And I think I'll just sit on this table right here. That way I won't have that far to get up when I want to stand." Slowly he lowered himself down and sat on the edge of the table. "There. And hey!" He pointed to his cup that Sandra still held. "I seem to remember having one of those." He looked around absently. "Somewhere, somewhere, somewhere."

"Here," Sandra said, holding out the cup to him.

"Why thank you," he said. "That's most considerate. But what about you?" He turned to Alva. "And what about you?"

Sandra turned to Alva. "You stay with him. I'll go get us something. What would you like?"

"A Coke would be fine, if they have it."

"Ah, a Coke," Kerry echoed. "Very good. Very good. Accept no substitutes. And screw Pepsi."

"I'll be back," Sandra said.

Alva sat next to Kerry. Turning her head, she watched as he sat there staring blankly ahead as if his thoughts were carrying him someplace other than where he was. Although she wanted to talk to him, if only to make small talk, she was not comfortable about *intruding*. It wasn't until Kerry closed his eyes that she felt that she should say something, anything.

"Would you like to dance?"

For a moment Kerry continued to sit there with his eyes closed. Then, without opening his eyes, he smiled. "That's not quite the style of humor that I would have expected from you, Alva. You are kidding, right? Dance? Me?"

"Yes," Alva lied, "I was just kidding."

Opening his eyes, Kerry turned to her. "No," he said, "you did mean it, didn't you?"

Alva nodded, embarrassed.

"Well, that's nice. Ain't you sweet? Actually, I have been known to *cut-a-rug* from time to time. But right now," he shook his head and laughed, "it could be disastrous, lethal even. I'll take a rain check on the offer though." Closing his eyes again, he turned his head away. "Yes, Alva, you are sweet. Sweet enough to marry." And then, as if the notion took him by surprise, he opened his eyes and quickly looked at her. "Yes. You are sweet enough to marry. How about it? Will you marry me?"

For a moment Alva just sat there. "Yes," she said seriously. "I will."

Kerry blinked. And then he blinked again.

"This time you *are* kidding," Kerry said, "right?"

"Yes," Alva said quietly, embarrassed. "I was just kidding." Turning away quickly she looked around the room.

"For a second there you had me going," Kerry said shaking his head as if trying to clear it.

"You really should be careful about asking someone that," Alva said, still looking around the room. Then she turned to him. "You should only ask it if you mean it."

Kerry looked at her, nodding his head slowly. "You know, if anyone else had taken me to task for that, I'd suggest that they could go…that they lighten up some. But…"

"But what?"

"But you're right. I shouldn't say things just to get a reaction. I should know better."

"Know better about what?" Sandra asked smiling as she returned, a cup in each hand.

"Alva here asked me to dance and…and I would have. Really, but…well…"

Sandra frowned. Then, shaking her head, she turned to Alva. "Here's your Coke."

"Thanks."

For an uncomfortable moment, no one said anything. Finally, setting her Coke down on the table beside her, Alva got up.

"Excuse me," she said with a smile. "I need to use the ladies' room." She looked around. "Can you tell me where it is?"

Sandra turned to point in the direction from which she had just come. "It's right behind the refreshment area."

"Thank you," Alva said, starting off. "I'll be right back."

Chapter 51

Coming out of the restroom, Alva happened to notice a set of sliding glass doors off to her left. Beyond them there were a dozen or so of people standing around outside smoking. She was surprised to see that most of them were out there without coats or hats.

Despite knowing how cold it had to be out there especially so underdressed, Alva suddenly felt the need for some fresh air. Detouring to the sliders, she opened one, stepped outside and then closed the slider behind her. Wanting to keep away from all of the smoke, she walked a short way and stood off to one side. Standing there watching the others, it struck her odd that some of them were sharing their cigarettes with others, a cigarette passing from one person to the next.

Out there without a coat on, the cold soon got to her. First, she folded her arms to keep warm. When that proved to be insufficient, she started doing small hops, alternating between hopping in place and bouncing back and forth from one foot to the other. Even with all that, she found herself shivering and she was just about to turn and head back in when...

"I thought that was you."

Turning she found Steve standing there with what she took to be a cigarette in one hand.

"Oh. Hi."

"Speaking of high," he held his *cigarette* towards her. "Have a hit."

"A what?"

"A toke. A hit. A… Oh," he said, nodding his head slowly. "You don't…I take it you don't partake," he said letting his hand fall to his side.

"Partake in what?"

"Never mind. What are you doing out here in the cold?"

"Just getting some fresh air."

Steve looked around slowly to where the others were standing. "Well, I guess there might be some in this corner, but," he turned back to Alva, "aren't you freezing?"

"I guess I am. If you'll excuse me…"

"Hey, Steve."

They turned to find the remainder of Kerry's entourage, except for Hawk, approaching.

"Hey," Joey said, "don't bogart that joint man."

Steve passed it to him. "What's up guys?"

"We're ready to go," Sammy said, taking the joint from Joey. "Where's Kerry?"

Joey smiled. "He's kind of incapacitated at the moment. Sandra ain't letting him go anywhere."

"Like I've told him before," said Sammy, "you can do that alcohol, but don't mix it up with seconal. Alcohol yes, reds yes, alcohol and reds no." With that he handed the joint back to Steve.

"Where's Hawk?"

"He's with Sandra and Kerry. He thought he'd stick around

for a while and keep an eye on him before heading over to a friend's place at those apartments across the way."

"What about you two?"

"We're bored. Let's hit The Mighty O and play some air hockey."

"And what about Kerry?"

"Sandra said that she'd get him home," Joey said. "In fact, she kind of insisted." He smiled. "She seems a little pissed."

"A little!" Sammy echoed. "She got real testy, like it's our fault for the shape that Kerry is in. Yeah right, like he hasn't done this to himself before."

Steve turned to Alva. "Do you think we should hang around? He's probably better off with just you and Sandra and Hawk."

Alva almost laughed at the 'probably.' "I think Sandra knows best."

Steve nodded. "Yeah, she always does." Tossing what was left of his joint into the snow, he turned to his cronies. "Okay gentlemen. Suit up and let's go."

With that, the three of them and Alva stepped inside.

Parting from them, Alva went back to where she had left Sandra and Kerry. When she got there, she found Sandra sitting alone on the edge of one of the tables.

"Where's Kerry?"

"In the men's room."

"Is he okay?"

Sandra frowned and shrugged. "Hawk's with him."

Alva sat down next to Sandra. "I'm sorry. I didn't mean to desert you."

"What? Oh." She shook her head. "No problem. It's not like there was anything you could do, or that *any of us* can do."

Alva noticed the note of disgust and frustration in her tone. "Are you okay?"

"Yeah. I'm fine."

"You look upset."

Sandra nodded. "I am."

"What are reds?"

Sandra turned quickly to her. "Who said anything about reds? Joey?"

"No, the other one. Sammy?"

Sandra nodded. "So that's what it is." She shook her head. "Once again. Sleeping pills and alcohol."

Suddenly, Sandra jumped up from where she sat on the table and started to go through the pile of coats that lay on the table. Grabbing Kerry's long wool coat, she searched through its pockets, producing a quart bottle that was nearly empty. Laying the coat back down, she stood there looking down at the bottle. "Richards," she said to herself.

"What is it?" Alva asked.

"Wine. A cheap wine. Cheap, but effective."

Shaking her head, Sandra walked over to a nearby trashcan and dropped the bottle into it. Returning to where Alva stood, she picked up Kerry's coat and started going through its pockets again. This time she came up with a small, aluminum film canister. Unscrewing the cap, she tipped the contents into the palm of her hand. Alva saw four red capsules there.

"Take this," Sandra said, screwing the cap back on to the canister and handing it to Alva, "and toss it in the trash while I flush these away."

"Should I wait here?"

Sandra smiled. "Yes. God, I'm glad you're here."

With that she turned and headed off in the direction of the restrooms.

A minute or so later, Hawk came up to Alva, a cup of beer in hand.

"Where's Kerry?" he asked.

"Sandra said that he was with you."

Hawk looked around. "He said he was feeling good enough to head back here, so I went to get this." He held up the cup. "Maybe he's still in the men's room."

"He's not," Sandra, suddenly appearing, said with some heat. "I checked."

"Well, his coat and things are still here," Alva said. "He must be around somewhere."

"He isn't."

The three of them turned to find the young woman who had been minding the door standing there. "You're talking about Kerry, right?"

"Yes," Sandra said with some impatience. "Where is he?"

"I was told that he was outside on top of that mountain of snow in the corner of the parking lot."

Sandra turned quickly to Alva. "You suit up and grab his things and meet us out there. C'mon Hawk."

Chapter 52

When Alva caught up with them, Hawk and Kerry were wrestling on top of the pile of snow. Sandra was up there too, trying to pull Kerry away and pin his arms.

"Un-hand me you *minions* of the dark one!" Kerry roared. "I am a saint! I am *the* saint. I am the *saint* of the mountain!"

A small crowd was gathered at the base of the pile of snow. Alva was shocked to see that they were all looking up and smiling, as if they had never seen anything so amusing before.

"Fight on your holiness!" one of them shouted, eliciting a wave of laughter from the observers.

"Stop it!" Sandra shouted at them. "What's wrong with you! He could die of exposure out here!"

"Lighten up, lady," the one who had urged Kerry to fight on said. "He looks like he has plenty enough antifreeze in *his* system."

Again, there was laughter.

"Animals," Alva said with undisguised disgust, and not entirely under her breath. Turning, she started to climb the pile of snow.

With the steepness of the climb, the unsure footing and being burdened with Kerry's things, Alva found the going difficult and slow, and it was a couple minutes before she reached the summit. By the time she got there, Hawk was sitting on Kerry and had his arms pinned. Sandra, kneeling at Kerry's head, was pressing down on his shoulders. To Alva's surprise, though definitely showing wear from the struggle, both of them were smiling, and broadly at that.

"Leave me be," Kerry gasped, as he struggled to free himself. "Leave me and my sainthood here on the mountain top. Don't drag me down into that vale of iniquity, or all is lost."

"God," Hawk said, "he can't be in too bad of shape if he can put up this kind of a struggle."

"I guess not," Sandra said with a laugh. But then, looking down at Kerry, her expression turned serious. "Kerry," she said, "listen to me. This cold is brutal. We've got to get you dressed." She gave his shoulders a shake. "Do you hear me?"

"Yes. Yes. I hear you. But it's hard to take you seriously when you're upside-down like you are."

"Kerry, stop! I'm serious. You could die out here. And we could too."

Kerry looked at her and then at Hawk. "Your things. You came out without your things... Just to..." He nodded his head. "I see. And I'm sorry. I'll behave. I promise." Hawk and Sandra exchanged looks of skepticism. "You have the word of a saint," he said.

With some difficulty they got Kerry to his feet and his coat and things on. With even greater difficulty the three of them managed without mishap to get him down from the pile of snow and into the back seat of Sandra's car.

"You get in there with him," Sandra said to Alva, "while we go get our things. We'll be right back."

Nodding once, Alva climbed in closing the door behind her. For a moment or two neither of them said anything. Then Kerry turned to Alva.

"I guess they couldn't turn the engine on and leave it running, asphyxiation and all that. But God, it's cold."

Inching over to him, Alva put an arm around Kerry's shoulders and drew him closer to her. "Is this better?"

Kerry nodded. "Well…yes. It is. It's nice. It's real nice."

"May I ask you something?"

Kerry groaned. "You're not going to ask me to dance again, are you?"

Alva laughed. "No," she said. "Why do you do this?"

"Why do I do what?"

"Alcohol and pills."

"So that I don't have to dance."

"That's not funny."

Kerry let out a long sigh. "No," he said, "I guess it's not. Sorry." He sighed again. "But it might be the truth in a way…like it's a fending off…a fending off of something…whatever. Like just putting everything on hold, really on hold." He shook his head.

"Is that supposed to sound deep, profound?" Alva asked.

"Nah. It's just a tactic, a diversion, a distraction." He turned to Alva. "Simply put, I do it out of sheer stupidity." Kerry looked forward again and closed his eyes. "That's it really. I'm stupid, and I've grown real comfortable with my stupidity. Real comfortable."

"I'm sorry to hear that," Alva said quietly.

Eyes still closed, Kerry nodded. "That does not surprise me. You, you and Sandra." He paused. "I don't know why… No, check that. I do know why. The two of you, you're…well, special. And you shouldn't be putting up with this nonsense of mine. And…

and yet...you do."

Alva felt Kerry shudder violently.

"Alva," he said hoarsely, "I need to lie down."

Drawing her arm back quickly, Alva straightened up and slid over next to the far door. "Go ahead."

Leaning away from Alva and lying down, Kerry positioned himself so that the top of his head touched the other door. After that he drew up his knees so that he wouldn't touch Alva with his boots.

"You could lie this way and put your head on my lap."

"Thanks," Kerry said with a hoarse chuckle, "but odds are you'd end up with a lap full of puke."

Alva was going to repeat her offer when the driver's side door opened up and Sandra poked her head in. "How's he doing?"

"*He* couldn't be better," Kerry said, remaining motionless where he lay, "or any worse."

"He just started feeling nauseous."

Sandra nodded. "That's not surprising."

"Where's Hawk?"

"He took off. He's staying with friends tonight at one of the apartments across the way."

"Should I come up front?"

"I'd prefer it if you would stay back there with him. Just in case...well, something."

"Sure. No problem."

Climbing in and shutting her door, Sandra started the engine and put the car in reverse.

"Do turn the heat on, darling Sandra," Kerry called.

"Will do, your majesty, will do."

Chapter 53

By the time they reached the main road, the heat was going full blast. It was at that point that Kerry, with a groan, reached over his head with one hand and struggled to lower the window. "Fresh air," he said. "I need some fresh air."

"Do you want me to pull over?" Sandra asked, glancing at the rearview mirror.

"No. No. Keep going, please," he said as he pulled himself up to the now open window. "The faster I get home, the better."

As little traffic as there was on the drive over earlier, the roads now, in comparison, were completely dead. From the back seat, Alva felt like she was being chauffeured home after a long, evening soiree. Although the streets bore less than little of anything in the way of resemblance to those of New York City, Alva gave her imagination free reign and saw the scene being one of tall, tall buildings, yellow cabs, traffic lights at the end of each block, and *limos like hers* with *bon vivants* like herself and her companions here inside.

Her reverie was broken suddenly and completely when...

"Oh, sweet Jesus please," Kerry moaned.

To her horror Alva saw him open the door and then, holding

on to the door's inner handle with one hand and the doorjamb with the other, lean out.

"Sandra! Pull over!" she yelled, diving towards Kerry and grabbing his legs.

"No!" Kerry roared. "Keep driving! Keep driving!"

He said it with such force that it felt like there was no way he was going to stand being disobeyed.

With that, with his head just a foot or so above the rapidly passing pavement, he vomited, and he continued to do so for a good couple blocks as they rode along, with Alva frantically hanging on to him.

Finally, having finished, Kerry inched his way back in, closing the door once he was totally inside.

"Thank you, ladies," he said turning over onto one side. "Well done."

Sitting there, still holding on to Kerry's legs, Alva felt her heart pumping away from the excitement and the exertion of keeping him from falling out of the car. A few moments later, to her astonishment, she heard him snore. Letting go of his legs, Alva sat back and tried to relax.

When she felt calm enough, she leaned forward and touched Sandra on the shoulder. "How far away does he live?"

"He's staying with us tonight. Someone has to keep an eye on him."

"Can we do that?"

Sandra shrugged. "We haven't much choice."

"Do you think he can make it from the parking garage to the Cottage."

"I'll just park where I did earlier this evening, by the loading dock. It's the weekend. There won't be any deliveries or trash pick-up. The trick will be getting him up all the stairs, but the two of us can give it a go. We'll manage."

Chapter 54

It proved to be no easy task to get Kerry up the stairs, but, with considerable effort, Sandra and Alva did finally manage it. Once in Sandra's room, they got him out of his coat and boots and onto Sandra's bed.

"He can sleep in his clothes," Sandra said as she folded Kerry's coat and set it on her easy chair. "Stay with him a second while I go brush my teeth." With that she turned and left the room.

A few moments later she returned with a tall glass of water in one hand and a small plastic basin in the other. Setting the glass on her desk she turned to Alva and held up the basin.

"Just in case," she said setting the basin on the floor next to the head of the bed.

Alva nodded.

"That should do it," Sandra said.

Alva and Sandra stood there looking down at the sleeping Kerry. As they did, he started to snore.

Sandra smiled. "Well, that's a good sign. He'll probably sleep through to morning now."

"What about you? Where will you sleep?"

"In here," Sandra said continuing to gaze down on Kerry.

"Really?"

"Mmm," Sandra said without looking up. "I've got a yoga mat and an extra pillow."

"Oh…and…and you're okay with that?"

"I'll be fine." She looked up at Alva. "Like I said, he'll more than likely just sleep through until morning, but he still shouldn't be left alone." She looked down again at the sleeping Kerry. "Just in case."

Alva nodded. "Okay. Sure. I guess that makes sense."

For a moment the two of them just stood there.

"Well," Alva said finally, "then I guess I'll go to bed. I'm kind of tired."

"Kind of," Sandra repeated, looking up at Alva with a smile. "It *has* been quite the evening, hasn't it?" She looked down at Kerry. "And then some."

Alva looked at her. "Come get me if you need me."

"Thanks Alva. You are a comfort. You really are."

Chapter 55

A little later, having climbed into bed, Alva found herself unable to stop thinking about Kerry and Sandra spending the night together in the same room. Finding herself unable to let it go, it occurred to her that maybe her having a problem with the situation had less to do with the idea of any two unmarried people doing something like that than it was really about this being Kerry and Sandra, Kerry and Sandra *together*, that it indicated the significance of the connection between them, that there was something beyond that of Kerry and Sandra merely being friends.

Alva started. It suddenly occurred to her that, with this seeming so definitely to be the case, that the issue here really had to do with her, that, what really made it impossible for her to let go, was that she was jealous, jealous of Sandra being *that connected* with Kerry and with her, Alva, *not* being that connected with him.

But then, considering what Sandra had become for her over the course of the semester, Alva suddenly felt ashamed by her pettiness and ingratitude.

"This, this will not do," she said quietly but angrily to herself, "it just will not do."

Chapter 56

The following morning, Alva woke to find her room cold and silent. Both aspects seemed so intense that it felt to her as if there were a presence in the room, a presence with a degree of menace to it. As if trying to escape from it, she burrowed down beneath her quilt and lay there as quietly and as still as she could. Even so, the presence persisted, and it didn't let up until, to her immense relief, she heard the low rumble of the furnace in the basement kick in.

Feeling the *burden* lift, Alva poked her head out from beneath the quilt, took a deep breath and let it go with an audible sigh. She looked around the room. There was light enough, but it was an early winter morning kind of light, one that allowed for nothing in the way of color, the kind of light that reveals a world with little, if anything, in the way of inducement to rise up and go forth, and so, making herself comfortable, she continued to lie there.

As she did so, the events of the previous evening came back to her one by one like moments that, though connected, were also complete in their own way – she and Sandra navigating the back, unshoveled stairs to where Sandra's car was parked and idling, the warmth of the interior of the car, the empty streets on the way to the lodge, Kerry's friends and their king of the mountain battle followed by their suicide acrobatics down the pile of snow, the fire and vigorous warmth inside the lodge, and others. Each one, she thought, was like an individual bead on a necklace or a rosary.

She thought of how the evening had ended with Kerry and Sandra sleeping in the same room together. She thought of how she, in her own bed, had found herself jealous of Sandra, and how that had led to the shame of thinking so poorly of Sandra that came upon her. But then she remembered how, recalling her determination to rid herself of her ingratitude and pettiness, she had let the jealousy and the shame pass.

Still, she thought of Sandra and Kerry being across the way in the same room. She thought of him lying there, still dressed, on Sandra's bed. She thought of Sandra lying there, also fully dressed, on the floor, lying there on her yoga mat, next to the bed. She pictured how they would look asleep like that, and she smiled to herself. It was innocent, she thought, all so innocent. The arrangement was just one of convenience. Kerry needed someone to watch over him, and he and Sandra needed to sleep. That was, Alva told herself, all there was to it, nothing more. And since that was so, it meant that there was no *special* connection between Sandra and Kerry. Taking a deep breath, Alva sighed with contentment.

And then Alva remembered Kerry asking her to marry him.

For a moment she just lay there, visualizing how that went, how he had told her that she was sweet, sweet enough to marry. And then he did it, he actually asked her to marry him. He wasn't being serious, of course. She knew that then, and she knew it now. Just as she knew that she wasn't being serious when she said 'yes.' She knew that then too and…

Alva stopped. Lying there, the thought occurred to her that maybe, in some way, she hadn't been kidding, that, maybe, she might have actually meant it when she said 'yes.' And then she wondered if, in the same light, maybe there might have been something to his asking her to marry him. Lying there, considering this, she shook her head, deciding that this line of thinking was just fantasy, a romanticizing on her part, and she decided to drop it at once. Certainly, she thought, they were two completely different people, probably too completely different for any type of relationship to work, to say nothing of marriage.

And then she thought of Lily.

"But someone like me might be good for someone like him," Alva said quietly to herself, paraphrasing Lily. She recalled how Lily admitted that she and Arvel were two very different kinds of people, about her being *lively* by nature, and he more reserved. Alva laughed to herself remembering how Lily thought she could *liven* Arvel up and *round him out*. But then Alva thought 'why not.' Certainly she had to admit that *she* had changed this semester, that, owing mostly to her friendship with Sandra and her *connections* with others, she *had* changed.

And then she thought of Kerry.

Again, she started going over the events of the prior evening, this time those centering on Kerry. There was his more than obvious state of inebriation and the near empty bottle of cheap wine they found in his coat pocket. There was that coupled with finding, also in one of his coat pockets, the film canister containing the red capsules which, she was sure, were illegal, and that he had partaken of them that evening. There was his venturing out into the bitter cold without any outerwear and, worse, not telling anyone that he had left. And after all of that, there was his hanging out of the open door of a moving car and vomiting.

What troubled Alva most was the knowledge that this was not an isolated occurrence. Others had commented on his dissolute ways. There was the black gentleman, Robert, that first morning on the loading dock. There was Lily who echoed Robert's sentiments. There was also, ironically, the drunk at the bar on Tipperary Hill that she had doused with the glass of water. Even the night before, at the party, his fellow reprobates had mentioned Kerry's propensity for drugs and alcohol.

The most damning evidence as far as Alva was concerned was Sandra's comment the evening before.

"Again. Sleeping pills and alcohol," Alva said quietly to herself, quoting Sandra, stressing the word 'again.'

More than that was the way Sandra had said it with disgust, with sadness and with anger. Alva couldn't remember Sandra ever speaking that harshly of anyone or anything before.

Had she tried, Alva wondered, to get him away from that behavior? Was Kerry, Alva wondered, too set in this destructive lifestyle of his to be helped? She didn't want to believe that. Hadn't he remembered her and her poetry from sophomore year? And then there was Halloween and how much she had enjoyed being with him, even with the water flinging incident at the bar. And wasn't he genuinely contrite afterwards about making her come with him into the bar and, worse, having left her there? Even the night before, when he was in what she only could imagine was the worst shape he could possibly be in, he had, when she scolded him about proposing marriage without meaning it, instead of suggesting that she *lighten up*, he had agreed with her and apologized, admitting that he did it mostly to get a rise out of people, and that it was wrong of him to do so.

"That counts," she said to herself quietly, thinking that his *problem* might not be an inherent one on his part, that maybe it was something more along the lines of a bad habit. And habits, she told herself could be broken. Sometimes a person with a problem just needs someone to provide a good influence. It was at that moment that the notion occurred to Alva that, considering how he had acquiesced to her taking him to task, she might be that good influence.

"Yes," she said. "Yes! Maybe I can. Certainly, I could try. Maybe poetry could provide means to his reclamation. Maybe, *maybe* we could be poets, poets together."

Lying there, thinking about Kerry being, at that moment, just a dozen or so feet away, she felt compelled to leap out of bed and go to him. Certainly, after the state he was in the previous night, he would be in tough shape this morning, but…

'I can tend to him. I can give him the support he needs, the right support and help him,' she thought. 'I can start helping him right now.'

Throwing off the bedclothes, Alva sat up and slid into her slippers. Padding quietly to her closet, she retrieved her robe and put it on. From there she went to her bedroom door, opened it, and stood there listening. Except for the rumble of the furnace below, all was quiet. Across the way she saw that Sandra's door was open. Slowly and quietly she made her way over to it, stopping just outside and leaning around the jamb to look in.

Alva inhaled sharply.

They were both there, Sandra and Kerry. Sandra's yoga mat

was there on the floor next to the bed. On it was a blanket and a pillow, and that was all. Kerry was there in the bed with his eyes closed. He was lying on his back. Sandra was there too, nestled beside him, her head on his shoulder. One arm was across his chest. Kerry's arm was around her shoulder. They were both asleep. Kerry's long, wool coat covered the two of them.

Alva was just about to back away when Kerry's eyes suddenly opened. For a moment he looked slowly around the room as if he were trying to orient himself. Then, seeing Alva, he smiled. Lifting his free hand, he gave her a weak wave. With a forced smile Alva waved back.

Glancing down at Sandra, Kerry looked at her with a puzzled expression. Then, sizing up the situation, he nodded his head slowly. Looking back at Alva, he raised his free hand again and put a finger to his lips.

Alva nodded, slowly mouthing the words, "I'll close the door."

"Thank you," Kerry mouthed back, and then he closed his eyes.

Back in her room, Alva, without consciously deciding to do so, let her robe drop to the floor and crawled back into bed pulling the bedclothes up to her chin.

A series of emotions ran through her as she lay there. They ranged from the totally unwarranted, like betrayal, which she quickly dismissed, to jealousy, to frustration, to a quiet sadness. Sorting all of these out, she was left finally with disappointment. At first it was with Sandra and Kerry, that they should resort to sleeping together like they were only because of the events of the previous evening, that Sandra had taken advantage of the situation, and that Kerry had let himself get taken. To see them both end up so vulnerable like that, just seemed so tawdry and beneath them both and so cruel to herself.

Yes, it was disappointment that she felt, and a palpable one at that. But right away she knew and admitted to herself that it had more to do with her *aspirations* in regard to Kerry being quashed, aspirations that were really no more than *precious* fancies on her part, than they were anything else.

"Poets," she said with disdain and self-loathing. "Poets *together*. How *precious*. How stupid." She shook her head. "Guess I still have some way to go yet. Maybe…" she said, her tone touched with irony, "the Middle East will be far enough."

Chapter 57

"Guess what I got! Guess what I got!" Lily crowed as, without bothering to knock, she barreled into Alva's room waving a small envelope over her head.

It was the second Wednesday following Thanksgiving. Final exams were underway.

Alva, who was sitting at her desk writing a letter to her brother, turned around and smiled. "It looks a lot like a letter."

Lily frowned, "Very funny. But..." she beamed, "Yes! It is indeed a letter, but from whom? Try and guess."

"My brother, Arvel?"

Lily's smile faded in an instant and she stood there just staring at Alva for a good long moment.

Picking up a piece of stationery that was lying on her desk next to the letter that she was writing, Alva waved it over her head. "Guess who?"

Lily smiled. "Well, aren't we the lucky two."

"What did he have to say in yours?"

"Oh no," Lily teasingly protested. "You go first."

"Okay, but he didn't write much, just to say that he received an *interesting* letter from you, and to thank me for giving you his address."

"That's it?" Lily frowned.

Alva shrugged. "He mentioned your interest in signing up with the Peace Corps."

"And?"

"Sorry. That was pretty much it. What did he write in yours?"

"That he appreciated getting the letter from me. He did tease me about writing when I should be studying for exams. But mostly he wrote about the Peace Corps, and how one goes about signing up." Lily frowned. "It's pretty involved and takes *months*. He pointed out that since I only had one more semester to go that I should finish up here first. He said having a degree would give me an edge when applying. Which I guess makes sense, but..."

"Whoa," Alva cut in. "Hold on. You weren't thinking of dropping out here? Were you?"

"Well, yeah, I was," Lily said matter-of-factly. "I thought I could just sign up and we, Arvel and me, could go do the Peace Corps thing somewhere like Tahiti or maybe southern France, and..."

"Tahiti?" Alva cut in again. "Southern France? Seriously?"

"Yeah." Lily smiled. "Especially France, like on the Riviera."

Alva, stunned by this revelation, stared at Lily. "I don't think there's much need for the Peace Corps in places like that," she said quietly.

Lily frowned. "Yeah, that's what your brother said. But, no matter, just as long as it ain't some place like Antarctica or the North Pole. Freezing my ass...my bottom off...helping poor people hardly falls under the heading of romantic."

Alva shook her head. "No, I suppose not, but..." She shook her head again.

"What?"

"Well, I guess Arvel wasn't kidding when he said that he found your letter *interesting*."

"Yeah. I bet he found it a real treat."

"Oh," Alva said smiling and shaking her head. "It certainly sounded like he did."

Lily frowned again. "You know," she said, "I'm really disappointed that you're not going to be here next semester. Since I'm stuck here for the time being anyway, we could get together a lot and talk about Arvel, and you could tell me all about him, you know, what he likes, what he likes to do and all."

Alva nodded. "Yes. That would be..." she smiled, "that would be fun. Well, we've got a little time left."

Lily shook her head. "Not for me. I've got to hit the books or... My God. *Hit the books*? How Archie and Veronica is that, for Christ's...for crying out loud?"

"Sounds more like something I would say, doesn't it?"

"Yeah, exactly." And then, "I mean..."

"No offense taken. Although Betty was my favorite."

"Yeah. Veronica," Lily said with some disgust. "What a rich bitch, huh."

Alva laughed. "That certainly was her, alright."

Lily smiled. "You know," she said nodding her head slowly, "you've changed. Not that we've corrupted you or anything... okay...maybe a little, but...you have changed."

"I'll take that as a compliment."

"Oh, it is. For sure. And...well, I'm going to miss you next semester."

"Same here."

"Well, before I get any mushier, I really have to hit...to

crack... Oh God. That's just as bad. Okay. I'm outta here. Bye."

"Bye."

After Lily left, Alva turned back to the letter to her brother that she was writing. Picking up her pen, she was about to continue when she paused. Going over what had just occurred, she smiled. Yes, she felt some sadness at being reminded that she would not be around for the next and last semester. But being told that she had changed, changed in, what others thought, a good way, left her feeling genuinely warm about everything that had happened that semester – about herself, and about how things had turned out. And, although she wasn't sure exactly why, she was pleased that it was Lily who had made note of it.

Turning back to the letter, she looked at the unfinished line, but instead of continuing, she decided to leave it unfinished and to start a new paragraph. With thoughts about this Arvel/Lily connection, about Tahiti and the Riviera, she began.

Oh, dear brother! I just had a visitor...

Chapter 58

Alva was just coming down the front steps of the Cottage when, glancing up, she saw Kerry approaching. It was a surprisingly mild day for December. It was also the first time she had seen him since that morning after the food service Christmas party when he was lying there with Sandra in her bed.

His hands were in the pockets of his long wool coat, which was open in the front. His pack was slung over one shoulder. He was not wearing a hat and she saw that his long hair was not pulled back into its usual ponytail. Seeing her, he smiled and waved. When she got to the bottom of the steps she stopped and waited for him.

"One fine day, isn't it," he said as he came up to her.

She nodded. "That it is."

"Not quite the usual brutal winter day for these parts. But then...is it winter yet...true winter?"

"No, but close enough."

"Ah.

"Sandra's not in."

"No?"

Alva shook her head.

"Well, actually, I came to see you."

"Oh," Alva said, mildly surprised, "really?"

Kerry smiled. "Does that seem so strange?"

Alva shrugged. "I guess not," she said with a shy smile.

"You're on your way out, so I'll make it quick. It's just a couple of things. Two to be exact."

"I'm in no hurry," Alva said quickly. "I'm just going down to the post office." She held up an envelope that was in her hand.

"There's a mailbox right over there on the corner," Kerry said pointing to it.

"I know. But I feel like a walk."

"Well, it's a good afternoon for that *for a change*. Can you stand some company?"

"Okay."

"Okay," Kerry repeated with a smile. "I don't want to intrude."

"No, no, it'd be nice."

Kerry nodded. "Well...nice is good. I'll take it."

Alva laughed.

"A letter," Kerry said, pointing to Alva's envelope. "Some correspondence?"

"To my brother."

"Ah. I used to *correspond*. A couple different times way back when."

"Girlfriends?"

"Well, in a way."

"In a way?"

Kerry shrugged. "Yeah," he said smiling, "yeah, in a way. The first was my best friend's girlfriend." He saw Alva raise her eyebrows. "Oh, it was all above board. He was in boot camp and I was away for the summer."

"And the other?"

"I met her that same summer."

When he didn't say any more, Alva turned and saw that he was obviously remembering something. Although he wasn't frowning or anything, she could see that he wasn't exactly smiling either. She waited.

"Anyway," he said, finally snapping out of it. He turned to Alva and smiled. "It was a good summer. There were…" He smiled wistfully. "There were moments."

"What happened?" She stopped and shook her head. "I'm sorry," she said quickly. "I don't mean to pry."

"No, no," Kerry said. "Not at all. It just…" He shrugged. "Summer just ended. That's all."

"I'm sorry."

"Oh no," Kerry said quickly. "Nothing bad or anything went down. She was a year older and she went to school in Europe. She ended up staying there the next summer after she graduated, so things just kind of wound down until it was over."

They walked along without speaking for a bit.

"You had moments," Alva said. "Good moments?"

Kerry nodded. "They were special. I have no real regrets, more just good memories." He looked at Alva. "Next topic?"

"Sure. You said that you had a couple things to tell me."

"Right. Well…" He smiled. "You doing anything after the post office?"

"Nothing that I can't be led astray from." Alva started, surprised at what she considered boldness on her part. By Kerry's expression she saw that he had a similar reaction. But, though surprised, she felt no urge to backpedal.

"Well, good. You ever go to Charlie's?"

Alva nodded. "For coffee, and sometimes a pastry."

"Perfect. Why don't we go there when you're done with your post office business?"

"I'd like that."

"Good. We can sit, sip our coffee, and talk about what I have to tell you."

"Yes, that sounds…" Alva smiled. "Nice."

Chapter 59

"Looks like we have the place to ourselves," Kerry said after they got their coffee. "Where should we sit?"

"Over there," Alva said, gesturing towards the table that she had always sat at. "It's *my* table."

"*Your* table," Kerry said. "Then *your* table it is."

After taking off their coats and hanging them from the backs of their chairs, they sat down.

"Talk about dead."

Alva nodded. "There's only two days left to exams. A lot of people have already left for winter break."

"True. True. And I guess everyone else is studying. Hmm," he said. "So, what does that say about us?"

"I've finished. I'm just wrapping things up at my job in the library." Alva wondered if Kerry knew about her Middle East position the coming spring semester. She thought about bringing the subject up, but decided against it. "What about you, slacker?"

"That's *Mister* Slacker to you. And I'll have you know that I finished my exams two days ago. Mind you, I didn't say I passed them, but I took them."

"So why are you still here?"

"I had to meet with Mr. Phillips and go over my work this past semester. That's where I was coming from when we met up. And that brings us to one of the things that I wanted to tell you. First though," Kerry reached into the inner pocket of his coat and pulled out a long envelope. "Mr. Phillips asked me to give you this. He said it was your poems and some thoughts he had on them."

Alva took the envelope. "Okay," she said, more curious and eager at that moment to hear what Kerry had to tell her.

"Well, we were discussing poems, mostly mine, of course, but others from other people in the class, and I brought up your poem, the one I told you that we discussed in class when we were talking about voice. I mentioned that I knew you, and…well, he said that he'd been trying to remember to contact you."

"Why?" Alva asked, now even more curious and definitely more eager.

"Well," Kerry said with a smile, "he told me to tell you that he's keeping a slot open for you in next semester's poetry writing workshop, that is if you're still interested. Which is cool as I'm going to be in it too, so we…" Kerry stopped suddenly. For a moment he just stared at her. "You're frowning," he said. "In fact, it looks like you're deflating."

"Why now?" Alva said mostly to herself.

"What's wrong?"

"I've been trying and trying to get into his workshop for two years now, and I couldn't because space was given to English majors first, and there was never an empty slot. But now there is and…" She sat there shaking her head.

"Right. But now there is. So…?"

"I won't be here next semester."

"What?"

"I'm going to the Middle East."

"The Middle East. What for?"

"I'm going with the group from the project I worked on this semester."

Kerry frowned. "I thought that kind of thing was only open to grad students."

"It is, but…but I've fulfilled all of my requirements, and I already have enough credits to graduate."

"But what about GREs and being accepted into grad school and all?"

"Professor Nagy, who's in charge, pushed all of that through, so…"

Kerry smirked. "Yeah," he said. "They never have a problem fast tracking things when it's in their own interest. And…" Kerry caught himself. "Sorry," he said. "I…" He shook his head. Alva could see that he was embarrassed. "I'm sorry. What was I thinking? How rude of me. That's great. I mean it. I mean it sounds like a real special opportunity. How could you *not* take it, right?"

Alva nodded. "I can think of some good reasons not to, but…" She shrugged.

"Right. Well. Wow. I certainly wasn't expecting all of this. Congratulations." Reaching across the table, he took her hand. "Big time congratulations."

So sudden and so unexpected was this physical contact that, for one brief moment, Alva felt it almost difficult to breathe. But even with that, she didn't want the moment to end.

"You know," Kerry said smiling and taking his hand away. "I just had a thought. To return to an earlier conversation…maybe *we* could correspond. That is if you'd like to. No pressure. Just if you'd like to."

Alva smiled. "I would."

"Well, good. That's good. And I could share what you're up to over there with...well, Sandra, of course, and Lily. Even Mr. Phillips. I bet he'd be interested. And I'll let him know that you're not going to be around next semester."

"And I'd like to hear what's going on here with everybody."

"It's a deal. Shall we shake on it?"

"Let's."

And they did.

"You mentioned that there was something else you wanted to talk to me about."

"Oh yeah," Kerry said. Leaning forward slightly, he folded his hands. "It's about the Christmas party up at the lodge." Pausing, he frowned and let out a quick laugh. "It's...it's just that, I'm..." He shook his head. "I really don't remember everything clearly about that night, but I remember enough to know that I was a jerk and, well, I just wanted to apologize for ruining the evening for you and everybody."

"I think 'ruin' is putting it kind of strong. Things could have turned out worse. Especially for you."

"Yeah, good point, I guess they could have, and would have if it hadn't been for you and Sandra, and Hawk too. I'm lucky the three of you were there. Grateful really. Big time grateful. And so, I'm really sorry."

"Okay. Have you spoken to Sandra about all of this?"

Kerry smiled. "Oh...yeah. There was some pretty serious pillow talk that next morning."

"Really? Sandra? That doesn't sound like her."

"It doesn't, does it? Let me tell you, she's the first person I've ever met who can yell at you without raising their voice above a whisper. Believe me, she didn't spare any punches."

"Don't you think you deserved that?"

"Oh…yeah."

"Can I ask you something, something personal?"

"Uh-oh," Kerry said sliding his chair backwards an inch. "Well, normally, when someone asks me that, I give them one big 'no,' but…" He shrugged. "Shoot."

"Do you…are you in any way in love with Sandra?"

"Oh my," Kerry said with a look of surprise.

"You don't have to answer that."

"No, no, no. It's okay." He let out a quiet laugh. "But first tell me, why do you ask?"

"That morning…that morning after the party. I saw you two."

"I remember. You came in and then very discretely went away. A most mature thing to have done given the circumstances."

"It was just because of the way she was sleeping with you, close and all. And the way she got angry at the party about the state you were in. I just think…I think she cares for you. Seriously cares."

Pulling his chair back up to the table, Kerry folded his hands. He sat there for a moment looking down at them. "Well," he said finally, looking up, "I'd be lying if I said that I didn't…didn't get a sense of that."

"A sense of that," Alva repeated in a mildly derisive tone.

"Right. Right. Right. Yes, she cares. She's never said as much, or even implied anything, but…but yes. I know that she cares." He shrugged. "She's a caring person. You've probably heard about me asking her to marry me."

"I did. From you."

"Oh. That's right. Well, I did."

"Without meaning it," Alva repeated with a note of derision.

"So. You're really going to take me to task here. You know, if it was anyone else, I'd say something snide and cut you off. Or, if I was in *mature mode*, I'd get up and just walk away." He looked at Alva with narrowed eyes. "There is something about you."

"Don't change the subject."

"Right. *Without meaning it*. Well, let me tell you something about that. There's this gentleman, Robert, whom I work with, and, because of my lackadaisical attendance habits at work..."

"The complete opposite of Sandra's, I would imagine."

"Hey, let up a little here. Because of my *less than stellar* attendance habits, this gentleman, Robert, takes it upon himself to note my faults in this matter, and when I say 'note' I am using the word euphemistically. Like the man is on a mission. But you know what, besides being used to it, I'm okay with that. He has a right to. We do work together. Or at least we do when I manage to show up for work.

"Anyway, this one morning Robert and I are working the scrappers. We grab the trays and dishes as they come in on this belt, and we wipe what's left on them into garbage disposals and stack everything so that they can be fed into the dish machine, which consists of a long belt and works like a car wash. When it's slow, one of us will feed the machine, but when things pick up somebody will come in off one of the serving lines to do the feed. Often, it's Sandra.

"On this particular morning, Robert was really irked with me, like really worked up and that's when he said that I should marry Sandra so that she could straighten me out. Well, right in the middle of his tirade Sandra shows up to load the dish machine and Robert goes all quiet like. So, just to make him feel truly uncomfortable, I turned to Sandra and asked her to marry me."

"Without meaning it."

For a moment Kerry just sat there and glared at Alva. "*And I asked her to marry me.*" He paused again, and then went on, "And, well you know Sandra, right away she figures out what's going on, and for one long moment she just looks at me, and then she says quite matter-of-factly 'no, no thank you,' like I had offered her a stick of gum or something. So, it wasn't like I was jerking her around, if you'll pardon the expression, or anything. She knew what was going on."

Alva nodded. "Still, you asked her, you asked someone whom you know cares about you. Did you ever think that, at some level, the notion of marrying you was something that might mean something to her?"

Shaking his head, Kerry looked down at his hands again and smiled. "It's funny that you should bring that up."

"Why?"

Kerry looked up at her. "Because even asking something like that, even if only to needle somebody else…well, it gets one thinking about it too *at some level*, like *what if*. But…" He shrugged. "What can I say?"

"You can answer my question. Do you love her? Do you care for her?"

"My, my. You are a pit bull, aren't you?"

"Do you?"

"Yeah, I *care* for her." Kerry said calmly. "Of course, I do. In fact, I care for her a lot, so much so that I don't let myself get that *involved* with her. You've seen what I can be like. You certainly saw it at the party and afterwards. Why would I want to *inflict* myself on somebody as special as her? We're friends. That works well, well enough."

For a moment the two of them sat there in silence. Finally, Kerry picked up his coffee and took a sip. "Ugh," he said making a face. "Cold. Yours must be too." Rising from his seat he reached across the table and took her cup. "I'll be right back." With that he turned and headed for the counter.

"You know," Alva said quietly to him when he returned, "you're not always what you were like at the party. Like right now."

"Yeah, but I *am* like that at times, and not all that infrequently, or so others tell me."

"I think you're afraid, afraid to take a chance, afraid to be vulnerable."

"Oh, here we go," Kerry said, rolling his eyes. "I thought Lily was the psych person. Look, right now this is just the way things are, good, bad, *and* indifferent."

"I think you're missing out on something pretty special."

"It's not the first time."

"You're being very foolish."

"No argument there."

She gave him a searching look. "Or is this just a self-definition thing where you're devising this *persona* for yourself? Are you hung up on being the *dissolute*, the *self-tortured poet*?"

"That sounds more like an accusation than a question. But I'll admit, it *is* an interesting notion. Let's just suppose…"

"Stop," Alva said with noticeable exasperation. "Let's not *just suppose* anything. Stop trying to derail this conversation. This is serious."

"What... Who do you...?" Kerry stopped. For a moment he sat there staring at Alva. Then, nodding his head slowly. "Wait a minute," he said slowly. "I remember now. I also asked you to marry me." He smiled. "And you...*you* said 'yes.' Now I see. This is about the whole *at some level* thing. Sandra said 'no,' but you said 'yes.' What does that say about you *at some level?*"

"But then I said that I was kidding," Alva protested, suddenly uneasy about where the conversation was going.

"But...you...said...'yes.'"

Alva turned away. "Don't. Just don't."

"But...you...said..."

"Please don't," Alva pleaded quietly, still turned away.

For a moment Kerry sat there looking at Alva, not knowing what to do or say.

"Hey Alva," he said in almost a whisper. "I'm sorry. That was..."

"The word is 'cruel.'"

"Yeah. Once again, I end up being a jerk. And this time it's without the benefit of external stimulants. This is the real deal. This, this is what I've been telling you about inflicting myself on Sandra and...and you. I'm sorry. God, I come to see you to say I'm sorry about one thing and then I end up being stupid and having to apologize a second time for something else. What is wrong with me?"

For a long while they sat there not saying anything, just drinking their coffee, their eyes never making contact until, finally, Alva turned to Kerry.

"You know," she said quietly, "you still owe me a drive out to see that traffic light, the one that's upside down."

"Oh yeah," Kerry said with nothing in the way of enthusiasm.

"I do, don't I. Unfortunately, Stu is having problems."

"Stu? Oh, the car. Right?"

Kerry nodded. "Steve is waiting on a transmission part. From someplace out in Indiana or Ohio, I think. We're probably talking sometime…" He shrugged. "It could end up being next spring before we can work on it. So, we'll have to wait until then to…" He frowned. "Well, that ain't gonna work, is it?"

Alva smiled and shook her head. "I'm afraid not."

"And you're not going to be back at all next semester?"

"Maybe around graduation. But l can't say for sure. I haven't seen our itinerary yet."

"Well, we're gonna keep in touch, right? We *are* going to correspond, right?"

Alva smiled. "Yes."

"Promise?"

Alva laughed. "Sure, but…" She laughed again. "Do you?"

Kerry nodded. "Right. Okay. *I* promise. Or at least I promise to try."

"I can't ask for more than that, except…"

"Except what?"

"Except my coffee is cold again."

Kerry stood up and took her cup. "Allow me."

Alva looked up and smiled at him. "Thank you."

"Yes ma'am."

Chapter 60

"You know," Uncle Ward said as he and Alva came up the last set of stairs to Alva's room. "It's gotta be, what, forty, maybe fifty, degrees cooler than it was that day we moved you in here, and I've still managed to work up a sweat."

"I'm sorry," Alva said smiling sympathetically. "I really appreciate all that you're doing."

"Oh, don't mind me. I'm just an old whiner. And a sweaty old whiner at that."

When they reached the landing, Alva took his arm and, turning him around, gave him a quick hug. "You go right ahead and whine all you want."

"Thank you, my wonderful niece." They stepped into her room. "What's left?"

"Just the one box and my suitcase."

"That's it?"

"That's it."

"Shall I take the box while you say a last good-bye to...to your first home on your own."

Alva rubbed his upper arm. "That's not necessary. I'm ready to go."

"Still, you should at least have a moment alone here with the room, a moment of gratitude."

"You're right," Alva said with a nod. "You're right."

"Then I'll take the box and wait for you downstairs."

"Okay. I'll only be a moment."

"No rush."

After her uncle left, Alva picked up her suitcase from where it lay on her bed and walked to the doorway. Turning back to the room, she set the suitcase down on the floor and put her hands together in a prayer position in front of her chest. Bowing slightly, she stood there. As she did so, a plenitude of different thoughts of gratitude came quickly and they kept coming non-stop. Finally, deciding that enough was enough, she smiled.

"Thank you," she said slowly looking around the room and taking it all in. "Thank you for everything. For everything."

She was just about to pick up her suitcase when she happened to glance across the room to the dormer window. From where she stood, she could see the houses of Fraternity Row. Seeing them, she remembered her first day there at the Cottage when Bernie recommended getting curtains for the window. Standing there now, she was glad that she didn't, glad that she had followed through on her resolve not to be cowed by persons unknown and unseen, glad to have made that first of many resolutions, glad and grateful for the changes that had come her way because of them.

Looking again across the way to Fraternity Row, she stuck out her tongue and let loose a resounding raspberry.

"There," she said with a smile. "Take that."

Picking up her suitcase, Alva turned to leave. When she reached the top of the stairs, she glanced over to Sandra's room.

The door was open. Even knowing that she wasn't in, Alva felt a sudden urge just to see Sandra's room one last time. Setting her suitcase down again, she walked over and stood in the doorway. Looking in, she was surprised to see three good sized empty boxes on the floor and a suitcase open and empty on the bed. It seemed odd to Alva that Sandra would be taking anything more than a suitcase home for the winter break. Obviously, there was an explanation and Alva told herself that she would have to remember to ask her about it before she left.

Earlier, Sandra had told her that she had a last errand to run out at the Jewish home, but that she would be back by three. Looking at her watch, Alva was slightly concerned when she saw that it was already a quarter past the hour. With a shrug, she walked back to where her suitcase was, picked it up and started down.

When she reached the bottom of the stairs, she came upon her uncle and Bernie standing in the foyer talking. They both turned to Alva as she descended the last few steps.

"So," Bernie said, "I guess this is it. I was just telling Ward that we're going to miss your quiet and calm manner around here." She turned to Ward. "And that goes for her neighbor up there in the attic. Hopefully we'll get another quiet pair up there next semester."

"Well, Bernie," Uncle Ward said laying a hand on her shoulder, "you know as well as I do that change is the name of the game around here."

"That it is. That it is."

As startled as she was to hear Bernie address her uncle by his first name and then for him to respond in, what Alva considered, a *familiar* manner, she was more surprised by this news that

Sandra wouldn't be returning to the Cottage next semester either. Obviously, that explained the empty boxes and suitcase in Sandra's room.

"Well," Bernie said turning to Alva and extending a hand, "it's been a pleasure having you here." They shook hands. "And good luck with the gig in the Middle East."

"Thank you."

Reaching forward, Uncle Ward took Alva's suitcase from her. "Shall we?"

Alva nodded.

"Don't be a stranger, Ward," Bernie called after them as they went out the front door.

"Oh, don't worry, I'll be around."

After stowing Alva's suitcase in the trunk, Uncle Ward turned to her. "Climb in."

"I...I'm going to have to hang around here for a little bit," Alva said. "I haven't said goodbye to my friend Sandra yet. We were supposed to meet here at three. I guess she's running late."

Uncle Ward looked at his watch. "Well, she's not all that late. Why don't we wait in the car?"

"Oh, I don't want to keep you. I'll just sit out here on the steps and wait for her. It's nice enough for that today."

"You sure? I don't mind waiting."

"Please. I'll be fine. I'll walk over after I see her."

"Well, put your hat and mittens on."

Alva nodded and pulled the items from the pockets of her coat.

Sitting on the top step, Alva found herself pleased by how things had worked out with Sandra being late and all. Now, she realized, with no one else around, they wouldn't have to rush their goodbyes.

As it turned out, it was only a few minutes later that she saw Sandra's car turn at the corner and come up and park in front of the Cottage.

"Sorry I'm late," Sandra said climbing out. "Everybody wanted hugs. That's my only excuse."

"That's not an excuse. That's a reason, a good reason."

"Oh, I am going to miss you," Sandra said coming up the steps and sitting down next to Alva. "But let's not get into all that quite yet. First things first. Do you want to go down to Charlie's for coffee?"

"I think I'd just like to stay right here, if you don't mind."

"That works for me. Speaking of Charlie's, I heard that you had quite the talk there with Kerry." She laughed. "He said that he felt like he was being double-teamed by the two of us."

"Maybe that's what it's going to take."

"Maybe. But..." Sandra shrugged. "You *are* going to have to keep up your share in it, even if it is by long distance."

"And maybe you should plan on dogging him like a pit bull," Alva said. "You know, like not letting him out of your sight."

Expecting Sandra to laugh along with her or, at least, smile, Alva was surprised to see Sandra's expression turn to one of unease.

"What's the matter?" Alva asked.

"Nothing, not really," Sandra said with a slight shrug and a trace of a smile. "It's just that there's something I need to tell you."

When Sandra didn't continue right away, Alva took one of Sandra's hands.

"I heard," Alva said reassuringly. "Bernie just told me that you were moving out for next semester. And I saw the empty boxes and suitcase in your room."

Sandra frowned. "Yeah. Part of it was…" She squeezed Alva's hand. "I didn't want to be around here with you gone."

Alva suddenly remembered Kerry telling her about Sandra's friend Margaret, the woman that she roomed with the last three years, the one with MS. This, Alva assumed, was probably a big factor.

"Sure," Alva said sympathetically. "I can see why you might want to move on." She released Sandra's hand. "So, do you have a new place already?"

Sandra frowned again. "Yeah," she said, "I do."

"Well, great. You must be excited. Where is it?"

"It's off campus. A few blocks away from the park."

"Well, that will be a change. Wow. Great. Is it an apartment or a room in…"

"It's where Kerry lives," Sandra cut in.

For a moment Alva just sat there somewhat stunned. "Oh," she said trying to get a handle on this piece of news. "That…that *will* be different. I wouldn't have thought…" She shook her head and smiled. "Well of course I wouldn't have." She shook her head again. "I guess there's still a lot of the old Alva left." She looked at Sandra. "Don't mind me," she said dismissively. "So…so is it a house with a lot of bedrooms?"

"Yes. Yes, it is. There are half a dozen people living there already."

"So, someone has moved out and you're taking their…"

"I'm moving in with Kerry."

"Oh. Like living together?"

Sandra nodded. When a good long moment went by without

Alva saying anything else, Sandra pressed on.

"He's got a room on the top floor, the attic really. It's nice. And very private."

"It...it sounds nice." Alva said quietly and then, doing her best to come up with a smile. "Trading one attic for another, huh."

"Yeah, I guess so. We're just giving it a try. No commitment. Just...just giving it a try, taking it slow."

"Sure," Alva said. "That's smart, I guess."

"I guess?" Sandra repeated in a mildly teasing tone.

Alva shrugged and frowned. "What do I know?"

"Hey," Sandra said abruptly, "don't do that. Don't sell yourself short. I appreciate your take on things. Seriously. This hasn't been a one-way street with the two of us."

"Thank you," Alva said quietly. "Actually, I guess it could be a really good thing for him, for Kerry. In fact, I know it would be, if...if he..."

Sandra smiled. "Again, with the *I guess*."

"Sorry."

"No. I want to know how you feel about this. I've come to depend on your judgment and, even more so, your honesty. And you're right. One can't *make* people change. It's up to them to do the actual work. They have to *want* to do the work. And yes, it really is up to Kerry. The same goes for me."

"What do you mean?" Alva asked, surprised.

"I need to...I need to make some changes too."

"I don't understand. Like what?"

"I need to stop keeping things...I need to stop keeping people at a distance like I've been doing for...well, for quite a while now. I need to learn how to take a chance with people again, and not always be on my guard about getting too close to anyone and risk getting hurt. I need to stop obsessing about leaving myself vulnerable."

Alva looked at Sandra and shook her head. "I haven't seen that at all with you. You've been nothing but a good friend, a *really* good friend. The best. And that has meant so much to me."

"Thanks, but this *has* been a two-way street. Right from the start I felt that the whole vulnerability thing was not going to be an issue with you, and that we were going to get along well, real well. And we have."

Alva smiled and nodded.

"And," Sandra went on, "it had been a good long while since I felt that way about anyone. And now, thanks to you, *really*, thanks to you, I'm ready to risk being close with people again. I'm ready to risk it. And so…"

"Kerry."

Sandra nodded.

"What if it doesn't work out?"

"I'll be the first to admit that it might not." Sandra laughed, "his track record being what it is. *But*…but there's something about him, something *there* at times that makes me think that it could work out."

Alva nodded. "I know what you mean. I don't think he's hopeless."

"I'm glad to hear you say that. But again, it might not work out, but now…but now I feel that I can get through it if it doesn't. I've changed. And if I've learned anything from you, it's that change is possible, and the risk is worth taking."

For a while the two of them sat there without saying anything. Being close to the solstice, evening was already beginning to settle in and, with the slowly fading light, the air became chillier. The streetlights came on.

Sandra shivered. "Is it me, or did the temperature just drop a few degrees?"

"It's not you."

"Are you *sure* you couldn't do with a cup of hot, *hot* coffee."

"Black?"

"Of course."

"I can be tempted."

"Consider yourself tempted."

"Okay," Alva said with a laugh. "I'm tempted. But, before we go, can I tell you something?"

"Of course."

Alva took a deep breath and let it out slowly. "I'm jealous."

"What do you mean?"

"I'm jealous of you."

"Why?"

"Because, you'll be able to do it. I just know you'll be able to do it, to make things work with Kerry. I really believe that. It's going to work out."

"Well, I appreciate your vote of confidence, but...why jealous?"

"Because I would like to have been the person to make that happen."

Sandra nodded her head slowly. "I see," she said in a quiet voice. "I guess I've been fairly obtuse not to see that...that you were...interested in him. I'm sorry."

"Don't be," Alva said quickly and with a quiet intensity. "No. It's right that it's working out this way. I would've ended up romanticizing the..."

"The heck?"

Alva laughed. "No, let's say *the realness* right out of it. I would've ended up making it something that wasn't real, and it could never work that way. Not with me. And I know that, but I'm still jealous. Maybe, maybe if the last three years had been more normal for me, maybe then I..." She shook her head. "But the last three years were what they were, and I am where I am now. And that's okay. I'm good with this. This is where I am now."

"And you're moving on to what is next for you, for you, Alva, and that, I think, is all that really matters, isn't it?"

Alva nodded. "Yes. And I just wanted you to know this...this me that I am, this me where I am right now. And do you want to know what I really want right now?"

"I'm hoping you're going to say a cup of hot coffee."

"Exactly."

Alva and Sandra both rose slowly to their feet.

"Oh," Alva said with a slight groan. "We've been sitting on these cold steps a little too long."

"I hear you. But," Sandra shrugged, "in a way I think, long enough..." She smiled. "Long enough for now."

Alva nodded. "Long enough for now."

"Shall we?"

"Let's."

And with that they descended the steps and started off up the street.

Chapter 61

"We're not going to say goodbye," Sandra said matter-of-factly as they walked slowly up Market Street.

Evening had settled in fully by the time they left Charlie's. The lightest of snow was falling, the kind that you could only see by looking up at the streetlights, the kind of snow that you only felt as the barest touch on your face.

"We're not, you know."

Alva turned to Sandra and smiled. "No," she said quietly. "No, no we're not."

"And so, we're not going to stretch this…this *parting for the moment* all out of proportion, are we?"

"Certainly not."

"Good. Are you coming back to the Cottage?"

"No. I'm all moved out."

"That's good. Everything's at your aunt and uncle's?"

Alva nodded. "Yes, and I'm sure my Uncle Ward has all the boxes stowed away by now. All that's left is to pack up my suitcase and head to the airport in the morning. Back to Kentucky for Christmas."

"Well then you'll want to turn in early tonight."

"I hope I'll be able to sleep. I'm kind of worked up."

"Who wouldn't be? Especially with just having had coffee this late in the day. What were we thinking?"

They both laughed.

"My Aunt Lillian will probably have me drink some warm milk…by the gallon."

Sandra glanced at Alva. "Speaking of stowing your things away, I should have told you that you could have stored your things with us. We have plenty of room in the attic. I'm sorry that I didn't mention it sooner."

Alva noted Sandra's use of the words 'we' and 'us,' and then, with a smile, she let it go.

"That's alright. There's plenty of room at my aunt and uncle's place. *Plenty*."

"Well, it's just that I thought that maybe, maybe when you got back you might want to move in. Some folks will be gone for the summer. So, if you needed a room…" Sandra shrugged.

"Are you going to be around?" Alva asked, somewhat surprised.

"Yeah, I thought I would stay at least for the summer. The folks at the Jewish home have offered me a position, sort of an activities coordinator. It's just for the summer, and so, since I already have a place to stay, I thought I'd take them up on it. And it wouldn't look bad on the old resumé."

"That's great. And we are *supposed* to be back here sometime in June." Alva laughed. "No one is too keen on doing the Middle East in the summer."

"So why don't you move in with Kerry and me?"

"Well, that's tempting, but…"

"But?"

"But I think my Aunt Lillian would be disappointed, and

that's putting it mildly. And…and I don't want to disappoint her *again*."

Sandra nodded. "Sure. You're right. But maybe you could stay over with us once in a while."

"Sure," Alva said with a smile. "I'd like that. I'd like it a lot."

"Good. Let's plan on that."

For the rest of the way along Market Street they continued on slowly and silently until they reached the next intersection where there was a traffic light. It was red and so they stopped at the curb when they reached it.

"Sandra?" Alva asked. "Can I ask a favor?"

"Of course."

"Well, I have to warn you. It's kind of silly."

Sandra smiled. "I can't wait to hear."

"Can I take… Can *we take* each other's arm for the rest of the way, until we have to part?"

Sandra laughed good-naturedly. "Well…sure."

"I know. I know. It's silly. Forget it. Forget I brought it up. It was…"

"No," Sandra said quickly. "No, we can do that. Just…where did this come from?"

"The Amerio aunts, great-aunts actually, of Marie, a childhood friend. They were from Italy. Sicily. *The Great Aunts*. Neither of them spoke any English beyond 'hello' and 'good-bye.' They didn't even talk much to each other, even on their daily walks. And they would walk, arm in arm, for miles, never really going anywhere in particular, just walking. They were two old women dressed in black. And they were short, not even five feet tall. But there was something about them that made them real special to me. Like there was something…well, most people just thought they were cute, quaint, but I think they had something way more than that."

"A type of dignity?"

Alva turned quickly to Sandra. "Yes," she said surprised. "I think that's it. How did you know?"

Sandra smiled and shrugged. "It's like that with some of the folks at the Jewish home. They have this sense of their own dignity, their own *wholeness*, a quiet sense, like they don't really need to say anything just for the sake of saying it, that some things for them are just understood. They are wise, wise enough to be content to go on quietly. So…"

Moving closer, Sandra took Alva's arm. Nodding once, Alva took Sandra's. The light turned green. With that they looked both ways. Seeing that the road was clear of traffic, they continued on.

JOHN MULLER graduated from Syracuse University with a degree in English and Journalism. He currently resides in Florida. His first novel, *Island Moments*, is available to purchase online.

www.ingramcontent.com/pod-product-compliance
Lightning Source LLC
Chambersburg PA
CBHW020214260626
47156CB00002B/372